MW00915983

THE DESERT
OF GLASS

By
Michael C. Grumley

Copyright © 2021 Michael C. Grumley

i.ii

BY MICHAEL C. GRUMLEY

The Last Monument

The Desert of Glass

DEDICATION

To my Mom.
An incredible woman who has given me so much.

Prologue

July 1977

There was no sound.
No crickets, no insects, no anything...
but dry, dead air.

Utter silence. Unmoving. Slowing time and existence to a crawl through endless days of searing heat and suffocating air followed by long, empty black nights.
No movement of any kind.

Until it happened—
Almost instantaneously.

Grains of sand began to move across the trembling ground a split second before a massive explosion of sound and speed. Overhead, it was sudden, thunderous, and gone as quickly as it came.

Barely three hundred feet above the ground, with hands gripping the control column like vices, a lone pilot peered intently through the cockpit window into the darkness in front of him, feeling every vibration traveling up through his trembling arms.

The aircraft was under enormous strain, pushed to its limit by twin turbojet engines at the tail of the craft, sending it hurtling forward just below the speed of sound, ensconced in total and utter darkness.

All navigation lights had been turned off, including the

interior lights, leaving the only illumination of the pilot's face coming from the instruments themselves, the only lights keeping the small cockpit from pitch blackness. Except perhaps the dim scattering of stars across the ebony sky above.

A thousand kilometers was all he needed. Due East. Below the radar horizon. Enough to give him a fighting chance.

Fear coursed through his body, down his arms in the same path as the vibrations and into his hands, which remained wrapped around the controls in a death grip. He was fearful of making the slightest mistake, as it would take almost nothing at his velocity and altitude to slam the aircraft directly into the earth at full speed.

His thoughts briefly drifted to the rest of the craft behind him—to his cargo. He almost turned his head as if needing to verify it was still there.

Don't look! Pay attention!

He squinted tighter and continued peering through the tiny windshield, searching for anything in his way.

But he knew the truth. At this speed, anything he saw would hit him before he could even react, leaving his desperate plight fixed solely upon hope and prayer.

Hope that there was nothing in the way.

And the prayer that he would reach salvation in time.

What the lone pilot could not know, what he couldn't see, was the sky behind him, which was also black and dotted by a multitude of faint stars appearing like a giant shimmering blanket overhead, with more than enough twinkling lights to hide what was approaching from the rear.

Navigation lights from another jet.

In the lead cockpit, the man released one hand long enough to wipe the sweat from his forehead before immediately returning it to the controls, blinking wide and staring into the night. Each passing minute gave him another minute of hope.

If he could just—

He never heard the launch of the missile behind him—or its impact when the entire Learjet instantly exploded into a brilliant ball of orange flame.

1

Present Day

The mighty Pacific winds buffeted the small car as though trying to push it from the narrow gravel road upon which it was traveling alone, struggling through continual waves of dust clouds passing over the plains of Baja. Over thirty miles of barren hills and valleys before the powerful gusts finally rising up and over the open waters of Mexico's Gulf of California.

The car didn't surrender. Instead, it held its ground and stubbornly continued along the dirt-strewn road until reaching and turning onto an abandoned set of worn tire tracks heading toward the distant cliffs.

The tracks grew less visible as the small automobile wound back and forth over rugged terrain, reaching with difficulty the remnants of an old structure severely damaged but still technically standing in its own relentless fight against the elements.

The white car stopped and remained for several moments before the driver's side door opened, and Joe Rickards stepped out onto the hard ground.

Dressed in a light jacket, jeans and boots, he fought against the mighty wind to force his door closed and stood for several minutes staring at what was left of the old house. He then stepped out from around the car and approached. The house's entire roof was collapsed, with half of it missing entirely. What sections remained were wedged between several stone walls that managed to remain standing against all odds. Windows whose glass was broken and missing remained embedded within the stone in empty wooden frames.

Debris was scattered everywhere—large stone chunks down to small rocks and pebbles covered the entire stone foundation, obscuring what appeared to be broken dishes and a plumbing conduit.

Behind the structure lay perhaps another mile of rolling hills which eventually dropped off and began a meandering descent to the aqua-colored waters of the gulf several hundred feet below.

Rickards studied the abandoned dwelling and gradually began to circle, viewing it from all sides, his brown hair whipping wildly in the wind.

He stepped forward to move onto the house's foundation but stopped himself, deciding against it. He didn't want to desecrate the place any more than it already was.

Twenty-six years.

Twenty-six years had entirely destroyed the house, along with the family who'd once lived there.

He stepped back and scanned the horizon, finding nothing but dry grass waving under the forceful breeze. With hands in both pockets, he turned back to the remains and continued staring.

Loss was painful, but regret was forever.

2

Several days later, Angela Reed found Rickards on a bench in Denver's Bear Creek Park, quietly overlooking a small playground filled with children scampering about, squealing with laughter and chasing one another in a game of tag.

Angela slowed several feet from the bench when Joe turned and glanced up at her.

"I've been trying to get ahold of you."

"Sorry," he replied. "Been a little busy."

She stepped forward and eased herself down onto the other half of the bench. "Everything okay?"

"As well as it can be."

"When you disappear, you really disappear."

"Sorry," he said again, briefly glancing back at the playground. It used to be his daughter's favorite.

Angela lowered her large purse beside her and watched the children with a smile. "How did it go with your mother-in-law?"

"Interesting."

"Just interesting?"

He thought a moment and turned back. "She was more than a little reluctant. But I convinced her."

"How?"

"I told her I'd just keep coming back to visit her until she agreed."

"I'll bet that did the trick," Angela said with a laugh. "And?"

"I took her," he said simply, "to Bolivia."

"And did she go in?"

"Eventually, but it took a while. She thought I was insane."

"And?"

"Well, she doesn't think I'm insane anymore."

"What happened?"

He gave a soft shrug. "She went in—and came out thirty minutes later crying."

Angela inhaled. "What did she see?"

"I don't know. She wouldn't say."

"At all?"

Rickards shook his head.

"So… you have no idea what—?"

"No. But something happened. After that, she didn't hate me anymore."

"Well, that's good."

He nodded solemnly. "Yeah."

They both fell quiet, listening only to the sound of the children playing.

"Are you back to work?"

Rickards shook his head again. "I quit."

"You quit?"

He raised his head and looked at her. "Kind of hard to go back. Things are too different now."

"I can understand that."

"How about you?"

Angela nodded beneath a head of light-brown hair. "I'm back teaching at the university. But it *is* different." She looked out over a group of pine trees, their needles twinkling in the light spring breeze. "Surreal, really. It's as if very little in the world matters anymore."

"Yep."

"I turn on the TV and listen to the news, and it all feels so, I don't know, juvenile. Everyone just arguing over things that don't matter—at all. But they don't know it."

Rickards gazed absently at the ground. "That's about it."

She grinned and brushed a strand of hair behind her ear. "Half the time my students ask me a question, and I just want to answer, 'Who cares?'"

Rickards smiled.

"I feel strange," she went on. "As if I'm in this place between the life I've lived and the life I'm supposed to live now."

"I get that."

"You're probably the only one who does, which is why I've been calling. I was worried something had happened to you."

"I just needed some time."

"I'm happy you're okay."

"You don't have to worry, Angela. I'm not... you know."

She watched as a couple strolled past. "Well, that was *one* of the reasons. To make sure you're okay." She turned and picked up her purse. "The other reason was to show you something."

"What's that?"

She reached in and retrieved a thick manila envelope.

Rickards looked at her curiously and then at the envelope until she pushed it forward and into his hands.

He took it and studied it before flipping it over. "What is this?"

Angela didn't answer. Instead, she motioned to the envelope and waited until he'd opened the flap and pulled out the top piece of paper.

It took only a moment for his expression to change and his eyes to widen as he read the paper.

He didn't speak, but instead read the entire page. Then, when he'd finished, he sat in stunned silence.

"Is this real?"

"Yes."

"From Mike Morton?"

"Yes."

"How is that possible?"

"Look at the date on that email. He sent it the night we met. I'm guessing he had a satellite connection or something."

"But..."

"I know. I couldn't believe it, either."

Rickards repeatedly blinked at the sheet before finally pulling out the rest of the papers inside, page after page filled with what looked to be computer data and mathematical computations, including images from different maps.

He turned to Angela. "How long have you had this?"

"Since I got back."

"Have you told anyone?"

"No one else would believe me. Only you."

"And this is why you've been calling me?"

She winked. "One of the reasons."

3

"Something tells me you haven't been idle," said Rickards.

She grinned. "I've located the person Mike references in his letter."

"Who is it?"

"An old colleague who worked at NASA with him. Maybe on the same project."

"Mike said no one else believed him."

Angela shrugged.

"So who is he?"

"His name is Leonard Townsend. He's retired and teaches college math and physics."

"Have you contacted him?"

"No."

"But you plan to."

"I was waiting to talk to you first."

Rickards returned the pages to the envelope and sighed, leaning back against the wooden bench. "Another location."

"Sounds like it."

"That does what?"

She shook her head. "I have no idea."

After a long pause, Rickards took a breath and exhaled slowly. "I say leave it alone."

"What?"

"Angela," he said, turning, "you *do* understand the significance here."

"I do."

"Are you sure? Because what we already know is enough to change everything."

"I understand that."

"Then you also understand it's only a matter of time before others find out."

"Yes."

He held up the papers. "And you still want to find this?"

"Mike obviously did."

"Mike didn't even know what the first one *was*," exclaimed Rickards. "What it was *or* what it could do. This is big, Angela—bigger than either of us. Jesus, it's bigger than *all* of us."

"I know that, Joe."

"Really? Because it seems to me as if maybe you don't."

"What's that supposed to mean?"

"What I mean is this thing is beyond…"

"What?"

Rickards struggled for the right word. "I don't know— *comprehension*. And it's dangerous. What happens when everybody else finds out?"

"And uses it for something bad?"

"Exactly."

"I don't see how they could do that."

"Anything can be exploited, Angela. *Anything*. Every object on this planet has been used for something terrible at one time or another."

"Just because something can be abused doesn't destroy the good it can do."

"You're an anthropologist. You, more than anyone, should understand what people are capable of. How many times has a country, or a race, wiped out another, be it oil, land, or just ideology? Don't tell me you think this would be any different."

Angela contemplated before finally answering. "Yes. I'll admit it has and does happen. A lot."

"But now—"

"Let me finish," she said, cutting him off. "Yes. You're right," she acknowledged. "You're right. History is littered with terrible acts against one another. Without a doubt. Will it ever change? I don't know. Maybe it will, and maybe it won't. But good God, Joe. Look at the world today. Look at the fighting and the vitriol. It's everywhere! Is this our future? Is this the way you *want* the world to be? Because I don't."

She took the envelope and shoved it back into her open purse. "The world is lost, Joe. *Lost*. No one knows what's real anymore. No one tries to listen. It's as if the whole world is trapped in some constant, never-ending fight with itself where no one ever wins. They just incessantly attack each other."

"You're making my point for me."

"No, I'm not," she said. "Here we are, you and me, sitting on a park bench knowing something no one else knows. Something that could fundamentally affect people's lives, change them deeply, right down to their cores, and we think it may be too dangerous? Too dangerous for what? Do you really think it could make things *worse* than they are now?"

"Angela—"

"No. Say it, Joe. Say you think the greatest potential discovery—maybe *ever*—is actually going to make things worse."

"What I'm saying," he replied slowly, "is there is something powerful about that place. About that thing. And sooner or later, someone will try to exploit it. Harness it. Use it for their own self-interests."

"So, then *no one* should benefit? Because eventually someone will exploit it?"

Rickards sighed.

She softened her voice. "What do *you* want the world to be like?"

"It doesn't matter what I want."

"How can you say that?"

"Because I don't have any incentive to make it any better. Not anymore."

"None at all?"

"No."

Angela looked around. Her gaze stopped on the playground again and she pointed at the playing children. "Not even for them?"

There was no answer.

"What if your daughter were still here?"

Rickards suddenly shot her a stern glare. "Don't!"

"You said yourself this is bigger than all of us. You, me, anyone."

"That's not what I meant."

"Then tell me this," she said, looking back at the children. "With the path this world is on, do you think things will be better for them... or worse?"

4

Hard polished gray tiles stretched the entire length of the long hallway, creating a loud echo from the woman's heels as she walked.

Nearly every door she passed revealed another elderly patient lying in bed or sitting idly in a wheelchair with old, frail hands folded limply in their laps. Some shook uncontrollably, all against a backdrop of distant coughing.

These patients were all in their final waning days and years. Heads down. Sitting and waiting.

With each door the young woman passed, she briefly glanced in—sympathetically and respectfully—before eventually slowing as she reached the second to the last door, every one of them painted in a muted beige amongst perfectly matching walls.

She glanced in through the small window and, seeing nothing, reached forward to pull open the door, suddenly jumping when it was immediately pushed open from the inside, revealing a black-bearded man dressed in a light tunic and white skull cap.

Squeezing through the door, he promptly greeted the woman.

"A 'Salaam Alaikum."

"Alaikum a 'Salaam." The woman nodded and bowed respectfully, speaking in Arabic. "You were the one who phoned me?"

"Yes, yes. Thank you for coming. We do not have much time."

The young woman, dressed in a plain red dress instead of a traditional hijab, stepped back and peered curiously through the window again. "Time for what?"

"Please," the man answered, widening the door behind

him. "Come. He is very weak."

The woman cautiously followed, unsure of what or who was waiting on the other side of the wooden door. She'd been told almost nothing on the phone, only that it was an urgent matter and she needed to come quickly. Even in modern-day Egypt, when an imam summoned, you were expected to respond.

Inside the small room was a single hospital bed occupied by an older man. Tubes ran from his left arm up to a hanging IV bag, while a mask over his nose and mouth fed his thin, frail body fresh oxygen.

The man remained motionless, watching with a pair of sunken eyes as she entered the room.

"Sit down. Please," urged the imam, who circled the bed and took a seat on the opposite side.

Uncertain, the woman stepped over to the empty chair and eased herself down.

After an uncomfortable silence, she introduced herself in a polite tone, unsure how well the man could hear. "A 'Salaam Alaikum. My name is Mona Baraka. I am a journalist—"

The religious leader interrupted with a reassuring gesture of his hand. "It is okay. He knows who you are. He is the one who asked for you."

With some difficulty, the patient raised a hand and pulled the oxygen mask from his mouth, briefly licking his lips and inhaling before speaking in a low, raspy voice.

"Thank you," he said weakly, "for coming."

"You're welcome," Mona replied, glancing briefly around the room. "What, exactly, am I here for?"

With a heaving chest, the man glanced at the imam to his left, who answered for him. "Tawbah."

Mona blinked and turned back to the old man, studying him.

Tawbah was the Islamic word for 'repentance.'

"My name is Abasi Hamed," he began, inhaling between sentences. "I was born and raised... in a village outside Kharga."

Mona's brief hesitation went unnoticed by both men before she reached into her handbag to retrieve a small audio recorder. "May I record this?"

Hamed, the older man, nodded.

It wasn't the first bedside confession for which she'd been summoned. Quite the contrary—though rarely did they prove to be newsworthy. They were often little more than an unburdening from the person facing the certainty of the great beyond, even from some of the most ardent and faithful believers. It was something to help them feel at ease with their indiscretions or regrets. While these deathbed confessions were critical in helping another human clear their conscience, it was hardly justification for Mona to suddenly drop whatever she was working on. Regardless, she gave a polite smile and offered no hint of annoyance, quietly pressing the small round button on the handheld unit and setting it on her lap.

"I am," the old man corrected himself, "*was* a captain in the Egyptian Air Force from 1963 to 1995." His eyes rolled and peered at the ceiling as he spoke. "Accepted when I was twenty-four years old."

Mona thought for a moment. "You are now 82?"

The old man didn't respond, instead using his energy to inhale again.

"Yes," confirmed the imam.

Hamed nodded. "I served for thirty-two years. I flew F-16 Falcons and later MiG-23s."

Mona was impressed. "That is admirable," she said, but to her surprise, the old man merely shook his head.

"I have served my country," he replied. "Faithfully." After another short breath, he added, "*Mostly*."

He watched while she glanced at the imam. "There are many things of which I am proud," he whispered. "But some of which I am not." Another pause to breathe. He was staring at her now. "By not proud... I mean *ashamed*."

Mona Baraka was unsurprised at the change in subject. "What are you ashamed of?"

It took the man a long time to respond. "I participated in many battles... things they now call *conflicts*. The Romani ambush... The Battle of Suez... The Four-Day War. Many more."

"You served your country well."

Hamed did not respond.

"You need not be ashamed," she offered.

"We are all ashamed," he mumbled.

"If you were—"

The man held up a finger and suddenly coughed violently, prompting the imam to rise and hold a small towel to Hamed's mouth until he gently pushed it away.

"Listen," he said. "Before it is too late."

"Of course."

"Soldiers are not given explanations. We follow orders. That is all." His dark eyes had returned to the ceiling. "But some orders," he said, now almost whispering. "Some orders felt wrong."

"Wrong in what way?"

"I am no longer fearful," he said, changing topics. "My family is now gone. In Jannah." He turned back to the imam. "But for me... it will be Sijjin."

The Islamic equivalent of hell.

Mona followed his gaze to the younger man at his side, staring back at Hamed. "What did you do?" she quietly asked.

"I sought."

She frowned.

"I sought," he repeated.

"Sought what?"

"To know the truth of what I had done." His words stopped until his eyes returned to Mona. "Firing on an enemy you know is easy, at least during combat. But other times..."

20

"You did what you were told," said the imam.

"It will not be enough," the old man croaked. "Not in the eyes of Allah."

"It will be enough," the imam assured him.

Hamed feebly shook his head. "Not this." He turned back to Mona and said, "Sometimes knowledge is worse."

"What do you mean?"

He replied almost painfully. "In 1977, I shot down a private jet."

After a long moment, Mona asked, "Who was in it?"

Hamed's eyes became glassy as though he were staring through her. "*Allah.*"

5

She stared at him with a confused expression. "You shot down Allah?"

The old man nodded.

"What does that mean?"

"It means Sijjin."

The man was beginning to talk in circles.

"Who was on the plane?"

"I did not know," he mumbled, staring through her. "I could not have known."

When she looked at the imam, he shrugged and returned a blank expression.

"It took years," breathed Hamed.

"For what?"

"To find out."

"To find out what?"

Again, he inhaled deeply, desperate for oxygen. "Whose plane it was."

Now Mona leaned forward. "Who?"

"*Shaitan.*"

She looked to the imam for clarification but received none.

Demons?

"I don't understand."

Hamed coughed again, this time with more spittle, caught once again by the imam's cloth. "You will."

No sooner had the words left his mouth that the old man's eyes widened, and his chest heaved without warning.

Once, then twice, before collapsing back into his frail body. In an instant, his eyes, dark and sullen, became lifeless.

Hamed was gone. Two nurses were in the room within seconds and together made a final, desperate effort to resuscitate him, until finally giving up and checking his pulse one last time. One of the two women turned and glanced between the imam and Mona, standing back against the wall, while the other gently reached down and closed Hamed's eyes.

A stunned Mona watched in eerie silence as though she were disconnected from the scene in front of her, while the imam dutifully stepped forward and began reciting a prayer from his open Quran.

Immediately following the prayers, and without a word, Mona was led out of the room and down the small hospital's hallway until the imam found an unoccupied room.

He pulled her inside and closed the door behind them. "His Tawbah is complete."

Mona was still reeling. "What?"

"He travels beyond now… unburdened."

"But he didn't finish."

The imam seemed not to hear her. "His burden has been passed to you."

"I don't–"

The leader finally stared at her and replied, "You will carry this forward."

"Carry what forward? He didn't finish. He didn't tell me *anything*."

The imam reached into his tunic and pulled something out—a large leather binder, aged and tattered.

"What is that?"

"It is for you," the imam said, placing it in her hands. "His instructions."

"Wait, wait," Mona said, stepping back and blinking

several times. "What is happening? What is this?"

"Here," he said of the binder, "are your answers."

"I can't. I was just—"

"You must take it forward now."

"Take *what* forward?"

The imam reached out and simply placed his hand on the binder. "This."

6

Joe Rickards sat solemnly and silently in his car, his hands resting on each side of the steering wheel as he waited behind a long line of cars at the intersection of East Colfax and Colorado Boulevard. It was a testament to Denver's rapidly growing population, now making daytime traffic through the city almost unbearable.

At the moment, it went largely unnoticed by Rickards.

Instead, he remained motionless, lost in thought over what Angela had said to him, coupled with the memory of a recent conversation he'd had with a priest in Bolivia.

It had been a discussion about suffering and loss and the often-inescapable trap of misery. Of true regret. A trap from which no amount of time or grief could free a person. No amount of reflection or therapy. Not even alcohol.

For there were some parts of the human heart that simply would not let go.

Ever.

Unaffected by reckoning or penance, there were places where some wounds never healed, and the only hope was in everlasting diversion.

In all the years the priest had consoled people through pain and loss, the one thing he'd told Rickards that would help–the only thing–was *purpose*.

Purpose alone.

The soul's one and only path for escape from the black hole of true misery.

Purpose.

He thought again of the playground, remembering back to one of the many days he'd been there with his daughter, watching her laugh and play with the other children, running in and out through the metal poles of the play structure until coming upon a smaller boy who'd fallen. He'd sat in the soft layer of wood chips crying and calling for his mother.

The boy was unhurt, but Rickards remembered watching his young daughter wrap her tiny arms around him and help him up. It was one of the sweetest things Rickards had ever witnessed. His daughter's genuine, untainted care for someone she didn't even know still touched him to that day, still resonated with him.

How proud he was of that little heart of hers.

He was so lost in thought that he did not immediately hear it—a noise outside. There was a commotion somewhere in the traffic behind him, within the endless line of cars waiting to inch forward beneath the stifling sun.

What he eventually heard was yelling, followed by the slamming of a door, prompting Rickards to turn and look over his shoulder a few cars back to two men who'd climbed out of their vehicles and were continuing to yell at each other.

Both appeared to be in their forties or fifties. Rickards watched as one man approached the second, yelling and waving his arms in unintelligible acrimony, spewing vitriol until just a few feet away and mere moments before the second man suddenly lashed out, punching him in the face and immediately sending him onto the hard pavement like a large bag of sand toppling over.

Almost simultaneously, honks erupted from all directions as the light turned green and dozens of cars impatiently pushed forward.

Rickards leaned and checked his side mirror to watch the fallen man slowly rise back to his feet and stumble away, returning to his vehicle.

It was a minor clash lasting mere seconds, and yet, for Rickards, the brutality lay not in the skirmish itself but in the reality of it. The vitriol. Without choreography or TV-like glorification. An actual assault in broad daylight at a stoplight.

There it was. Vitriol. The word Angela had used. Cruelty and bitterness.

7

She opened the door to find Rickards standing on her front step, pensive and sullen, staring back at Angela and her look of surprise.

"Okay."

She frowned. "Excuse me?"

"I said okay."

"What are you talking about?"

"I'll help."

Angela's face lit up. "Just like that?"

"Just like that."

"I'm... surprised."

"At finding me on your porch or that I've agreed to help?"

She grinned. "Both."

"Well, at least I didn't do it at seven o'clock in the morning."

***

Inside, Angela placed a glass of water on the coffee table in front of him and then walked around to the opposite side.

She sat, resting both hands on her knees and continuing to grin. "I still can't believe you're here."

He was slow to answer. "I've been thinking about what you said."

"And that convinced you?!"

Rickards picked up the water and took a sip. "Let's not beat a dead horse. I'm here."

"No beating," she mused. "Or flogging. I'm just happy you changed your mind."

"So, what all did you find out about Mike Morton's

friend?"

"As I said, he's retired and teaches now. College level, following a long career at NASA, just as Mike did."

"I guess they take their work seriously. Where's he at?"

Angela beamed back at him. "That's the best part. He lives in Hawaii."

"Hawaii?"

She nodded. "Maui."

"Not a bad place to retire."

"Exactly. Who wouldn't want to live in paradise? Have you ever been?"

Rickards shook his head and reached for another drink. "You?"

"Once," she said, smiling. "It's beautiful."

"At least there's an upside, I guess."

"Right. But here's the thing… I was thinking it might be better not to call him first."

"Why is that?"

"Mike said this man Townsend was the only other person who should see the data, but we don't know what kind of relationship they had."

"You don't think they got along?"

"I really don't know." Angela shrugged. "But Mike did say everyone else thought he was crazy all those years. That may include Townsend. Hopefully not, but if it does, what if he shoots us down before we even get there?"

"Like on the phone."

"Right."

"Then case closed."

"Wait, that's it? Everything just stops?"

"If the guy's not interested…"

Angela folded her arms. "Uh, yeah. No. If he rejects the idea, he can do it right in front of us—*after* we've shown him Mike's data."

Rickards shrugged. "We could end up taking a long plane ride for nothing."

"I wouldn't call it for nothing," she winked. "They have movies on the flight. And peanuts."

8

A world away and late at night, Mona Baraka sat quietly in her Cairo apartment studying the contents of the strange binder given to her by the imam. Cracked and peeling at each corner, it now lay spread across her small kitchen table filled with several dozen documents, letters, and photos. Some were originals and some Xeroxed, with a few even appearing to be copies of copies, all in what first appeared to be random order, but upon closer inspection looked primarily chronological.

But she still had no idea what it was all supposed to be.

There were documents on more than a dozen international companies, along with some of their financial filings, five of which had gone out of business years ago. Then there were the barely legible, handwritten letters and almost a hundred different Xeroxed pictures and newspaper clippings. But there was no apparent connection to all of them. None that she could see.

Why didn't the imam just tell her what this was all about? Clearly, the old man had revealed more to him than Mona. So why not just tell her what she was searching for?

All she knew was that it had something to do with a plane in 1977, owned by someone, or something, that took Abasi Hamed years to piece together. But so far, she couldn't find a single reference to the airplane incident. Not even in the hundred or so photocopied articles. Did the old man think she could read minds?

And why her? There were hundreds of journalists in Egypt, many of whom were far more prominent, with teams of people or staff who could make much faster work of this than she.

Mona leaned back in her chair and sighed before rubbing her face and pushing her chair back from the table. She stood and strolled into her apartment's modest kitchen.

She opened a colored glass cabinet and withdrew a small packet and teabag, filled the steel kettle with water, placed it on a burner, twisting the dial until a large puff of blue flame leaped out and promptly turned it down.

She leaned against the narrow counter and absently stared at the stove.

Why her? Why not one of the hundreds of male journalists who had access to so many more resources? Or even a man in her own office?

Mona's eyes wandered, and she spotted her dim reflection in the glass pane of the adjacent cabinet, her arms folded and a frown on her lips.

Life in Egypt was hard enough for a woman, especially one trying to establish a career. Between the incessant sexual harassment from her coworkers, the pressure from her entire family to get married and the constant derision from every corner of society for things as trivial as how she wore her hair, it often felt like too much.

Too much to make the constant struggle worthwhile.

Still watching herself in the glass, she reached up with her right hand and released the tight bun behind her head, letting her black hair fall around her shoulders in a private act of defiance.

She didn't have time for this. She already had too much work to do—assignments and stories that none of the male reporters wanted and likely no one would read anyway. All for a meager salary that barely paid for her tiny apartment.

How much longer could she endure it all? How much–

She suddenly stopped in mid-thought.

In the reflection, Mona slowly tilted her head, returning to a thought just a moment ago.

Why… Her?

One of the breaking stories currently being covered by multiple outlets was yet another corruption scandal, this one allegedly involving the Egyptian Prime Minister and two of his cabinet members. It was hardly a surprise to anyone, given the deep history of corruption in the country, but what stood out this time was the involvement of three different well-known journalists who'd participated in the coverup, skimming millions of Egyptian pounds through agricultural land ownership and reclamation fees. The story didn't just highlight another channel of corruption within the government but how easily journalists and reporters could also be bought.

The story had been going on for weeks and now suggested that at least two of the journalists involved had not been bribed but *blackmailed*. They were successful, well-known men with everything to lose if they didn't cooperate. Evidently, someone had something on both of them.

Which prompted Mona to ask her question one more time.

Why… Her?

Was it possible the old man—Abasi Hamed—wanted to give his information to someone who could not be blackmailed? Because in Mona's case, she had nothing to be blackmailed over. Literally. No scandals. No money. Not even a reputation to speak of. At least not yet.

She continued staring forward in a trance for a long time before suddenly turning back to the stove when her tea kettle began to whistle. She stepped forward and quickly took it off the flame.

Absently, she continued to ponder as she turned off the stove.

Could that be it? Could Hamed have chosen her because she had nothing to lose?

Pouring the water into a flower-covered teacup and placing the kettle back atop the stove, then through the trail of rising steam, turned to view the binder again on the table.

News and the momentum of a story could be highly unpredictable. So much so that the attention over the prime minister's allegations was already being overlooked following the new revelations about the three journalists.

Perhaps that was what Abasi Hamed was trying to avoid with her.

But if that were true, he had to have known the challenges she would face as a woman, just how little time and resources a single female reporter would have—especially if he needed a country controlled by men to believe whatever it was he'd given her.

Unless he didn't.

9

"Hello?"

"Omar, it's Mona. Are you awake?"

Following a long pause, the man finally replied. "Who is it?"

"It's Mona. Mona Baraka. Did I wake you?"

"Who?"

"MONA!"

On the other end, Omar Maher frowned and propped himself up on one elbow in his bed, emerging beneath a single silk sheet.

"Take it easy. I'm joking," he replied. "What time is it?"

"A little after 1:00."

Maher momentarily pulled the phone away from his ear and glanced at it. "In the morning?"

"Should I call back?"

"Why?" he sighed. "I was only in paradise, surrounded by my seventy-two Houri."

Mona smiled. "Sorry. I thought you might still be up."

"I am now. What is it?"

"I need some help from the smartest financial analyst I know."

"Of course you do. I'll make it easy. Gold and local bonds."

"That's not the sort of help I'm looking for."

"How about some real estate? I have a nice pyramid I can sell you."

"I'm serious. I need help looking into some companies—international companies."

"This for a story?"

"Yes. And it may be important."

"Let me guess," he said, exhaling. "Someone, somewhere, did something bad."

"Are you done?"

Maher managed a tired smile. "I think so. How many companies?"

"Fourteen. I have a bunch of financial statements, but I don't know what to make of them."

"What kind of statements."

"I'm not sure. Maybe income statements?"

"Digital?"

"Paper. But I've scanned them."

"Okay. Send them over. How urgent is this?"

"It's hard to say until I know more."

"Fine. I'll try to take a look at them tomorrow if I can."

"Perfect. Thank you, Omar."

"What are friends for," he replied sarcastically, "but to wake up in the middle of the night for something that doesn't involve them at all?"

This time, Mona laughed. "I owe you a favor."

"You owe me a lot of favors."

"Then I owe you *another* one."

"Can I go back to sleep?"

"Yes. Thank you."

With that, the call ended, leaving Mona scrolling through her giant scanned file on her computer. Forty-two pages in all. Page after page of numbers and columns, several of which had been circled on different pages, presumably by Hamed. Different columns, different numbers and different dates.

On her screen, she clicked out of the file and back to her browser, where a picture of a much younger Abasi Hamed was displayed.

Taken decades before, he was dressed in a tan military uniform and a dark blue cap and was staring intently toward the camera. He was almost unrecognizable from the man

Mona had met in the hospital, except for the eyes. Those same dark, fierce eyes.

10

The seven-hour trip to Maui was utterly uneventful—at least so far, with Joe Rickards and Angela Reed seated near the back of the plane and just thirty minutes left until touchdown.

Through the small window, Joe could make out the cloudy outline of the largest island of *Hawaii* in the distance as if slowly floating by on the gray-blue horizon.

The landing was bumpy as expected, with Maui's Kahului Airport nestled between the island's two largest mountains, both covered in lush-green vegetation. Together they produced a funnel of warm ocean air through the middle of the island's valley and a final layer of turbulence for the pilots as they moved through it to drop the aircraft the last hundred feet onto Kahului's gray runway with a firm bounce.

Immediately, the engine thrust was redirected to slow the plane while inside an unfazed Rickards continued staring through the window, noting the fields of tall grass just beyond the airport's runway as the plane shook from side to side. The grass bobbed heavily to one side under the island's natural wind tunnel, creating waves of rolling green.

Next to him, Angela grinned from her seat while reaching forward to retrieve her cell phone. "Much better than last time."

The last time had been to Peru, and the flight had been fraught with turbulence and sudden, albeit brief, drops in elevation—enough to make half the plane nervous and the other half nauseated.

"Try not to look like a tourist."

"What?"

"I'm joking," she said. "In Hawaii, you're *supposed* to look like a tourist." She looked him over in his gray polo shirt and blue jeans as if only now noticing his attire. "Never mind."

Once inside the open-air terminal, they each towed a small suitcase behind them and followed the flow of passengers along an open walkway and then down a narrow escalator, passing Baggage Claim and heading for the automated shuttle.

Ten minutes later, the two exited a two-story building in search of their rental car, a blue Toyota Camry they found waiting for them in the building's large underground parking lot.

With a heft of their bags and the trunk closed, Rickards opened the driver's door and made a brief 360-degree scan before sliding in and starting the car.

"Sorry," Angela said, turning on the air conditioning. "I should have warned you about the humidity. Very different than Denver."

"That's okay. I enjoy clothes that stick. So—where to, Professor?"

"The college," she said, opening a navigation app on her phone and waiting for it to pinpoint their location.

***

The University of Hawaii Maui was less than five miles from the Kahului Airport and took just fifteen minutes to reach through the island's afternoon traffic. Situated on one of the most beautiful islands in the world, the small college was an outgrowth of the island's original vocational college built in the 1930s. Now providing several bachelor programs and dozens of associates, the college was spread over a square kilometer in the form of two dozen buildings, all painted matching white under tropical green shingled roofs.

IKE, the science and math building, was located on the western edge of the campus next to its adjacent and virtually empty parking lot.

Rickards glanced at the clock on their Camry's dash as he pulled to a stop next to the only two remaining cars. "Looks like class is out."

"Most of them end before 3:00 p.m. Hopefully, our Mr. Townsend is still around."

Together, they climbed out and approached the main entrance, crossing an open patch of Hawaii's thick zoysia grass where two glass doors were propped open, welcoming in the afternoon breeze.

Scanning a small directory, they located the mathematics classrooms without difficulty and peeked inside each one. All three were empty. Finding nothing and no one else, the two climbed a set of wide stairs to the second floor, where more rooms lined the hallway, along with several offices, one bearing Townsend's name on a light-colored plate.

"Locked."

Angela frowned and looked up and down the hall. Hearing someone talking near the far end, she and Rickards followed the noise and reached the final classroom, finding two students conversing.

"Excuse me," Angela interrupted. "Do you know if Professor Townsend is around?"

One of the two girls, attractive with distinct Polynesian features, shook her head. "He usually leaves around two o'clock."

"Every day?"

"Like clockwork." The girl nodded.

"Do you know what time he arrives in the morning?"

"I think his first class is at eleven. So probably about 10:30, unless there's a faculty meeting."

"I see." Angela smiled. "Thank you."

Both girls politely returned a smile and resumed their conversation, leaving Angela and Rickards falling back into the darkened hallway.

"That was quick."

"I guess it's onto Plan B. Unless you want to wait until tomorrow."

"What's Plan B?"

Angela reached down and pulled her phone from her purse. "I have his home address."

***

Forty minutes away by car and along the island's west coast, Lahaina had once served as the capital of the Kingdom of Hawaii. In present day, the city still rested upon the ruins of Lahaina Fort, which dated back two hundred years and held the distinction of being the island's largest census-designated place, or CDP.

With 11,000 permanent residents, the district often swelled to over 40,000 during peak tourist season, with an epicenter precisely two miles north on the same road onto which Joe and Angela had just turned. They slowed, looking for Townsend's address.

The house was smaller than either were expecting, built upon a small, narrow lot that looked as though it had been squeezed between two much larger homes.

Rickards and Angela parked and approached the house, stopping in front of its waist-high chain-link fence. On the other side, a modest green lawn appeared long and unkept and in the process of being slowly retaken by dozens of nearby bushes. Multiple potted plants lined the porch, all wilted and browning.

The two looked at each other before Rickards raised the metal clasp of the gate and swung it open. They made their way over the overgrown walkway leading to the porch.

Once on the porch, they gave each other one last glance before Rickards pulled the wooden screen door open and knocked loudly.

11

There was no answer.

After a long silence, he opened the screen and knocked again.

Still nothing.

"Hmm." He stepped to the side and peered in through the front window into a darkened living room.

"What do you see?"

"Not much. Furniture. Pictures. An old piano. And some of the kitchen."

Angela stepped in next to him and raised both hands to block the reflection. "Looks clean and neat."

"And old."

She nodded. "Like the furniture my parents would have. Or my grandparents."

Rickards straightened and knocked a third time, unsurprised by the silence that followed. "Okay, time for Plan C."

Angela glanced up at him. "I don't have a Plan C."

"No C?"

"Nope."

"How about a D?"

"Is this your idea of humor?"

He turned around, scanning the street and watching as a car drove past. Then he checked his watch.

"Are you sure we have the right house?"

"Pretty sure," Angela said, double-checking her phone. At the same time, Joe noticed something. He descended the stairs and strode across the thick grass and back out through the gate, following the short fence to a mailbox at the far end near the driveway where he proceeded to open the front flap and look inside.

He reached in and withdrew three envelopes.

"What are you doing? Isn't that illegal?"

"Not unless I open them." Rickards rotated one of the envelopes. "It's definitely his house. This is addressed to him and his wife."

"Maybe they're just out, then."

He nodded and returned the letters. "Probably."

Scanning the street again, Rickards noticed a neighbor watching them from a few doors down. He grinned politely and turned back around. "I don't suppose you have his phone number."

"I do. But I wanted to talk in person, remember?"

"Right. I guess it's either later tonight or tomorrow, then."

"To be honest, I'm getting a little tired, and it's almost eight o'clock our time. Why don't we check into the hotel and try the school again tomorrow?"

After checking in to their hotel, they found the Mexican restaurant recommended by the front desk clerk. As they sat waiting for their food, they watched the sun slowly descend over the island of Molokai and the small evening waves lapping at the shore nearby.

"This is nice," said Angela with a sigh before picking up and sipping her wine.

Staring out over the glittering water, Rickards nodded without a sound.

Nice had become a meaningless term—at least for him. There was so little in the world he was able to enjoy without his wife and daughter. Instead, each day merely felt like the one before, a long series of unending days and nights. Some, like this one, were even beautiful enough for him to feel guilty over witnessing it without them.

Across the table, Angela could read the expression in his eyes, momentarily sparkling blue beneath the sun's dying rays.

"Are you okay?"

Rickards nodded.

"Thinking about your family?"

He looked at her, this time without nodding.

"They're here with you, Joe. You know that."

He turned back to the water, pondering, unable to keep from thinking of all the days they would miss—that everyone would miss once their time was up. Thousands, millions of beautiful days like this. Somewhere in the world.

Unexpectedly, he thought of his parents, both passed on. *His mother loved the rain. And the snow. How many days had she missed? How many beautiful snowfalls?*

Sometimes he was just unable to accept the full magnitude of the loss and the painful reality that the world simply moved on without them. And it always would.

Which returned him to a question he still asked himself every day.

Why in the hell was he still here?

12

It was magical.

The rolling waves upon the rock-strewn shore with bubbling sounds as though from a gentle brook. Beautiful, but louder.

Still on Denver time, Angela was up before 6:00 a.m. and decided to take a walk in the cool, early dawn air. It had been years since she'd been to Hawaii and she'd forgotten one of her favorite things about it—the air. The Hawaiian air, with its sweet and unmistakably dewy scent. There was simply nothing else like it.

Few cars and even fewer people were out this early, allowing her a comfortable walk in the street without a sidewalk, where she noticed a brief clearing of reddish dirt and foliage between houses and a small concrete bench.

She sat down and quietly peered out over the water, calm and shimmering under the rising sun behind her. In the distance, dozens of small boats rocked on their moors, their masts swaying back and forth like wobbling tops that refused to fall.

Angela inhaled deeply, allowing the dew-filled air to flow through her nose and into her lungs and then back out again. Unlike Rickards, she was feeling more at peace every day, content with what had happened and stronger from having experienced it.

In truth, she and Joe were searching for the same thing, just from different directions.

Meaning.

She knew about his conversation with the priest in South America and about his explanation to Joe, that purpose and meaning relied on one common denominator.

Responsibility.

And it was true.

Responsibility led to purpose, and purpose led to meaning. It was as easy as that—almost silly in its simplicity, though harder in execution.

But she was trying. Trying to dedicate herself to something meaningful. Something important. Maybe bigger.

What they'd found in Bolivia was astonishing enough, but the magnitude of it all was almost mind-boggling. Impossible. And yet, from what Mike Morton had sent them, maybe not impossible at all.

A second location with perhaps the same incredible properties.

She had no idea what was out there—or whether it was similar to the first…

Or completely and utterly different.

***

They arrived back at the college just past noon, hoping Townsend's first class had let out or shortly would. They stood in the hall as the door finally opened and a small stream of students poured out, eventually followed by a tall, thin black man with glasses and short white hair dressed in comfortable shirt and slacks.

Clearly distracted, he glanced only briefly in their direction, and promptly strode to his office door across the hall, stepping in and quietly closing it behind him.

"Chatty fellow."

Angela grinned. "You just look scary. More like *mean*," she teased and walked toward the office.

He was peering at his laptop screen when the door opened, and the woman from the hall peeked in. "Professor Townsend?"

"Can I help you?"

She glanced back as Townsend studied her and then the larger man as he stepped in.

"May we have a word with you?" Angela asked.

The older man checked his watch and nodded, staring up as both she and Rickards stepped closer.

"We've come to talk to you about something."

He clasped his hands together and placed them on the desk in front of him. "What can I help you with?"

"Well," Angela took a deep breath. "It's actually, more like *who*. An old friend of yours."

Townsend's expression turned curious.

"His name is Mike Morton."

If Rickards and Angela were expecting a reaction, they didn't get one. Townsend's expression never changed.

"Okay."

"Um," she glanced again at Rickards, "do you remember him?"

Townsend stared at her for a long moment. "Yes, I do." His attention moved to Rickards. "Are you from the government or something?"

"Sort of."

"Is he in some kind of trouble?"

Angela started to speak but stopped. She didn't know how to say this. "I'm... afraid he's passed away."

Townsend stared at her again, his mouth falling into a frown. "I'm very sorry to hear that." Again, he turned to Rickards. "I haven't spoken to him in some time, if that's what you're here for."

"Not exactly. May we sit down?"

The professor motioned to two chairs, his gaze following them as they sat.

"Do you recall the last time you spoke with him?"

Townsend pursed his lips thoughtfully and eased back. "A long time ago. Probably seven or eight years."

"Nothing since then?"

"No."

"Was there a problem between you two?"

"Not really." He shrugged. "His wife had just died."

"Did you know his wife?"

"Yes. Very well. She and my wife were friends."

"And you and Mike?"

"Also friends. We worked together most of our careers."

"That was at NASA?"

His face returned to a curious expression. "Did something unusual happen to him?"

"It's a longer story than you may think. Are we keeping you from anything?"

Townsend shook his head. "I'm on my lunch break. My next class isn't until 1:00."

"Good." Angela exhaled. "Mr. Townsend, we're here because Mike Morton requested that we find you."

"He did?"

"Sort of," replied Joe.

Townsend's eyes moved to Rickards. "He sort of told you to find me, or he told you to sort of find me?"

Angela grinned and continued. "The former. You see, we knew Mike briefly before he died."

"Were you with him?"

"Sort of."

Again, Townsend looked at Rickards. "You seem to be in a perpetual state of uncertainty."

Glancing sarcastically at Angela, Rickards nodded. "You have no idea."

"Mr. Townsend, we met Mike largely by accident while traveling in South America."

The professor's brow rose. "South America?"

"That's right."

"How long ago was this?"

"Several months."

"When did he die?"

Angela cleared her throat. "Shortly afterward. Just a few days later."

"From?"

"A heart attack, we think."

Townsend slowly nodded his head. "I'm very sorry to hear that. So, why did he want you to find me, *sort of?*"

"Mike was retired and was in South America after his wife had passed. He was looking for something."

"Like what?"

"Before we get to that, can you tell us in what capacity you and Mike worked together?"

Townsend shrugged and leaned farther back in his chair. "We worked together a lot, actually."

As he spoke, Rickards glanced around the office, noting the waist-high bookcases filled with textbooks, a large blackboard half-covered in scribbled equations, a window and several black-and-white posters of old but smart-looking men and women. Then he turned his gaze back to the large wooden desk beneath a short stack of books and the man's laptop in the middle.

"We joined NASA about the same time," continued Townsend. "The first two black mathematicians to join the rocket and propulsion team." He grinned. "It was a different world back then."

Angela's mouth fell open, unsure what to say.

"Relax." Townsend's grin widened. "That was a long time ago. And truth be told, those men weren't really bigots. We eventually won them over."

"H-how?"

Townsend's lips suddenly grew into a wider grin. "Hubris."

"Excuse me?"

"Hubris," he repeated.

She glanced at Joe. "I don't–"

"Ever hear of John Houbolt?"

"No."

Townsend looked to Rickards, who shook his head.

"How about Wernher von Braun?"

They both shook their heads again.

Townsend rolled his eyes. "Have you ever heard of the Apollo Mission?"

"As in the moon?"

"Yes. The moon. Neil Armstrong?"

"Of course, we've heard of Neil Armstrong."

"Well," said Townsend, "it was the Apollo Mission that got him there. And Wernher von Braun and John Houbolt were a large part of it."

"Von Braun," he continued, "was a famous German rocket scientist during World War II."

"A Nazi?"

"Von Braun was no Nazi. He was merely raised there. Trapped. Not unlike those fellas at NASA, being raised without ever meeting a black person."

"I'm not sure I'm following."

He looked at Angela. "Von Braun was stolen from the Nazis at the end of the war. Let's call it *rescued*. Located and skirted out with hundreds of other scientists for their expertise before the Russians could get them. Von Braun was the brains behind those V2 rockets fired at England. Those were unfortunate but used revolutionary concepts." He looked back and forth at them. "Don't you two ever read any history books?"

Rickards pointed his thumb at Angela. "She's the know-it-all."

"Von Braun and Houbolt helped lead the early Apollo program. But they became adversaries over the best way to get to the moon—more specifically, how to land on it. Von Braun wanted to use a gargantuan rocket to do it, while Houbolt argued it would be too dangerous and take too long."

"And?"

"Houbolt was right. And Von Braun eventually came around, though quite reluctantly."

"What does all this have to do with you and Mike Morton?"

Townsend smiled, displaying a set of perfect white teeth. "Who do you think was on Houbolt's team?"

"You and Mike?"

"Correct. We were part of the team to argue the use of a much smaller lander. The math proved it was the most practical way to go—and ultimately the safest."

"And… the bigotry?"

"I was just making a point—that differences, even in race, are quickly torn down once one side helps the other. Our team was no different. Sure, they were difficult at first, until the first major crack in the wall came, when Mike discovered a math error that could have killed the Apollo 11 launch team. That destroyed a lot of that old-school hubris and we eventually became friends. I still talk with a few of those fellas today. There's not many of us left, and I'll tell you this, there's not an ounce of racism in them anymore."

"That's great." Angela smiled.

"Don't get me wrong—it wasn't like that everywhere, just on our immediate team. But it was a step. And an important lesson in being human."

"You said you still talk to some of these old colleagues?" asked Rickards.

"That's right."

"How often?"

"I don't know. Every six months or so, I guess."

"But not Mike?"

Townsend shrugged. "I didn't know where he was. And besides, he always got talking about other things. Strange things. Theories the rest of us didn't particularly share."

"Do you remember his work on satellites?"

"Of course. I was in a different department in those days, but I assisted him on a few of his birds."

"Do you remember helping him on a project called CERES?"

Townsend's brow dropped into a serious stare. "I do. Why are you asking?"

"Because it's part of the reason we're here."

The professor's expression was beginning to border on dubious as he watched Angela carefully reach into her purse to pull out a large manilla envelope. Without a word, she leaned forward and placed it on his desk.

"What is this?"

Rickards spoke up. "It may be better if you just take a look."

The older man turned his gaze to the desk and picked up the envelope. Opening the flap, he reached in and slid out the packet of papers. On top was Mike Morton's email to Angela.

"He sent that to me the night before he died," she said. "I didn't know until weeks later."

It was unclear whether Townsend had heard her. Instead, he remained quiet, reading.

When he finished the one-page letter, he silently and delicately lifted the page from the stack to reveal the rest of the printed data, carefully examining the first few pages and then flipping through the rest.

Slowly, the professor frowned and dropped his hands on either side of the paper. "I hope," he said with a frown, "you didn't come all the way to Hawaii for this."

"What?"

"Please tell me you're also here on vacation."

"What do you mean?"

Townsend continued frowning and leaned back again, causing his wooden chair to squeak. "I know what this is."

"You do?"

"It's one of the things Mike always tried to talk to us about. Me and the other engineers."

"You didn't believe him?"

The old professor sighed, carefully choosing his words. "It's not that we didn't *believe* him. It's just that some of his ideas were a little... out there."

"Like this?" asked Rickards, nodding at the papers.

"Like this. And other things."

"If you didn't believe him, then why–"

Townsend interrupted Angela. "I just said it wasn't that I didn't believe him. It's because all this CERES business was disproven back in the 70s."

"By whom?"

"Almost everyone on our team. And other teams.

Everyone concurred throughout the department. Except Mike, who was adamant. He wouldn't let it go. He just couldn't accept that it was a glitch in one of his own systems." Townsend looked back and forth at them. "He didn't tell you that, did he?"

"Actually," replied Angela, "he did."

"He did?"

"He told us no one believed him. Then or now."

Townsend began to look perplexed. "And he was still looking for it when he died?"

"In a manner of speaking."

"What does that mean?"

Angela glanced hesitantly at Rickards, who gave her a slight nod.

"What it means, Professor, is that Mike Morton *was right.*"

13

"Pardon?"

"I said… he was right."

Townsend looked over at Rickards, who simply shrugged.

"What do you mean he was right?"

Angela tilted her head sarcastically. "What does it normally mean when a person says someone was right?"

"You're not implying–"

"I'm not implying anything, Doctor. I'm *telling* you he was right. And you were wrong."

Townsend stared at her, confounded. "I don't—"

"Don't what? Believe you can be wrong?"

He stopped to rethink. To compose himself. "What do you mean *exactly* when you say he was right?"

"She means," said Rickards, "that it's real."

"It's real," Townsend echoed.

"Yes," nodded Rickards.

"It's real," repeated Townsend.

"Yes."

"*Real.*"

"You can say it a hundred times, but it won't change anything."

"I'm not, I'm not trying–" he said, pausing again. "By real you mean… what?"

"We saw it."

Townsend peered at Angela with a look of apprehension. "You *saw* it?"

"Correct."

"YOU SAW IT?"

"Yep."

"What *exactly* did you see? Or think you saw?"

"Mike Morton said his instrumentation on the CERES satellite was designed to detect various forms of energy in and around the atmosphere, which it did. But he also said it detected a point of concentration where these different energies appeared to have coalesced and reached the planet's surface." She was now staring intently at Townsend. "Sound familiar?"

"And you're saying the three of you have found this supposed location?"

"No. Not the three of us. Just Joe and me, after Mike passed away."

Townsend blinked and folded his arms. "I see."

Rickards turned to Angela. "I don't think he sees."

Townsend then clasped his hands together in front of him and leaned forward onto the desk. "Okay. I *believe* you think you saw something—whatever that might be. And I also accept that Mike *believed* he'd found something. Or nearly did. But you have to understand," he said, once again glancing down at the papers, "what Mike was proposing flies in the face of almost a hundred years of known, accepted physics."

Angela's tone softened. "Well, we're not in a position to argue that. We're not physicists. Or engineers. All we can tell you is that we found the place Mike had been looking for. Believe me, there was absolutely no question. And now, in his letter to me, Mike claims there is another."

Townsend stared at them. "And you've come to me for—*what?* Validation?"

"No."

"Then what?"

"We want you to help us find it."

Townsend fell silent, continuing to blink as he peered at the two across his large desk.

"You want my help to find it."

"That's right."

"By going through this fifty-year-old data?"

"Yes."

Townsend shook his head in exasperation. "Why?"

"Because it's important."

This time it was the older man who became sarcastic. "Try again."

"Fine. We want to find it for Mike."

He shook his head a second time. "Your answers are getting worse."

"What does it matter *why*?" asked Rickards. "The fact of the matter is that Mike said you were the only one with whom to share this. Not just should but *could*. Which means to me that you may be the only other person who *can* go through all this and make sense of it." Rickards leaned forward, closer to Townsend's desk. "Which makes you, Professor, our only option."

Townsend fell quiet again, this time longer.

"You said yourself that you and Mike were friends," Angela finally said. "Isn't that worth something to you?"

There was no response.

"And your wives?"

Townsend held up a finger and waved it, silencing her. *There was something about the wives*, she thought.

After a long while, Townsend finally cleared his voice and spoke. "Tell me."

"Tell you what?"

"Tell me," he said, "what you *saw* in South America."

Joe and Angela glanced at each other. "And then you'll help us?"

"Maybe."

"Try again," mocked Angela.

"I will *try* to help you. For Mike."

"To begin with, we'll need to know its location," she said. "Which, judging from what little I can understand, may lie somewhere in the Middle East."

Townsend nodded.

After a brief silence, Angela nodded too. "Okay, we'll

tell you *exactly* what we saw. But don't stand up."

"Why not?"

"For *this*… you'll want to remain seated."

14

"Mona, it's Omar. Sorry for taking so long to call back. Things took longer than expected. I was waiting on a friend at the Ministry of Finance to pull some records."

"Did you find anything?"

"Yes, on all fourteen of your companies. As well as a few other things. You ready?"

"Yes!" she said, running back to her computer. "Go ahead."

"To begin with, it looks like six out of your fourteen companies are dead—not five. Completely shut down. But even for those, my friend was able to come up with some info, enough to see they're all connected."

"Connected, how?"

"They're all privately owned—by the same person."

"Really?!"

"Yep. And I had to do quite a bit of digging to find out who. Because they certainly didn't make it easy."

"Do you think that's on purpose?"

"I think so. This person is buried deep beneath dozens of different corporations, shell companies, subsidiaries and a host of other legal entities, all located—or should I say *distributed*—throughout the world. Which is why it took me so long to find a name."

"So, who is it?"

"Have you ever heard of a man named Mido Saad?"

Mona shook her head. "I don't think so. Should I have?"

"Don't know. I'd never heard of him, either, but he's worth a lot of money."

"How much?"

"Hundreds of millions."

"There's a lot of people in the world worth that much."

"True. But most are well known to a lot of people. This man Saad appears to be a mystery to everyone."

"Did your friend know who he was?"

"No," Omar answered. "No one I've asked does. This guy keeps a low profile. Very low. Not just personally, but professionally, too. Considering how opaque his companies are, I'm guessing few people know how much this guy is really worth."

"Exactly how much are we talking about?"

"I can only guess—not just based on numbers but the level of complexity involved in these businesses. His net worth could easily be in the billions."

"It goes that deep?"

"A lot of companies have complex structures, Mona. Either to spread out their risk or minimize their tax base, or both. But I've never seen a structure that goes this deep. We're talking many, many levels. Dozen more into which I didn't even have time to look."

"Do you think it's some kind of criminal organization?"

"Surprisingly, no. I haven't found any red flags. Granted, I couldn't get a heck of a lot of detail, but normally, things don't pass the smell test pretty quickly if something is off, even without hard evidence."

"So, nothing with Mido Saad?"

"All I'm saying is I didn't smell anything. So, either this guy is one of the smartest guys on the planet, or his companies are clean. But–" Omar clarified, "just because a company is clean doesn't mean they're not hiding something."

"Like what?"

"It could be anything. I may not have smelled anything, but the level of complexity this guy has gone to is weird. This amount of distribution and decentralization would have to result in a huge amount of inefficiency. And I mean *huge*. So, the question is, who would do that on purpose?"

"And why?"

"Right. And there's something else. I can't prove anything without more data, but it *feels* like Saad made his money rather quickly."

"What do you mean?"

"It doesn't feel as if this money goes back all that far. Not like aristocracies. Sure, he's made more over the years, but it seems like most of it happened in the 60s or 70s, which was much harder before Big Tech. And he's Egyptian, yet none of us have ever heard of him? Very strange in my opinion."

"You can't find anything on him?"

"I can search and find some stuff on him, but it's not much. At best, articles that are infrequent or sporadic. What little I did see talks mostly about his philanthropy."

"Philanthropy?"

"He's big on that. And you'll never guess where the guy spends a lot of his money. And I mean *a lot*."

"Where?"

"How about orphanages?"

"Really?"

"Yep. He spends a lot of money building and supporting private orphanages all over the continent, from South Africa to Egypt and everywhere in between."

"None of the companies I gave you were orphanages."

"Nope. Those were all for construction companies or utilities and a few smaller manufacturing plants. No orphanages. But they seem to make a lot of the money the orphanages receive. On the surface, it looks as if this guy is a true *wali*, the likes of which I've never seen."

Mona stopped typing on her keyboard. "So, this huge, ultra-complex system of companies does nothing but serve orphans?"

"Well, I wouldn't say that. A lot of money goes to them, but I'm sure not all of it does. Just a lot more than I've ever seen from *any* organization. At least that's the impression I've gotten after digging for a couple of days."

"Maybe that's intentional, too," Mona suggested.

"Maybe. But I'll leave the real digging to you."

She stared down at her phone pensively. "That's certainly more than I was expecting."

"I would be interested to hear what else you find, especially if you get ahold of any more financials. Something tells me this is only the tip of the iceberg."

"And nothing you saw smells fraudulent."

"Nothing nefarious. But remember, it was just a small whiff. If there is something, it would have to be much deeper and harder to find. Or..."

"Or what?"

"Or the guy is clean. A legitimate saint."

Having already typed Saad's name into her browser, Mona brought up a picture. "So, he's either one of the smartest people in the world or one of the most generous."

Omar laughed. "More or less. Good luck in finding out which."

"Thanks, Omar. I can't tell you how much I appreciate this."

"No problem. Just call me during the day next time instead of the middle of the night."

She smiled and ended the call, gently placing her phone down next to her computer. Then she opened an empty document and spent the next ten minutes typing, capturing as many details as she could from the conversation.

What Omar had found was not only unexpected but just the opposite of what she'd been hoping for. Part of her wanted both a simple answer and a quick resolution. She already had too much work on her plate and didn't have room to take on something new, especially like this.

But she also had to admit there was something undeniably titillating about what Omar had just told her—along with the binder itself—including a handwritten letter of which she was now able to read pieces. It appeared to be from the person who, decades ago, had sent the old man Abasi Hamed those financial records.

Maybe it was a hunch, or just a wisp of female intuition

combined with that innate desire of all good journalists to find the truth. Her instinct was telling Mona this was just the beginning of something much bigger.

No one knew just how big of a story a single clue might turn out to be, or how significant or profound. Some stories, even where least expected, turned out to be genuinely earth-shattering and enough to launch even the most minor career into the journalistic stratosphere.

Others were about life and death.

15

When the polished chrome elevator doors parted, Mido Saad looked different from the picture Mona had found. He was older by several years and now well into his seventies, when a person's physical appearance seemed to accelerate to the downside, fighting against both time and fate.

His dark face was overly sullen, with cheeks whose skin was thinning along with the rest of his face and body, covering lean muscles not as strong as they once were. His white hairline was visibly receding.

However, even with the malaise of old age well upon him, Saad's movements betrayed nothing of the sort as he stepped purposefully from the private elevator, walking smoothly and well-balanced down a long, empty hallway covered in polished marble below beige painted walls. Plain and unadorned, it extended almost a hundred feet to a secured doorway at the opposite end and located sixty feet below ground and more highly protected than many Swiss vaults.

Walking in silence, the only notable sound came from each step of his Berluti leather shoes off the marble flooring. He walked slowly and methodically until he reached the reinforced metal door, where he placed his palm upon a small scanner and waited for the giant lock to disengage. The door obediently slid open.

It was a simple room, formed from three feet of solid concrete and measuring thirty feet along each inside wall and painted in the same bright beige as the hallway. The room maintained a perfect 68-degree temperature and carried not so much as a whisper of sound.

They were called safe rooms by some. Panic rooms by

others. But to Saad, it was more than that. It was his *thinking* room.

A place utterly devoid of all distraction.

A large modern computer desk sat along one wall with its screen powered off. Next was a bar and an overhead television screen facing four plush leather chairs covered in smooth, black Royalin leather arranged in a semicircle in the center of the room.

These were demure and modest accommodations, given the significance of both the room and its owner, all of which were merely secondary in purpose.

The room's real purpose was dedicated almost exclusively to what covered the rest of the four walls.

Hundreds of pieces of standard 8½x11 inch sheets of paper filled nearly every square inch of available surface, each carefully and meticulously hung beside one another in a veritable mosaic of drawings. They were bright and vivid and each one hand colored.

But unlike paintings that reflected the hand of an adept and talented artist, these were nothing of the sort. Instead, they were wild and unrefined, amateurish, with objects and shapes lacking any sophistication or maturity. As if hastily and sloppily colored.

Hundreds of pictures displayed a cacophony of objects, shapes, pictures and numbers, some recognizable and some not. There were animals, human stick figures, cars and buildings. Clouds, flames and trees. Everything one could imagine. An actual menagerie of images drawn by young hands and stitched perfectly together into an attentive patchwork covering each wall.

Individual pages provided a glimpse inside the mind of a child. It was a collection only one other person in the world besides Saad knew existed.

That person was sitting in an equally comfortable group of chairs in Zambia in a bright and openly lit room just outside the ramshackle village of Kaindu, where large African tulip trees waved outside in the warm morning breeze.

The woman looked up from her computer tablet when the door finally opened, and a neatly uniformed staff member peeked her head in.

"Are you ready?" she asked in Arabic.

The older woman, in her late fifties, trim with long, black-dyed hair, nodded. She lowered her device and leaned back in the chair. "Send them in."

The younger woman nodded and momentarily disappeared before the door swung open wider, and she ushered several others inside.

She whispered and pointed forward, instructing the children to line up against the wall and allowing the dark-haired woman an unobstructed view of each.

One by one, they complied, walking in short steps until reaching their spot along the wall and sheepishly turning forward. They were all cleanly dressed. Girls between the ages of six and nine, as requested.

The dark-haired psychiatrist casually rose from her seat and walked several steps forward to the first girl in line, carefully examining her up and down before moving to the next.

Slowly. One at a time.

When finished with the initial inspection, she would take each into an isolated room for a more thorough examination, looking for marks to indicate signs of physical abuse. Then would come the questioning and assessment to determine whether any of the girls might require mental or emotional counseling, something that would take days before she would do the same with the boys.

16

Leonard Townsend's reaction to Angela and Joe's story was not at all what they were expecting. Rather than shock or even a laughing dismissal, he instead stared at them for an uncomfortably long time. No questions. No statements. He just stared at them with no movement of any kind.

When he finally did move, it was to lean down and quietly reach into one of the desk's side drawers to retrieve a piece of paper. He then picked up a pen and scribbled a message onto it before looking back at them and standing up.

He walked to the door, opened it, crossed the hall and using a push pin, he posted his message on a small bulletin board next to the classroom door.

He returned and picked up the stack of papers Angela had brought, sliding them carefully back into the envelope.

"Are you okay?" she asked.

Townsend paused to stare at her again before stating, "I need time to think about this."

"Shall we come back?"

"Where are you staying?"

"Uh, the Lahaina Coast Inn just off Front Street."

"If you'll excuse me." With that, Townsend closed and lifted his laptop, slipped it into his carrying case and exited the room, leaving Angela and Rickards alone in his office bemusedly staring at each other.

"What the hell was that?"

Joe Rickards frowned at the open doorway and gradually shook his head. "Well, that was weird."

Townsend's note on the board stated simply: *Class Cancelled* along with the day's date, again leaving both of his visitors standing bewildered in the empty hall.

***

It was another forty-five-minute drive back to Lahaina, where the two pulled into their modest hotel's lot and parked in one of only two remaining spots. During the trip, the two had run through scenarios of what Townsend might say—and ultimately do, leaving Angela worried and second-guessing her decision to surprise Townsend in person with the information.

"He did say he would help."

Rickards nodded. "Before we told him everything."

She turned to face him. "That shouldn't matter. He said–"

Rickards surprised Angela, not by interrupting, but by laughing. "Shouldn't matter? Think about what we just told him, Angela. And about what we saw. Unfortunately, he doesn't exactly strike me as the believing sort."

"But…"

"But what?"

"We told him everything exactly as it happened."

"And think about how we must have sounded."

"Who in their right mind would make up something like that?"

"Have you ever heard an alien abduction story?"

When Angela glowered, he continued. "This isn't about originality. It's about believability. And we just spent an hour telling the guy that the laws of physics as he knows them may not apply in a tiny canyon in South America. If you were him, wouldn't that strike you as more than a little ridiculous?"

"I suppose. But this isn't just from us. It's also from–"

"Mike Morton. Yes, I know. But you heard the man. Morton wasn't exactly a ringing endorsement of sensibility in their field."

"Well, he has the data now."

"He does—which is what you were hoping to accomplish. And you did."

Angela frowned. "So, what are you saying? Just forget about it?"

"I'm saying it's out of your hands. Now all you can do is wait and see what happens."

"But what if he *does* think we're crazy? We have to–"

"No," said Rickards, raising a cautionary hand. "We don't have to do anything. If someone thinks you're crazy, trying to convince them otherwise in a fit of desperation never helps. Trust me."

She opened her mouth to speak but stopped and closed it again, frustrated, but reluctantly agreeing.

"I don't like this."

"Neither do I," said Rickards. "And I didn't even want to come."

She turned with a quip but found him grinning at her.

"Look, it is what it is. Just let it be and see what happens. And hope he finds something in Morton's data that changes his mind—or at the very least stirs some curiosity."

Angela folded her arms and turned to look out her side window. "What do we do until then?"

Rickards shrugged. "I could eat."

***

In the ten minutes it took to drive to reach Kaanapali Beach north of Lahaina, something changed.

From the passenger seat, Angela could sense a difference in Joe. He seemed to grow quiet and anxious, judging by his driving, which now was beginning to seem a little erratic, as though he was irritated. There was a notable difference from the longer drive they'd just made from the college.

She remained quiet in her seat, watching him from the side and saying nothing while he accelerated in and out of the cars on the two-lane highway, only to calm down again and move back to the right-hand lane.

"Everything okay?" she finally asked.

"Fine."

Reaching Kaanapali, he turned left with the other cars and wound around the large section of golf course. But when they reached Whalers Village, he continued driving, completely missing or else ignoring the GPS instructions from her phone to make a turn.

Instead, Joe turned another direction and headed up a steep incline onto Kekaa Drive, where he turned right and looped back onto the highway and then back toward the same turn they'd just made, now from the opposite direction.

"Joe?"

He didn't answer.

She decided not to press the issue. He was most likely growing tired. Or perhaps it was just the distinctly male habit of not wanting to ask directions after making a mistake.

Not that it mattered. This time he turned into the Whaler's parking garage as expected and found a spot on the bottom level.

Without speaking, they climbed out of the car and walked the two hundred or so yards toward the scattering of restaurants overlooking the beach and ocean.

After being seated, they ordered without conversation and eventually started to eat.

They were halfway through lunch when Rickards finally spoke, peering through the crowds of people strolling by.

"I need to tell you something," he said. "And I need you to stay calm."

Midbite, Angela swallowed part of her burger and nodded.

"I think we're being followed."

She stared across the table, unsure whether she'd heard him correctly. "What?"

"I said I think we're being followed."

"Why do you think that?"

"Because when we left the hotel, there was a car behind us that I've seen before. Twice."

She blinked at him. "Couldn't it just have been someone from the same hotel or a car that looked the same? A lot of rental companies—"

"I considered that," he said, "but I saw it near the college earlier. And it wasn't until I made that circle back out to the highway that they finally broke off." He picked up his glass of water and sipped, continuing to speak behind it. "Now there are two men outside this restaurant maintaining eyesight with us."

"Eyesight?"

"Yes."

She began to turn when Rickards suddenly raised his voice. "Stop! Don't turn around."

"What do we do?"

"Just finish your lunch while I talk," he answered. "Does anyone else know about the envelope you gave Townsend?"

She paused to think. "No."

"You're sure?"

"Yes. Why? Do you think—"

"Someone," he said flatly, "found out about this secret last time, and we didn't know until it was too late. We're not about to make that mistake again."

Angela took another small bite and chewed. "But the man who followed us before is dead. And so is the man he was working for."

"And that's all we know," added Rickards. "Not who else they were involved with."

"You think it's them again?!"

"I don't know who it is. All I know is those two are watching us." He turned and casually gazed around the restaurant. "Which means there may also be someone inside this restaurant with us."

"Oh my God."

"Relax. Nothing's going to happen here. Just stay calm."

"Are you sure nothing's going to happen?"

No. He wasn't sure. But it was unlikely.

"When you're done eating, I want you to go to the restroom. Understand?"

"And do what?"

"I don't know. Powder your nose or something."

"Powder my nose? What decade are we in?"

"Do *anything*," he growled. "Just stay in there."

"For how long?"

"Ten minutes. I want to see if anyone follows you in."

"Now I'm bait?"

"No," he said, before thinking and shrugging. "Well, maybe a little."

"I am *not* comfortable with this!"

He inhaled, still watching through the window. "Fine. Then stay at the table when I get up. You'll be safe in the middle of everyone."

"What are you going to do?"

He frowned, his gaze still on the window. "I'm going to the restroom. We just talked about this."

"That's not—will you just—"

Rickards suddenly stood up.

"Oh my God! Right now?!"

"If I'm not back in three minutes, call the police."

"The police?!"

"911. Tell them what I told you, and tell them what I'm wearing."

"Joe! Wait!"

"Relax," he said. "Don't act strange."

"Don't act strange. Are you kidding me?!"

Without another word, Rickards turned and casually walked away from the table, stopping a waitress and asking where the restroom was. When she pointed, he walked obligingly back toward the entrance and down a short set of

stairs to the men's door, then pushed through, letting it
swing closed behind him.

17

Inside, Joe moved to the urinal and stood in front of it for a moment before turning and walking back to the sink closest to the door, where he turned on the faucet and let it run.

He glanced under the two stall doors to make sure he was alone and then placed both hands near the water, pretending to wash.

Less than a minute later, the door to the restroom opened, and someone entered.

The man was barely inside when Rickards recognized him and lunged, grabbing the man's forward arm and yanking him as hard as he could inside.

Caught by surprise, the man stumbled forward, off-balance and out of control, falling past the urinals and into the side of a metal stall.

Rickards was immediately on top of him, pile driving into the man's side and smashing him into the tiled wall with a violent thud before he slumped to the floor with a groan.

Rickards was in midstride, charging the man again when the restroom door opened and the second person he'd seen entered. Spotting his partner on the floor, he instantly reached beneath his oversized Hawaiian shirt and withdrew a Smith & Wesson semi-automatic, pointing just as Joe reached him. Knocking the gun up and out of the way, Rickards shoved both of them back through the open doorway, smashing the man into the opposing wall, where they fell together in a tangled heap onto the hard floor.

Rickards was searching for the gun when he heard the distinct sound of its slide action directly behind him and the unmistakable sound of a bullet being chambered. The first man spoke.

"Freeze, goddamn it! Federal agents!"

Angela's heart jolted when she heard the noise from the restroom. Moments later, she heard the loud scuffle near the entrance, followed by a thunderous crash.

She couldn't see what was happening and instantly rose from her seat but was almost immediately met by the firm hand of a woman standing over her, one hand on Angela's shoulder and the other behind the woman's back.

"Don't move, Ms. Reed. Stay right where you are."

***

They were both handcuffed and escorted outside, down a set of steps and through the middle of the small, upscale shopping center until reaching the street entrance, where a light-gray GM Suburban was waiting.

Two men dressed in regular clothing opened the doors and Angela and Joe were pushed inside and over a bench seat. They faced a woman neatly dressed in a pressed, navy blue pantsuit.

Her face was anything but friendly as she stared at them through intense green eyes.

"Who the hell are you?" Rickards snapped.

Her eyes moved to Rickards without saying a word, simply staring at him with a look of extreme consternation.

"Let me be clear," she said in an icy snarl. "I could have you arrested for what you just did to my agents."

"They didn't identify themselves."

"That doesn't matter, and you know it. The only reason, and I mean the *only* reason you're not on your way to jail right now, is out of professional courtesy as a *former* federal investigator. A courtesy that is wearing damn thin with those first four words out of your mouth. So, if I were you, I would change my tone very quickly."

Rickards didn't respond. Even he knew when to keep

his mouth shut.

My name is Agent Hayton from the Honolulu field office. We've been watching you for two days."

"What for?"

She continued glaring at him. "Why don't you tell me?"

Rickards glanced at Angela. "How the hell should we know?"

"Do you know a Kathy Myers, Mr. Rickards?"

He squinted. "My mother-in-law?"

"Do you know her current whereabouts?"

"What?"

"I asked if you know where she is?"

"She's in Denver in a retirement home."

"No. She's not. Ms. Myers has been missing for four days."

The news was clearly a surprise to Rickards.

"Just a few months," said Hayton, "after making a trip to South America—with you."

"What is that supposed to mean?"

"Evidently, you were the last one to spend time with her outside her retirement home. Our Denver office was trying to locate you when we discovered your sudden trip here to Maui."

"My mother-in-law and I went on a vacation together. That's all."

"To South America."

"Bolivia."

"What for?"

"For grins and giggles."

Hayton was not amused. "Is that something you do often?"

"No."

"Then how often?"

"With her? Never."

"Never?"

Rickards frowned. Not because of the question, but because of his answer. "She used to hate me."

"And she no longer does?"

Rickards sighed and slumped in his seat. "It's a long story."

Agent Hayton crossed one leg in front of her and folded her arms. "I have plenty of time."

"Because I was an asshole," he said with a sigh.

"To her?"

"To everyone," said Rickards, turning and glancing embarrassingly at Angela.

"Obviously, this was before you became the charming person you are today?"

"That's right. Now I'm delightful."

Hayton ignored the sarcasm. "So, you have no idea where your mother-in-law is?"

"No, I don't. You said four days?"

"Correct."

Rickards glared at the woman until he detected a hint of curiosity in her eyes. "Something tells me you know already where she is."

"Pardon?"

"I said, I think you *know* where she is."

"Why would you say that?"

"Because you or the NCIC should have already run a trace on her—including bank records and passport activity."

There was no reply.

"And if you were genuinely concerned, I would have already received a phone call from one of you. So, if I had to guess, I'd say you've already found what you're looking for. And this charade of following me," he looked at Angela, "of following us, is your way of trying to find out something more."

The woman continued examining him and eventually nodded. "It seems your mother-in-law purchased a ticket back to Bolivia after your trip—with very little notice. Much like you two did in coming here."

"You think us coming here has something to do with

76

Kathy going to Bolivia?"

"*Back* to Bolivia," corrected Hayton. "And I don't know. Does it?"

"No. It doesn't."

"So, you have no idea why she immediately decided to fly all the way back down there."

"None," lied Rickards.

Agent Hayton continued studying him. "Bolivian immigration confirmed she arrived on her flight and went through customs two days ago. But at present they have no idea where she is."

"Then that makes three of us."

Hayton glanced down and casually examined her fingernails. "Sounds strange. Wouldn't you say?"

"What can I tell you? Women are enigmas."

"And I suppose none of this would have anything to do with your trips to Mexico."

Angela, who was intently listening, suddenly turned to Joe.

He didn't look back. "No."

Hayton's eyes moved to Angela. "Did you know about Mr. Rickards' trips to Mexico, Ms. Reed?"

"Uh…" she stammered. "It's not really any of my business."

"You sure about that? Would it surprise you to know that Mr. Rickards traveled to Mexico not once but twice immediately after *you and he* returned from Bolivia?"

Angela hesitated. "As I said, it's none of my business."

Hayton calmly glanced out of her window. "What exactly was the nature of your trip to Bolivia, Ms. Reed—with Mr. Rickards here?"

She looked nervously at Joe. "He was helping me investigate the death of my grandfather."

"When he was still an agent for the NTSB?"

"That's right."

"And how did the two of you end up down there?" asked Hayton.

"We discovered my grandfather had received a letter from his brother, with whom he'd lost contact. But my grandfather was killed in a plane crash before he could go there himself. Joe was assigned to the case."

The look on Hayton's face told Angela this was news to her.

"And Mr. Rickards here just up and left with you all the way to Bolivia to find this great uncle?"

"Something like that."

"Well, that's certainly beyond the call of duty."

"I told you," said Rickards. "I'm delightful."

"So, what?" Agent Hayton stated. "You two travel to South America and see something you thought your mother-in-law, who hates you, would want to see?"

"Believe it or not, that's precisely what happened."

"Just like that?"

"I wanted to show her something her daughter wanted her to see. My late wife. I was hoping it would help bridge the divide between us."

"I see. I understand some of her friends at the retirement home claimed your mother-in-law blamed *you* for her daughter's death."

Rickards slowly nodded.

"And you think your mother-in-law was so moved by what you showed her that she just forgave you and then decided to go back on her own."

"Yes."

A wary Hayton shook her head. "Something about this story of yours isn't adding up."

"It's the truth."

A very stretched truth, he thought.

"And your trips to Mexico?"

"It was one of my wife's favorite places."

Another lie.

Hayton seemed unconvinced but changed the subject with a sigh. "Well, Mr. Rickards, if what you say is true about your mother-in-law, there's still one big problem."

"What's that?"

"If she was so taken with whatever you showed her in Bolivia, that she just *had* to go back… why do you suppose she took four more people with her?"

18

The foyer was beautifully decorated, as always, with bright wallpaper and furniture and fresh flowers on a three-foot-long table available for anyone to take and enjoy. Leonard Townsend inhaled the scent as he passed them.

"Hello, Isabelle," he said warmly.

The nurse, dressed in light-pink scrubs, turned and smiled as he walked behind her. "Good afternoon, Mr. Townsend. How are you?"

"Very well, thank you."

Continuing forward, Townsend walked past a bulletin board covered with half a dozen colorful announcements and then through a set of propped open double doors before proceeding down the clean, wide hallway.

On his left, an even wider door opened into a dining room filled with two dozen round tables, scattered patients occupying each one.

Further, he passed another nurse and greeted her with the same warm smile before eventually reaching the nurse's station. Without hesitation, he then turned and entered room 112, where his last name was posted on a placard.

Inside, he lowered the items he was carrying onto a nearby table and smiled at the woman who looked up from her wheelchair.

"Hello, Florence."

The elderly woman was dressed in a green dress with her long gray hair tied back into a braid. She peered up at him with a look of surprise.

"Hello. Who are you?"

Townsend lowered himself into a chair and grinned at her as he folded his hands. "I'm your husband."

"My husband?" The woman blinked at him curiously.

"I'm not married."

"Of course you are, my dear. To me. Leonard. We were married in 1961."

"We were?"

"Yes."

The woman stared at him for a long time, searching for something that never came. "Was it a nice wedding?"

"It was a gorgeous wedding," he said, reaching into his pocket and retrieving, as he always did, an old worn photo. "This is our wedding picture."

Florence reached out and accepted it with frail fingers. "Oh my," she said, staring through a set of black-framed glasses. "This was me?"

"It's both of us."

"Well, I haven't been in a dress like that in... I don't know how long."

Townsend grinned and turned away, picking up a small box. "I brought you some chocolate truffles."

"Ooh, I do like truffles," she said with a smile and waited while Townsend unwrapped them.

He removed the top and handed her the bottom of the small box, allowing her to pluck one of the treats and happily take a bite.

"I also brought you a new gardening magazine."

His wife giggled. "I like to garden, too!"

"I know you do, sweetheart."

Outside, from the nurse's station, a young nurse watched the two through the open doorway, touched, yet wearing a soft, saddened expression.

Behind her, an older nurse passed and sat down before the computer. "Sweet, isn't it?"

The younger woman dropped a hand to her chest and frowned. "It really is. And yet so sad."

The older nurse began to type but stopped, leaning forward and watching through the doorway with her colleague. "I'm not so sure."

"Not so sure? What do you mean? He comes every day at the same time and has the same conversation. Over and over."

"True. Just like clockwork. Every day for almost three years."

"I just feel so bad for him."

The older nurse smiled. "I used to, until I finally asked."

"Asked what?"

"Exactly what you're thinking. What all of us are thinking whenever he comes in. How does he do it? How does he come back every day and have the same conversation when she doesn't remember him at all?"

They watched through the door as Townsend raised his phone, placed it on the table, and then pressed the tiny screen to play a song.

Brown-eyed girl.

His wife smiled again. "I *love* this song."

"I know," he said. "We danced to it at our wedding."

The nurses watched together before the younger of the two finally turned.

"So, what did he say?"

"What did he say when I asked him?"

"Yes."

The older nurse, with dark shoulder-length hair, beamed as if reliving something herself. "I asked, 'How do you keep doing it?' and he just looked at me and smiled, then said, 'She may not remember me, but I sure remember her.'"

19

"You okay?"

Rickards snapped out of his trance when Angela appeared on the balcony of her room with a cup of coffee.

"Just... thinking," he said, taking the cup. "Thank you."

"I don't know about you, but I'm still a little shaken up."

"From the FBI? Yeah, me too."

"They were pretty pissed at you."

He shrugged and sipped his coffee. "I probably had it coming."

Angela moved to the railing and looked out over the water at the outline of nearby Lanai Island. "What exactly were they after?"

"They're just fishing. They were probably trying to get ahold of me before they discovered where she'd gone and then decided to shake me down, anyway."

"For what?"

He stared out over the water with her. "Federal law enforcement doesn't like loose ends—or loose cannons."

"What does that have to do with–?"

"It's just how they work, Angela."

"Well, at least we didn't have to tell them everything. Do you think they'll try to find exactly where we went and what you took Kathy to see?"

"Don't know. Maybe. Telling them it was to see the ruins may have been enough. But even if it is, it's just a matter of time."

"Until they find out?"

"Until *someone* finds out. Eventually, all hell is going to break loose."

"Well, hopefully not before we can figure the rest out."

Rickards shrugged with indifference.

The phone in her hotel room rang loudly behind them, startling Angela and prompting her to trot inside to answer. After a few brief words, she returned to the balcony. "Speak of the devil. Guess who that was?"

"Leonard Townsend."

"Good guess. We've been invited to his house."

***

The sun was nearly down when they returned to Townsend's house and the familiar front porch. This time when they knocked on the door, it opened within a few moments, and the elderly man pushed open his screen door to welcome them in.

Inside the dimly lit room, the furniture appeared even older than it had from the outside. A long, upholstered couch with wooden arms and matching fabric, along with two rounded chairs that looked as though they'd been plucked directly from a 70s TV set.

Townsend eased himself into one of the chairs, while Angela and Joe sat beside each other on the couch. Before them, an empty, dark mahogany coffee table held the manila envelope with Mike Morton's data in it.

"I heard a man and a woman matching your description were arrested at Whaler's this afternoon."

Rickards glowered. "Not technically."

"What is *not technically* arrested?"

"Interrogated?" he offered. "Or... strongly talked to?"

"Are you mixed up in something illegal?"

"No. Nothing illegal."

"So, you were interrogated for no reason, then."

"It has to do with what we told you at your office," said Angela.

"What we didn't tell you," added Joe, "is that I took my mother-in-law to Bolivia to see *it*. And it seems she turned around and went back to see it again and was initially reported missing to the police and then the FBI."

"Along with a few friends."

To their surprise, Townsend didn't react. Instead, he remained still in his chair, gazing at them.

"Did you look at Mike's data?" asked Angela.

Townsend nodded. "Some."

"And?"

He grew silent again, as if mulling over a decision.

"Do either of you know anything about physics?"

"Sure. We're experts."

"Really?"

Rickards rolled his eyes and slumped back against the couch.

"Oh, you're being facetious."

Angela leaned forward. "No, we don't know anything about physics. Only what Mike told us."

"What exactly did he tell you?"

A surprised Angela straightened and thought back. "Well, for one, he said energy is not what it seems. That it's very strange and sometimes can be different things."

"Such as?"

She frowned. "Um, he said that in smaller, controlled circumstances, it was more predictable, I think. But in larger, more concentrated levels, it could change. And something about energy and mass being similar at extreme levels. I'm not sure if I'm remembering exactly right."

"You're close enough," said Townsend. "Do you recall when I told you about the hubris at NASA? That kept those fellas from having an open mind?"

"Yes."

He pursed his lips. "That can go both ways."

"What do you mean?"

Townsend was slow to reply. "What I mean is that Mike Morton may have been a bit eccentric, but he was no dummy."

"We certainly didn't think so."

The older man continued contemplating, biting his bottom lip. "In a lot of ways, I'm not... the man I used to be. In some ways, I'm the same. But others…"

He stared down at the envelope on the table.

"Just like everything in life—including physics."

"I'm not sure we're following," said Rickards.

"Everything changes," he replied. "And evolves over time." He continued staring at the envelope, then at the table. "There was a man named William Herschel who lived in the late eighteenth century. He was an astronomer who discovered the planet Uranus. Brilliant astronomer… but…" Townsend momentarily grinned to himself. "He also thought the Sun was very cold."

"Our sun?"

"Back then, it was believed by many scientists that our solar system was teeming with life, and Herschel believed the Sun was no different. That it was cold, and its inhabitants had just adjusted to the bright luminosity of their giant planet.

"Then there's the idea Albert Einstein had in the early 1900s of our universe being static and unchanging—until a man named Hubble proved that was not the case. Or the erroneous science behind combustion and oxidation. Or a thousand others." Townsend relaxed and placed both arms on his chair. "The same goes for quantum physics or quantum mechanics. A lot of mistakes were made, even by Einstein."

He looked at both of them. "Do you two know what an electron is?"

"Uh, yeah," Rickards mumbled.

Townsend nodded. "My point is that even mankind's brightest minds have been and still *are* proven wrong from time to time." He blinked and said simply, "*Hubris*."

"It happens to all of us," said Rickards, "not just scientists."

"Yes, it does."

Another long pause left them waiting.

"Electrons make up most of what we see around us. They are very small and very strange."

"Mike Morton said something like that."

"I'm sure he did. Even back at NASA, Mike had some odd ideas. Still grounded in fundamentals, but odd. *Kooky* is what I used to call them. But looking back, I think I was caught up in my own hubris."

"Are we still talking about electrons?"

"Yes—whose strangeness we have only recently come to realize and accept. And quite reluctantly, at that."

"Strange, as in…?"

"It turns out the universe is not at all what we thought." Townsend glanced at Angela, staring and thinking. "A man named Thomson discovered the first electron in 1897, and since then, we have come to understand just how strange they really are."

Townsend continued thinking before abruptly reaching into a pants pocket and retrieving a penny, which he fingered gingerly. "In the world we live in, the physical world, things are logical. Predictable. But in the quantum world, they are anything but."

He reached down to the table and moved the envelope. Then with a finger, he stood the penny on its edge and flicked it with his other hand, sending the coin spinning in a blur.

Townsend pointed to the coin. "What do you see?" he asked. "Heads or tails?"

Rickards stared at the whirling coin. "Both?"

"Exactly," said the older man. "Unlike our world, the quantum world is not predictable. It's just the opposite. It is extremely *unpredictable*. Or should I say—*unreliable*. Allowing for things to be in more than one state at a time. Like this penny."

Still watching the spinning penny, he said, "In the quantum world, this penny can be both heads and tails."

Without warning, he abruptly flattened the coin under his palm, "unless we measure it."

Angela and Joe remained quiet, intently listening.

Townsend slowly raised his hand, revealing the coin,

now still displaying its *head* side up.

"In the quantum world," he said, "things can be two things at once, or even more—until they're measured."

"Until it's measured?"

"Or observed. Believe it or not, because we cannot *know* what state an electron is in, or even where it is, it can be considered to be in all places at once."

They both stared at Townsend, perplexed. "But that's impossible."

"In our physical world, yes. But not in the quantum world. It has been proven many times over, yet no one accepts it easily. Not even Einstein."

"Einstein knew about this?"

"Oh yes. It was his ultimate nightmare. A sensible world built upon the foundation of an utterly nonsensical quantum world."

They both stared at Townsend, gaping as they tried to comprehend what he was saying.

"And Mike Morton...?"

The older man stared at Angela. "Einstein called the quantum world *spooky*. And it is. Extremely so. Very much how I considered Morton's ideas for all those years. But it turns out they weren't spooky. And neither was he. Electrons, or energy, are inherently unpredictable, and yet they compose most of the world we see around us, even at this very moment."

"So then, Morton was right?"

"At least much closer than I was willing to admit at the time," acknowledged Townsend. "Whatever the two of you saw in South America may seem spooky to you. And it would to most people. But it may not be as impossible as it sounds. The truth is that no one understands energy. And I mean no one. In fact, all physicists pretty much agree that *if you think you know quantum mechanics, then you don't.*"

"Then it's official," Angela joked. "Mike Morton was not crazy."

From his chair, Townsend's face lightened. "Young

lady, at the moment, we don't even know what crazy is."

A long silence ensued, with the only sound coming from the repeating ticktock of an old German-style pendulum clock hanging on the living room wall.

"So... now what?"

"Now," Townsend said, easing forward in his chair, "I will help you."

"You will?"

"Yes," he answered. "I will help you find Mike's second location..."

Excited, Angela prematurely began to rise from the couch before Townsend had finished.

"...after you show me the first one."

20

"Say what?"

"After you show me the first one," he repeated.

Rickards leaned forward. "You want us to show you the first one?"

"That's right. I want to see what you found."

"In Bolivia."

"Yes."

Rickards stared at Angela as if to say *you've got to be kidding*.

"Um, Professor, I don't... know if that's possible."

"Why not?"

"Well, I can't speak for Joe, but I don't have any intention of going back there. It wasn't the best experience."

Townsend nodded. "Yes, you explained that."

She grimaced over his response. "Evidently not well enough. We almost didn't make it back."

The professor turned to Rickards. "Did you not just say you made a second trip?"

Reluctantly, Rickards nodded.

"Was it a terrible trip the second time?"

He shrugged, still seated on the couch. "Well, I *was* with my mother-in-law."

Townsend responded with a broad smile, looking at them both. "I would very much like to see it."

Angela remained transfixed, blinking at the older man before turning back to Rickards. "Can I speak with you outside?"

"Please tell me you're not considering this," Angela murmured.

"I didn't even want to come here."

"So, you won't do it either."

"I wasn't planning to. But…"

"But what?!" she exclaimed.

"We're not exactly in the catbird seat here. He is."

"He doesn't have to see it to help us find the second location."

Rickards thought it over. "I don't know that for sure, do you?"

"Why would he?"

"Off the top of my head, he may have a better understanding of what is actually occurring in that canyon of yours."

"We told him everything!"

"True, but in light of the physics dissertation he just gave us, I'm starting to wonder."

Angela crossed her arms. "About what?"

"About that whole electron thing. With that much energy flowing through one single spot, are those electrons still operating in our world or quantum world?"

She stared at him without replying.

"Seems like maybe you're starting to think about it, too."

"What I'm also thinking about is getting thrown in jail again. If it weren't for Mike Morton, we might still be there today!"

"Perhaps."

"Perhaps?"

"The guys who were behind all that are dead, Angela. And the second time I went, with Kathy, no one seemed to notice me. There weren't any hassles at the airport, and no one followed us."

She remained quiet, searching for an argument but couldn't find one. If he'd been followed, Joe of all people would have noticed.

"What if you slipped through by accident?"

Rickards rolled his eyes. "What if I didn't? Or what if I get killed by an angry chicken? Playing *what if* is a pointless exercise. You can speculate forever, and nothing will be solved."

"Fine. So, your answer is just to go and hope nothing bad happens?"

"I'm not trying to convince you, Angela. All I'm saying is this depends on how much you want the man's help. Everything in life is a tradeoff."

She remained steadfast on the porch, frustrated.

She didn't want to go back. She'd had two traumatic experiences in Bolivia, both of which she desperately wanted to forget. She didn't need to add a third.

"The place between," Rickards said after a long silence.

"What?"

"What you said before. Being in that space between what your life was and what you're supposed to do now."

She glared at him in irritation. "Sometimes I hate telling you things."

***

When Townsend strode through the front door and down the hall again, the nurses glanced up at him in surprise.

"Mr. Townsend."

"Good morning."

"You're early. Is everything all right?"

He slowed before the entrance to his wife's room, staring briefly inside. "I hope so."

"Who are you?"

"I'm your husband, Florence."

"My husband? I'm not married."

"Of course, you are, dear. To me." He began unwrapping another small box of truffles and, when finished, handed it to her.

"I love truffles!"

With only a slight grin, Leonard Townsend retrieved his phone and pulled up his list of songs and placed it on the small table next to him. He pressed the play button and relaxed as *Save the Last Dance for Me* from The Drifters began.

Music memory was all he had left, shown to be one of the few memory centers still unaffected by Alzheimer's—at least until the very end.

The human memory system was a complex process of coding, storing and retrieving information. But while everyday memories dealt with information, music memory had continued to show that music recall was more than information.

It was an *experience*.

Experiences spread across a far greater synaptic plane and remained partially independent from other memory systems, allowing large swaths of music to remain intact even as different brain anatomy and cognitive functions were significantly impaired.

And Leonard Townsend was a believer. He'd seen firsthand the influence music had on his wife, allowing him occasional glimpses into the woman he married so many years ago. Sometimes these glimpses even allowed *her* to see *him*.

After the fourth song, one of those glimpses appeared— increasingly infrequent and fleeting, but still there. When *California Dreamin'* began to play, her beautiful brown eyes seemed to sharpen and briefly focus, seeing him once again.

"Do you still have that old Dodge Dart?" she asked.

Townsend instantly softened, almost to tears. "We sold it to put me through college."

She nodded, grinning. "I loved that car."

Two hours later, after playing the entire list, he watched as his wife's eyes grew tired. Without a word, he stood and took her hand, helping her frail frame up and onto her bed, where he settled on the edge beside her.

"Sweetheart, it may be a few days before I can come

back to see you."

Her eyes fluttered closed. "Okay."

"I have to go on a trip."

She nodded softly. "I love to travel."

Townsend raised a hand and gently stroked her cheek. "I know you do."

21

"See the enclosed. This is all I can provide without calling attention. Please do not contact me again."

Mona Baraka stared at her computer screen, finally able to read the handwritten letter in the binder. It was unintelligible not just from the poor penmanship, but from being written in a different language called Punjabi, which was spoken thousands of miles away primarily in India and Pakistan by Sikhs.

This left Mona to wonder if the different language had been intentional. Below the original faded text was a name written by another hand—possibly by the older Hamed, including what looked to be the person's name.

Harpreet Ahuja.

But if the person had sent something to Hamed, wouldn't they have had to communicate before that in a shared language? And yet, Harpreet still chose to write the letter in Punjabi. Were they intentionally trying to obscure their identities? If they were, why would Hamed, or someone else, later write his name right on the letter?

There could be dozens of explanations, but Mona sensed this was the most likely, even if she couldn't be sure of the person's motivation. Because if Harpreet Ahuja had indeed written the letter, it might explain what Mona had now uncovered.

Someone by the same name had worked for a large conglomerate associated with one of the fourteen companies about which Hamed had information. But that was almost thirty years ago. So, was Ahuja really the same person who'd sent those various financial records to Hamed?

And was this perhaps the same Harpreet Ahuja about whom Mona could find nothing else following the mid-1990s, as if he had simply disappeared from the world?

Here are the financial records, she thought. *Now don't contact me again. Because he didn't want to stir attention. About what? Fear of reprisal? But then he later disappears.*

Mona stared at the translated text, wondering if the man had disappeared by choice. And if so, was he still alive? Or had he been *found out* as feared?

And how did Hamed, an Egyptian fighter pilot, come into contact with Ahuja in the first place? Had he tracked the man down in his effort to understand what had happened in 1977?

And if Ahuja was indeed connected to one of Mido Saad's companies, could he also have been connected to more?

The pieces felt loose yet still seemed to fit. Or was she forcing them to fit?

And then there was Mido Saad himself. Deeply connected with the Egyptian government and possibly others, operating quietly and almost wholly unseen.

She hadn't found much more on him than her friend Omar had. Even using every search engine she could think of only produced a few dozen articles about his philanthropy and being recognized at various events—but even those were few and far between and extremely outdated.

The man was a mystery. Most people with that much money reveled in it, in the stardom and the prestige.

In the power.

However, Saad seemed just the opposite. His life was a series of short, brief appearances, staying just long enough to be honored. Long enough to dedicate a new building, usually an orphanage. And then he was gone, disappearing from the news for months at a time.

Sometimes years.

She *had* found other things. His place of birth if it was accurate. The small town a merchant father had raised him in. His dropping out of college, only to become abruptly rich several years later beyond most people's wildest dreams.

Mona clicked back to her notes on him, along with several pictures she'd found on the internet spanning perhaps a few decades.

And then nothing. Nothing at all.

She'd never found so little information on someone so rich. *Almost,* she thought, suddenly peering away from the screen, *as if his details had been scrubbed from public records.*

Was that crazy? Could someone do that? Had he been involved in something nefarious or illegal, which was the reason why he donated so much money to orphanages and children? But he'd been involved with them from the very beginning—almost immediately following his newfound wealth, as far as she could tell. Beginning somewhere in the 1960s.

Could it have been a preventive measure in case he was later caught, so he could fall back on his reputation as a humanitarian?

Mona shook her head. No. That was a stretch. Maybe Saad was simply a good man—perhaps even someone who participated in a little financial fraud and had to cover it up all for the greater good.

Which could easily explain Harpreet Ahuja sending copies of financial records to Hamed, attempting to expose a fraud. But even her friend Omar had said he hadn't found any red flags. If there were any, he'd said they'd have to be deeper. So why would Ahuja send financial records to Hamed if there was nothing obvious in them? Especially since Hamed was a pilot and probably unfamiliar with the ins and outs of corporate finances.

The puzzle was starting to fall apart again, as though she had to mentally glue the pieces in place just to keep them connected.

She was missing something.

Of that, she was sure.

22

Through a set of dark attractive eyes, the psychiatrist studied all nine girls through a square window in the door. All were seated at desks with their heads down, obedient and writing.

It was called psychometrics, a battery of qualitative tests used to assess intellectual, behavioral and communicative skills in both children and adults and ranging from verbal to nonverbal to physiological to emotional. It was a bevy of measurements to evaluate and identify a person's particular abilities and skills—even gifts, to ensure placement in the most conducive environments. Or, in the case of adults, the most applicable vocations.

Used worldwide, psychometrics, along with traditional clinical assessments and observation, gave professional psychiatrists and psychologists the tools they needed to study and understand a person deeper at all levels, particularly regarding behavior.

Which was precisely what Dr. Layla Abo was doing over the course of several days. Although, admittedly, her tests had to be significantly modified for orphaned girls. And the same for the boys.

She would take three of each. After multiple interviews, thorough psychometric testing and finally, behavior and social observations, she would select the best suited to weed out unforeseen issues or complications.

This was a long, arduous process that Abo had performed hundreds of times over her career, honing her technique to produce the best possible results. Of course, mistakes still occasionally occurred, but they had become increasingly less common, giving the doctor a gratifying feeling of achievement and efficiency.

"Is everything correct?" asked an approaching staff member.

Dr. Layla Abo nodded without turning around, continuing to stare through the small window. "Yes."

"Can I get you anything while you wait?"

She shook her head without a word.

Abo never grew tired of watching the children. Instead, she remained unmoving and transfixed—fascinated as she watched their slightest actions and motions during the tests. She studied to see which of them displayed signs of struggle or nervousness, who fidgeted or who tried to glance another's answers even after being explicitly warned not to.

She especially enjoyed examining them without their knowledge, appreciating the glimpses into their strengths and abilities but thriving at witnessing their weaknesses— the cracks in their intellectual or emotional states. These were the crevices that would eventually let Abo in to see who they really were.

Truly and deeply. Defenseless. Pure.

It was now an obsession, getting as far as she could into another person's psyche and then their souls filled her with a profound sense of divinity.

⁕⁕⁕

Several hours later, Mido Saad himself answered the phone when Abo called.

"Yes?"

"I should be done by Thursday," she reported, "and heading back."

"Wonderful. I will have everything ready."

23

"You're calling me during the day," Omar said, answering his phone. "Is everything okay?"

"You're so funny," Mona answered sarcastically. "Do you have time to talk, or are you busy being important?"

Omar laughed. "I have a meeting in about fifteen minutes."

"This should be quick. I just need someone to bounce something off of."

Omar nodded and rotated in his office chair. "Go ahead."

"I'm slowly piecing things together, but instead of becoming clearer, it feels as if it's getting stranger."

"I had a similar feeling going through those financials. Have you gotten any more?"

"No, not numbers. But other things are beginning to feel weird."

"Like what?"

"I found more on Mido Saad. Not surprisingly, there's very little on him."

"That's what I said."

"And I may know who sent those financial records to the army pilot—a man named Ahuja. But I can't find anything on him, either. And what little there is on Saad is decades old. The last article I found on him was seven years ago."

"What was it?"

"Another school being built for children. An academy. I can't tell if they're schools or orphanages, but that was it. The last article I could find. Another strange thing is *where* he's building the schools."

"Where?"

"I've read everything I can find on him over and over, but only a few mention locations. One location I had to deduce from a banner in the background of a photo. But they're all in strange locations. Not *strange* strange, just remote."

"How remote?"

"All over Africa, in tiny villages far away from everything."

On the other end, Omar stared forward, listening. "Isn't that where people need the most help?"

"Yes and no," she said. "Isolation would mean they have fewer resources. But these are also small buildings."

"I'm not following."

"This goes back to the money. If the corporations you investigated are making hundreds of millions of pounds a year, how much does it cost to build a small school or orphanage in the middle of Zambia?"

"I don't know, ten thousand?"

"At the most. So, with even a portion of the money, couldn't they be building hundreds of these places every year?"

"You'd think so."

"But it doesn't seem like they are. Which makes the locations seem even more odd."

Still in his seat, Omar raised a finger to scratch his upper lip. "That is interesting. Building places in larger cities *would* help more children."

"Exactly. But it feels like just the opposite."

"How many are out there?"

"I don't know. That's one of the things I'm trying to find out."

"Let me guess—another is where the money is going?"

"Not really," she replied. "People have been finding creative ways to hide money for thousands of years. So, where it's going wouldn't surprise me all that much no matter what I find. What I'm really curious to know is *when* did Mido Saad become rich?"

"When?"

She switched the phone to her other hand. "From what I can find from Saad's past, there was nothing really extraordinary about him. Average child. Average teenager. Average family. Dropped out of college."

"He dropped out of college?"

"Yes. Which was a bigger deal back then. It would have been hugely embarrassing, even disgraceful. Especially if your family had struggled to send you."

"And then what?"

"I don't find much on him until several years later when he was already a businessman."

"Okay, so how are you proposing to find out when he made his fortune?"

"I was hoping you could help."

On the other end of the call, Omar leaned back, thinking. "Well, from what I saw, those business structures seemed very sophisticated and go back a long time." He paused. "So, how does Mido Saad go from a dropout to a brilliant businessman in just a few years?"

"More specifically, *when* and *how fast?*"

"You want to know how fast?"

"Any ideas?"

He sighed. "The structures have been around for a while. How long, I'm not sure. He could have been hiding money from the beginning, if he was smart enough."

"Or experienced enough."

"Yeah, but who has that kind of experience at that age?"

"Maybe he was coached."

"If that's true, then if we could get his financial filings from that far back, they may not reveal much, especially if he was already hiding it."

"Is there another way?"

He looked up at the ceiling above him. "There could be."

"There has to be something he couldn't hide."

Omar blinked, then slowly eased forward. "Labor."

"Labor?"

"Labor. As in jobs. Assets and revenues can easily be manipulated and hidden. Jobs, not so much. If his wealth came from these businesses and you want to know *when*, one way might be to find out how many people were employed by those companies at any given time, and more importantly, how quickly the number of employees grew or shrank."

Mona smiled. "Omar, that's brilliant."

"I wouldn't say brilliant. It's not a perfect indicator, and labor always lags revenue, but it should give you a decent idea of the trajectory of how fast Saad's money grew. Any chance you know someone in the Ministry of Labor?"

***

Two hours later, in downtown Cairo, Omar Maher opened the door and stepped out of a small conference room. Tall and lean, in his late twenties, he straightened his suit and headed down a bright, clean hallway, stopping briefly to look for a colleague before continuing on when he found the person's office empty.

Reaching his own office, he pushed the door open and casually strode in, suddenly jumping at the sight of someone sitting quietly inside.

"Subhanallah! What are you doing here?"

Mona Baraka giggled as she stood up. "Sorry. I wasn't trying to scare you. Makes me wonder what you were up to in that meeting, though."

"Funny." He removed his suit jacket and whirled it around the back of his desk chair. "To what do I owe this surprise?"

Still grinning, she watched as he reached into his top desk drawer and withdrew a single cigarette. He lit it with a match and lowered himself onto the desk's front edge. "I have a favor to ask."

"What a surprise," he said, blowing out a stream of smoke.

She stood watching him, her long black hair pulled back into a bun. Her dress was conservative and straightforward but unable to completely hide her figure.

The truth was that Omar liked her, and had for a long time—enough to have his mother approach Mona's parents about a courtship. But the relationship had been short-lived. Mona cared for him but ultimately decided she wasn't ready for marriage, leaving the two as friends and growing closer.

Omar remained hopeful.

"So, what's the favor?" he asked.

"First, I actually do know someone in the Labor Ministry. My sister-in-law. I called her on the way here, and she's going to try to track down headcounts for those companies during the 60s and 70s."

"Great."

"I also thought maybe I could track down some of the actual employees."

"Good idea."

"See if any of them knew of or had met Saad."

"Makes sense."

"Maybe they know something."

Omar paused, staring at her curiously through the rising smoke, studying her. "You're stalling."

"What?"

"I said, you're stalling."

"What do you mean?"

His eyes narrowed. "Now you're stalling *while* stalling."

Mona opened her mouth to speak but stopped, abruptly closing it again. "Fine," she said with a sigh. "I'm stalling."

"This must be some favor."

She bit her lip apprehensively. "You could say that."

"Speak."

She reached out to the chair next to her and fiddled with one of its fabric corners.

"Monaaa?"

"Yes?"

"What… is… it?"

"I want to find out more about these orphanages."

"Okay."

"By going to one."

Omar was still listening. "And?"

She continued fidgeting. "And I need someone to go with me."

24

"Oh really?"

Mona folded her arms. "As you well know, a single Muslim woman can't just travel wherever she pleases."

"True."

"Especially where I want to go."

"What about your brother?"

"He's in Saudi Arabia, on business and won't be back for a few weeks."

"So, you want *me* to go with you."

She glared at him, trying to deter his look of satisfaction. "Don't let it go to your head."

He took a long drag from his cigarette. "You want *me* to go with *you* and pretend I'm your *husband*."

She rolled her eyes. "Not my husband."

"Then what?"

Mona hesitated, and after an excessive pause, exhaled. "My fiancée."

"Your fiancée?" he shouted.

She immediately groaned.

Given the restrictive laws and nature of courting, engagement was a significant event in Egypt and a status symbol in many ways, allowing for a single man and woman to openly spend time together without public scrutiny or judgment—particularly in heavily practicing Islamic communities.

"You know how much trouble you could get into."

"I do."

"That *both* of us could get into."

"I know!"

Omar thought it over. "Where do you want to go, Zambia?"

"Not quite that far. Kharga."

"That's a long way. When?"

"That depends on you and your work."

He feigned a look of shock. "Just like that, you assumed I would say yes?"

Another groan. "You're getting a lot of distance out of this, aren't you?"

"Yes," he stated proudly. "I am. But I don't know if I'm *ready* to be engaged."

"Stop it."

"I need to be… romanced."

"That's it," she said and turned toward the door.

"Fine. Fine!" He laughed.

"You'll do it?"

"Yes. But you do seem painfully unaware of how many favors I've done for you."

"Trust me, I know."

"Then you just don't care."

"Can we please move on?"

"Fine. Where in Kharga?"

"About an hour west."

Omar finished his cigarette and smoothly rose from the desk. "Let me see what I can move around."

25

After an adjustment period of several hours, the high pitch of the 737's roaring jet engines had become largely unnoticeable, leaving Joe Rickards seated in an aisle and staring absently at the seatback in front of him.

After a nearby snort, he turned and looked at the lightly snoring face of Leonard Townsend, his mouth turned upward as he leaned against the half-closed window next to him.

Between him and Townsend, Angela Reed watched as Rickards shook his head and turned forward again. "I wish I could sleep like that on a plane," she murmured.

He frowned. "I wish I could sleep like that in my own bed."

She closed her magazine, placing it on her lap. "I take it you can't sleep on a plane, either."

"No."

"Well, at least this is a better flight than the first time."

"That is true."

She glanced up as someone passed them in the aisle. "I have to admit, I'm surprised you came."

"That makes two of us."

"Maybe the old investigator in you just can't give up wanting to know."

He looked at her sarcastically. "Maybe it was your guilt trip that did it."

Angela was still grinning. "I'm happy with either."

Rickards paused to study her. "I thought you'd be a little more nervous."

"Me, too. But I'm not. I'm not sure why." She thought for a moment and changed the subject. "So was your boss surprised when you quit?"

"I think he was relieved."

"Relieved?"

"In case you hadn't noticed, I wasn't exactly a model employee."

"You'd been through a lot."

Rickards shrugged. "I'm glad you didn't quit."

"It gave me something to do. A way to take my mind off everything."

"Good."

She glanced briefly at Townsend, who was still softly snoring. "Do you think your mother-in-law is still in Bolivia?"

"I doubt it. It didn't take long when I brought her."

"How did you two get along before…"

"While my wife and daughter were here? Okay, I guess. She's pretty high-strung. We'd butt heads a lot until I finally learned to find other things to do when she came to visit. After that, it was fine."

"And how long ago did she move into the retirement home?"

"A few years ago. Just before the accident."

"I see." Angela pulled a small bottle of water from her seatback and took a sip. "The playground at the park. It was special to you, wasn't it?"

"Very much."

"I'm sorry I got mad at you there."

Rickards' eyes returned to her. "I probably deserved it."

She returned the bottle to the seatback. "Can I ask you something else?"

"No."

She continued staring until Joe finally relented. "What?"

"Did you really just come back from Mexico?"

"Yes."

"It was a favorite place for you and your wife?"

He shook his head. "Not really."

"No?"

"No."

"Even though you told–"

"Agent Hayton?" he said, raising an eyebrow. "I lied."

Angela gradually smiled. "Well, she deserved it."

Rickards smirked.

"Should I warn you about some of the local customs again?"

This time he laughed. "Didn't help all that much last time."

"What did you do in the Army?"

"Infantry."

"Which means?"

"Ever see a movie with thousands of soldiers marching across an open field?"

"Yes."

"That's us."

"I see. On the front line."

"Infantry *is* the front line."

Angela tilted her head. "Is that where you learned to fight?"

"No. Before that—when I was younger. You could say I grew up on the wrong side of the tracks and learned the hard way."

"Did you ever lose?"

"Many times."

"Well, even so, I'm glad you came."

Rickards eased his head back against the vinyl headrest. "Are you saying you need a bodyguard?"

"No. Just a friend. Someone I can talk to without judgment."

"I'm too old and too flawed to judge anyone."

"That's what I like about you," she said, smiling. "The non-judgment, not the flawed part."

He motioned past her toward the sleeping Townsend. "You think he's going to be able to help you decipher Morton's data?"

"I sure hope so."

With that, Rickards nodded and closed his eyes. "Just

remember the old saying, *be careful what you wish for.*"

***

Touching down in Bogota, Colombia, the three spent an hour in a remodeled section of the airport's terminal before boarding an Airbus A319 headed for La Paz. Landing two hours later, just past 9:00 p.m., they deboarded and walked the quarter mile to baggage claim.

Townsend's bag was bigger than either Joe or Angela was expecting. And heavy. It took up most of the trunk in their small rental car.

To Angela's relief, the arrival had been uneventful, including reaching the small hotel a few miles west of the airport, where Rickards trudged up the stairs carrying Townsend's heavy bag. He dropped it with relief outside the professor's assigned room.

"Thank you, Joe. That's very kind of you."

"Don't mention it. I hope there's a giant espresso machine inside. Something tells me I'll need one in the morning." He then approached Angela as she opened the adjacent door and briefly scanned the room inside. Satisfied, he waved at them both, picked up his own bag and strode to the next door.

***

Three hours later, they were all awakened by a sudden screaming outside, followed by a man intermittently yelling in Spanish. The ruckus culminated several minutes later in a thunderous slam of one of the hotel doors beneath them.

There was a long silence before the swearing resumed, and a car was started, backing up and peeling out of the small parking lot.

While watching the commotion from his room's window, Rickards heard his cell phone ding behind him, resting atop an old wooden bedstand. The sound prompted him to let the curtain fall back into place and then walk over to pick it up.

On the brightly lit screen was a text message from Angela.

Welcome back to Bolivia.

26

The morning was less eventful—barely. Rickards froze in his tracks the moment he opened his hotel room door. Below, positioned behind some of the parked cars, was a white Bolivian police truck. It stood unattended, with a wide green stripe traveling the length of the vehicle over the hood and cab and running beneath a set of red and blue flashing lights. Spanning both doors in giant green letters read *POLICIA BOLIVIANA*.

Rickards remained still, listening. Hearing nothing, he eased slightly forward and peered along the concrete walkway. First left, then right.

Moments later, Angela's door opened next to his, and he watched her discover the vehicle with wide eyes. She slowly turned toward Rickards.

"What do we do?" she mouthed.

Rickards' response was also silent. One slow word. "Calm."

Cautiously, he advanced and peered down over the white painted railing to find nothing. No people and no movement.

He turned back and began to speak when Townsend's door suddenly opened loudly before the man exited with a square metal sealed container.

"Not an espresso machine," he joked, "but almost as good."

"Shh!" Rickards ordered.

The older man looked around. "What's going on?"

Rickards placed a finger over his mouth and made a sign with his free hand to stop. When he pointed to the police vehicle, Townsend raised both eyebrows.

"What is it?" he whispered.

"No idea."

"They can't be here for us," Angela said in a hushed voice. "We haven't done anything."

Rickards nodded and looked back down.

It was true. They hadn't done anything. Not that they knew of. Were the police there for them or someone else?

He turned and eased his door closed behind him, quietly shutting it. Then he motioned for the others to do the same. As they did, he caught a sound of noise downstairs near the office.

Rickards' years of investigation training kicked in.

The truck had a double cab but still looked too small to take all three away in it. If the officers were indeed here for them, maybe it was only for questioning. To ask why they'd come back, or worse, where they were headed.

Calmly, he pointed to the far end of the walkway, ushering them toward a distant, second set of stairs. "That way. Quietly."

He eased forward and softly hefted Townsend's case with his left hand, following until the three reached the end and started down the concrete stairway.

They reached their car without seeing anyone and opened the doors, including the rear doors, where Rickards slid the case onto the back seat next to Townsend. He then straightened and turned around, ensuring they could squeeze out past the police truck.

Sliding into the driver's seat, he quietly pulled the door closed until it clicked and started the car, bringing the small motor to life and purring softly beneath the hood. Joe turned the steering wheel to the right and eased the car back, turning as tightly as he could without scraping the old Ford parked next to them.

Backing up, he straightened the wheel and drove forward outside the police vehicle and continuing toward the open street. As they passed, Angela spotted an officer inside the hotel's office speaking to someone at the front desk.

With little sound, they reached the road and turned right, gradually accelerating.

Still looking back, Leonard Townsend finally turned forward again in the rear seat. "I see you have a healthy skepticism of the authorities."

Rickards' eyes looked at him in the rearview mirror. "Fear might be a better word. At least out here."

"Our first trip didn't go well," said Angela.

Townsend nodded. "Yes, I remember you telling me. I guess there wasn't a lot of embellishment."

Turning to Rickards, she said, "If they were looking for us, they'll most likely be waiting when we get back."

"Then let's hope we aren't the ones they were after." He switched lanes and slowed as they approached a stop light, preparing to make a U-turn.

If the police were waiting when they returned, with any luck, it would be too late.

Townsend watched through his window as they turned around. "I guess we're skipping breakfast then."

Without a word, Angela opened her purse and dug out a tiny container of Tic Tacs, tossing them back to Townsend.

"So, what's in your case?" asked Rickards.

"An isotropic probe."

"For what, measuring energy?"

"More or less. Directly detecting energy is very difficult, so you measure the energy field instead. A physical field surrounds electrically charged particles and exerts force on those particles. Most likely that's what Mike Morton was trying to do with the pole you said he was carrying around."

"Is yours better?"

Townsend patted the metal container next to him. "Oh yeah. She's old, but she's a workhorse."

Rickards spotted another police car and watched as it passed, moving immediately to his side mirror to see if it slowed or turned. It didn't.

"Professor," said Angela, turning around. "Something we forgot to ask you is what kind of shape are you in?"

"Pardon?"

"For example, your heart? What kind of condition?"

"As far as I know, it's fine. I walk a mile and back every afternoon when I get home."

"Ever do any hiking?"

"Occasionally, with a few friends. You're asking because of the climb that killed Mike."

"Yes. It's not easy."

"Only one way to find out."

"How much does that probe of yours weigh?"

Townsend looked back at Rickards. "Thirty pounds or so."

Wonderful.

It took thirty minutes, headed due west on Bolivia's Route 1, to reach the first sighting of Lake Titicaca's southern edge.

The largest lake in South America, Titicaca was known as the highest navigable lake in the world and appeared in the distance more like a small ocean. Nestled amongst the famed Andes Mountains, its rich deep blue water sparkled brilliantly under a calm blue sky stretching nearly to the horizon. The lake was so large that it took almost two hours to pass along its western edge, leaving those in the car silent most of the time, with Angela staring through her side window taking in the magnificence of it all.

So many places of simple and exquisite beauty. Such an extraordinary planet, she thought to herself. *It was something she'd known for years but had never truly appreciated until now. This world was gradually feeling more superficial than exceptional, with billions of people arguing over places and things that, frankly, would be here thousands of years after everyone was gone.*

She thought about how short a human lifespan was on a planet like this. In a universe like this. Seventy or eighty years against millions or even billions, making the span of a human life little more than a speck—at best, a momentary flash in time compared to things like a lake or an ocean, whose waves and ripples felt timeless, ambivalent of what floated on or within them. It reminded Angela of the old saying that *an ocean had no memory.*

In reality, the only true *sense* of time was born through human consciousness, with human lives being just a momentary flash within it. So brief and so temporary, yet humans spent so much of their flash doing what? Arguing and fighting. Only to have their entire existence snuffed out seventy or eighty years later. Sometimes sooner, sometimes later.

Everything they felt. Everything they thought about or loved. Gone into the ether.

It made Angela stop and ponder.

Just how much of our lives did the average person spend in some form of confrontation with something or someone over what they thought was right either mentally or emotionally?

And most of it, she knew, being an anthropologist, *were the same arguments. The same worries and bickering that thousands of generations had before us. The same fears. The same controversies. The same disagreements. In many cases humans had fought over the very same resources.*

A perpetual argument. An endless cycle running repeatedly in a world that had not and would not change unless something interrupted the pattern. Something so meaningful and profound that it would make every person stop and reassess what the world meant to them and what life meant to them. To make them remember that our individual flashes in time were precious, never to repeat. Never to remember what we had done or learned even between the bickering.

Because this was it. Once we were gone, our lessons and memories were lost forever.

Angela was still gazing out the window when the morning sun rose enough that its sunlight hit the colossal expanse of water, reflecting out and over the patch of hillside they were traveling through, creating a stunning, shimmering glow off the gigantic lake.

"Did you know," said Angela softly, "that Lake Titicaca has long been believed to be a source of great power and energy?"

"Is that right?"

She nodded. "All the way back to the Incas."

"I guess they were only about fifty miles off," mused Joe.

There was silence in the back until Townsend added, "Energy never disappears."

Angela blinked, then turned around. "What was that?"

"Energy never disappears," he said again.

"Mike Morton said the same thing."

"Probably because it's true. Most scientists know it. Energy doesn't disappear. The most it ever does is change from one form to another."

"What are you saying? Energy is forever?"

"Essentially," said Townsend. "As I explained before, energy is very mysterious—and very unpredictable. It's probably one of the few things in our modern world that has become *more* mysterious the more we learn of it and has confounded a great many minds."

"Like Einstein."

"Not just Einstein. The greatest minds of today. Right now. No one understands it. And I do mean *no one*. Just in the last two decades, it has become clear that literally nothing is off the table when it comes to the quantum world. What we thought was impossible before, even ridiculous, no longer is."

Rickards and Angela glanced at each other.

"And it's not just that. It's also about how different energies react to each other. All those charged particles affect one another. Just like molecular biology. Understanding molecules and cells is one thing, but how they interact with each other and affect each other, that's where things become truly humbling."

"Scientists becoming *more* humbled."

He laughed. "Especially theoretical physicists and

neurobiologists."

This time Angela twisted all the way around. "As in brain surgeons?"

"Neurobiologists aren't merely surgeons. They study the physiology and biochemistry of—"

"The brain."

"Yes. But more than that," said Townsend. "Neurons."

"Which are in the brain."

He nodded. "They are in the brain, and they operate...using energy, which makes one stop to wonder. If *electrons* are mysterious and unpredictable at their most fundamental level, what does that then say about neurons?"

27

They reached the dirt road beneath a scattering of gray clouds that began dotting the windshield with tiny droplets, prompting Rickards to turn on his wipers as he slowed. The gravel road was smooth and long, traveling east and descending into a narrow canyon whose walls were colored in several different rock strata as they rose toward the darkening sky overhead.

After two slow miles of increasing raindrops, the road narrowed into a set of twin trails worn from years of tire treads. As they continued up an embankment and around a gentle curve, holes in the road increased both in depth and frequency, causing Townsend to reach for his bouncing case beside him and to lift it onto his lap to keep it secure.

"You sure we're on the right road?"

"Pretty sure."

Reaching and rounding the next bend, Rickards slowed the car and soon eased to a stop just outside a small village.

Dozens of huts constructed of adobe-like mud bricks and metal roofing lined both sides of the road. A few of the nearby structures sat open with no doors and several children began to gather, curiously peering out at the dirty rental car. Then several adults followed in the children's wake.

Rickards exhaled and opened his door, stepping out into the drizzle and nodding politely at the growing group of people, all of whom were dressed in colorful, modern clothing.

As the other two climbed out of the car, Rickards searched the dark faces of the Quechuan children, finding who he was looking for in a small boy who stepped forward, grinning.

The boy approached and stared at Rickards before speaking in English. "You are back."

Rickards returned the smile. "Hello, Julio." He then walked around the front of the car and motioned. "These are my friends Angela and Leonard."

The boy smiled politely at them before turning back to Rickards. "She is the one?"

He nodded. "She came with me the first time."

It seemed enough, at which point Julio turned and looked behind him, waving more children over and speaking in rapid Quechua.

"You've made some friends," said Angela.

"Julio is a bit of a prodigy with languages."

Behind Rickards, more Quechuans continued gathering and grinning, welcoming them forward into one of the open buildings to escape the rain.

Julio, who looked about twelve, turned back and stated with some excitement, "Your mother was here a few days ago."

"Mother-in-law," corrected Rickards. "I thought she might have been."

The three followed the others into the open structure where several children examined Townsend's shiny metal box, touching it and tapping on it.

Julio peered up at Townsend. "You have come to see the Wank'a."

The professor turned to Rickards as he bent down toward the boy. "Actually, I'd like to show *him*."

The boy nodded. "The Wank'a is for everyone, but we must visit Urcaguary and get her permission."

Rickards smiled appreciatively and checked his watch, then turned back to Angela and Townsend. "We'd better get a move on."

***

The second visit was different for Angela.

There were more houses scattered along the entire hillside than she remembered, reaching all the way to the base of the canyon. And more children. Lots more than the last time. And behind them, the dry open field stretched much farther than she recalled, from one canyon wall to the other, perhaps a half-mile as it climbed along the rough terrain before narrowing toward the mouth of the upper canyon.

Near the top, she remembered in better detail the houses where the elders stayed and the larger circular hut where they'd met and sat with Urcaguary during that uncomfortable but enlightening exchange.

Now, well into South America's winter, all the huts had streams of pale gray smoke ascending from thick outside mud stacks.

She'd forgotten about the stream, too, flowing from the base of the walls and meandering down through one side of the village.

"Coming back to you?" asked Rickards.

"Yes. A lot."

"Same thing happened to me when I came back with Kathy." He turned to find Townsend directly behind him and slowed, taking the older man's metal case.

As they made their way up the steep path, he and Angela continued studying the huts, remembering what they had been told. The Wank'a, as Julio had called it and loosely translating to *statue*, was for everyone—even if most people were not ready for it.

It was Urcaguary herself, old and with the same profoundly wrinkled skin, who opened the wooden door of the hut when they approached. Standing at a demure five feet tall, she didn't appear the slightest bit surprised at seeing them. Instead, she ambled out using her old legs and met them as they neared, almost blithely unaware of everyone bowing their heads around her. This respect was mimicked without hesitation by the three Americans.

When they rose, the old woman's eyes moved among them, passing over Joe and pausing briefly on Angela, and then on to Townsend, whom she studied for a long time. She reached her hand out, drawing him to take it, at which point she merely stood, staring quietly.

After a long hush, she spoke, while young Julio translated. "She says you are a very knowledgeable man."

"Probably depends on the topic," Townsend joked uncomfortably.

Urcaguary continued, then paused again, waiting for Julio.

"She says you carry much pain and grief."

Rickards and Angela studied him curiously as he replied, "Don't we all."

Urcaguary gave a broad smile and laughed.

"She says, 'Knowledgeable *and* wise.'"

***

The exchange was shorter than before, even briefer than either time Joe had been there, and with less said. But what the older woman did say gave both Joe and Angela a sad, chilling feeling.

"More are coming now," translated Julio. "As she knew they one day would. We shall now see what becomes of our world... and our spirits."

With that, the old woman blessed them with her frail hand and returned to the hut.

28

"That was a little odd."

Rickards gave the older man a fleeting smirk and continued walking. "Trust me—you got off easy."

The path slowly became arduous, extending another several hundred yards toward the upper canyon walls. The ground was precipitous as the light rain continued dampening the soil, eroding their traction.

Rickards slipped several times with the added weight of Townsend's probe, almost falling the third time but managing to support the case between both hands. Behind them, several of the children followed, including Julio, climbing with little effort.

When the trail finally leveled, the three adults stopped to catch their breath, looking down upon the Quechuan village and spotting dozens more houses extending farther downriver where the stream widened and wandered away.

The professor stared ahead, panting, following the trail forward as it continued up another, gentler rise. "How far did Mike make it?"

Joe looked at Angela with a pained expression.

"Right here," she answered.

A brief look of surprise flashed across Townsend's face before all expression left it, and he slowly peered down around his own feet. Examining the area, he gradually lowered himself onto one knee with his arms crossed and exhaled.

It was here. Here where his old friend had left this world forever, without ever knowing Townsend's regret. Without even the benefit of a simple apology.

As if reading his mind, Angela spoke softly. "He didn't seem the type to hold grudges."

"He wasn't," nodded Townsend, still kneeling. "But I would have liked to tell him I was sorry."

"All of us would have," replied Rickards dryly. "For a lot of things."

The older man remained motionless for a long time before breathing in deeply and rising to his feet. "We did have some fun together in those days. God, what an exciting time it was." He peered up at the patchy gray sky above them. "Even through all that civil rights mess. Lord, the things we talked about. The ideas we had. About the present. About the future. As if we were glimpsing the building blocks of the universe itself."

Angela beamed back at him until he looked down once more and mumbled something to himself.

Then, raising his head, Townsend immediately walked past them, leaving Angela and Joe to follow, briefly noting the children had stopped.

It was another long trek before they reached the familiar narrow gap between two giant boulders, where they rested, and Joe lowered the professor's case onto the hard ground.

"This is as far as we go. What you came for is just on the other side."

"You're not coming?"

"We've already been. If we come now, you won't see it." With that, Rickards reached down and hefted the case with Townsend's probe once again, pushing it up onto one shoulder and preparing to push it over the top of the gap, where there was a wider opening.

Townsend squeezed through and reached up to receive it, lowering it with some difficulty to the ground at his feet.

"So, what exactly am I looking for?"

"It's not far. And you'll know when you see it."

Without comment, the older man picked up his case and peered back at them through the narrow crack. The rain had stopped but left them staring at one another with wet hair and clothing.

A moment later, the professor nodded and turned away.

29

They knew when it started from the sounds bouncing off the walls and echoing back to where they were standing.

Just as they knew when it was over—when it all simply disappeared, leaving Angela and Rickards patiently waiting for Townsend's image to reappear around the distant outcropping of boulders.

But it never happened.

After a half hour, they finally advanced, squeezing through the opening and scraping against the hard rock.

Once through, they continued forward and eventually rounded the boulders to witness the familiar wide-open expanse stretching out before them. In the distance, a prominent crystal spire ascended well over a hundred feet into the air.

In the open area surrounding it was Leonard Townsend, sitting motionless, on the lightly colored dirt ground, unmoving and facing away from them.

They approached cautiously while scanning the area. Seeing only Townsend and his open metal case, they quickened their pace and were within shouting distance when Rickards called forward.

"Professor?"

There was no answer, only a faint echo, enveloped by silence.

"Professor?!" Rickards repeated.

"Dr. Townsend?! Are you okay?!"

Now almost trotting, they came to a sudden stop beside him, staring down at the older man's white hair. His face was unreadable. He was gazing forward as if in a trance.

Angela dropped to the ground beside him and touched his left shoulder. "Dr. Townsend?"

The older man remained frozen, his dark eyes intently focused ahead and nothing moving but his blinking eyelids.

"Doctor?"

She shook him again and was relieved when he finally turned to angle his head at her. For a moment he stared at Angela's face, then turned to Rickards above her.

"Are you okay?"

He simply stared at them before slowly turning to face forward again. "Everything we call real is made of things we cannot call real," he murmured.

"What was that?"

This time, gazing at something else, the older man gently leaned forward and pushed himself onto his knees.

He rose without another word and slowly walked forward in short, deliberate steps until his movements became smoother and his natural gait returned.

The professor was still intently staring at the giant spire positioned directly in the center of the open area and surrounded by canyon walls and an open stretch of dirt.

When Townsend reached the spire, he stopped and stood fixated. Entranced. He examined and peered inside the thick column of clear crystal.

Softly, his hand reached out until he touched it.

"It's hot."

"Are you okay?!"

It took the older man several moments to finally acknowledge her question.

"We thought something had happened."

"Oh," he said, peering up over his head, "something happened, all right."

***

Together, Angela and Rickards remained sitting in silence on the ground waiting for Townsend to come out of whatever trance he was still in, which took time—more than it had for either of them.

The older man was still gazing at the spire in fascination when he said, "I've never... seen anything... like that."

"You sure you're okay?" she murmured

He nodded his head of white hair.

"You're not hurt?"

"Not hurt," he said. "Just... surprised. Very, very surprised."

"You said you wanted to see it," said Rickards, from the ground next to him. His legs were up and crossed with one arm wrapped around each knee.

"I did."

Trying to lighten the mood, Angela then added with a grin, "Still think Mike was crazy?"

Townsend shook his head. "I never thought Mike was crazy. And certainly not now."

"Mike said that with so much energy flowing around and through the planet, it wasn't surprising there would be a place like this where they connected and converged."

The professor nodded. "But I'm sure even he hadn't imagined this. It's as if–" Townsend suddenly stopped when he thought of the case behind him. He rose and hurried over to it.

The metal case was splayed out, three elongated probes secured and pointing upward into a position of triangulation. Below them in the unit's base was an old magnetic tape drive with several chrome buttons in a line below it, reminiscent of an old VCR.

To their surprise, the entire case was charred and blackened. Each of the cylindrical probes had melted, while the tape drive appeared to be leaking thin wisps of smoke through its tiny rectangular door.

The rest of the unit's base was also scorched around its edges, leaving everyone standing over it studying the destruction. Half of the outer metal was warped.

Rickards raised his head and clapped Townsend lightly

on the shoulder in a conciliatory tone. "They don't make them like they used to."

The disappointment on the professor's face was palpable, leaving him crouching in silence and fingering the remains of the three probes.

"The amount of energy required to do this…" he said, trailing off.

"A lot."

Townsend chuckled beneath a dour expression. "More than a lot."

He examined the various pieces, deliberating, until finally standing back up. He adjusted his glasses and looked up at the nearest canyon wall, following it to the next, and then the next until completing a full circle and returning to the crystal spire in the center.

He approached it again in a straight line toward the pillar. He studied it one more time, more slowly, gazing closer and closer at the crystal column. He leaned back and followed it up, examining the outside layer, even removing his glasses to hold them up to the spire's surface as he would a magnifying glass.

Angela and Joe patiently watched and waited.

"Do you see something?"

The professor nodded and gently took a step to the side, examining another section.

"What is it?" Angela asked.

"This isn't crystal," said Townsend.

She glanced at Joe. "No?"

"Nope." They both watched the man shake his head. "Crystal is caused by a process called crystallization, when hot liquids cool and begin to harden, giving them their unusual clarity. But this…" he said, speaking while rubbing the tower's smooth surface, "is more opaque. Especially in certain sections. It reminds me more of silica."

"As in glass?"

"Yes. But glass is a non-crystalline, because it's formed from intense heat rather than cooling."

Townsend now placed his entire hand against the spire. "Still hot?"

He nodded. "But not hot enough to make glass."

"So, it's not glass."

"Remember, energy can have many different forms. Heat is just one of them."

"Meaning…"

"Meaning," said Townsend, "that if other forms of energy are also coalescing here, they may be assisting in the formation of the silica."

"You said different energies could turn into one another."

He dropped his gaze and turned to Angela, grinning approvingly. "That's right. Because energy never disappears."

30

After a dramatic afternoon, the three returned to the hotel before sunset, thankful to find no police waiting for them and allowing them all to relax together inside Joe Rickards' room.

Angela was propped up on the bed with her head against the headboard while Townsend sat in a cheap vinyl chair, with Rickards resting his hip against the edge of a short black and tan dresser—which, coincidentally, matched nothing else in the room.

The professor still had not revealed to them what he experienced in the canyon. Instead, he lingered quietly in the chair staring blankly at the wall.

"Still with us?" Rickards asked.

The question induced Townsend to calmly swivel in the chair toward them. "What?"

"Are you still with us?"

"Yes," answered Townsend, shaking the cobwebs from his head. "Sorry, I've just been thinking."

"Anything we can understand?" Angela quipped.

The older man grinned at her. "Just trying to figure it out."

"Which part?"

"How it works," he replied.

"The spire?"

"No," he said. "Everything. The whole thing. The whole experience. It's clearly real. But how?"

"I hope you're not asking us."

Townsend shook his head, then rolled himself toward the edge of the bed. "Energy never..." he paused, waiting for Angela to complete his sentence.

"Disappears."

"Excellent. It either remains or it transforms into another form." He glanced at the cheap lamp on the bedstand. "For example, when you turn on a light switch, the electrical energy is transformed into thermal energy inside the bulb. But either way, it's still here." He leaned forward and pressed a hand onto the top of the blanket. "Look. As I push down on this bed and remove my hand, what do you see?"

"Your handprint."

"Correct. Created by kinetic energy. Now step back and think of the bed as the universe, whereby using my own kinetic energy, I create an *imprint* of my hand. And when I remove it… it's still there."

"Until something changes it."

"Precisely. But until it does, my imprint on this blanket remains—potentially forever." He shrugged. "Or in this case, until the warmth in the room causes the fibers to slowly re-expand. It's not a perfect comparison because the universe is different. More lasting. But for the sake of argument, let's say my imprint remains for as long as this room remains undisturbed.

"The universe is an unlimited construct upon which impressions are constantly being made through means of energy. Different forms make and leave different signatures. But on a construct that eventually returns to how it was, like this blanket, it *doesn't*. Imagine instead that it has unlimited memory, so when one energy field leaves an imprint, even if that energy transforms into another form and even leaves a second imprint in the same place, traces of the original still exist."

Rickards squinted. "Kind of how a computer hard drive works."

"Very much so," said Townsend with a hint of excitement. "Even when data is written and rewritten over the same space, traces still exist of the original. A tiny example, but similar."

"So, the universe is a giant hard drive?"

"Of sorts." Townsend shrugged. "But limitless. Hard to believe, but true."

"And you think this somehow ties into that glass spire?"

"Maybe. You see, if energy never disappears and instead either remains or changes, then whatever it consisted of before would still exist, just in the form of rearranged electrons." Pausing to let the thought sink in, he continued. "Which would suggest they could be rearranged back into the original form by way of their original imprint."

"Rearranged?"

"Yes," said Townsend. "Back to its *original* state."

"But how would that be possible?"

The older man looked back at the blanket. "Because in the quantum world, electrons can have multiple states at once."

Rickards gave Angela a sarcastic grimace. "Well, that clears it up."

"I'm not telling you how that spire works; I'm telling you how it *could* work. How it would be possible based on what we know today and what we can observe. Most people who experienced what I just did would likely conclude it was some kind of trick or illusion. But I don't think so. I think something very real happened in that canyon. We just don't understand it yet."

"But whatever it is," said Angela, "is an individual experience. A one-time experience that's different for each person. How is that possible that it's so unique to us?"

Townsend thought it over. "Neurons."

"Neurons?"

"If electrons are somehow binding together in that place under extreme concentrations, why wouldn't all the nearby electrons be affected, including the ones in your head? After all, that's what neurons are—*electrons* within brain cells."

Angela sat motionless on the bed, dumbfounded. "Wow."

"What else?" said Rickards, causing the professor to

134

look back up.

"Excuse me?"

Rickards frowned. "Where are you going with this?"

Townsend stared at him, blinking, until glancing at Angela.

"Professor?"

He continued mulling. "The rest," he said, "has to do with Mike Morton's data."

Angela leaned forward.

"The glass," Townsend replied simply.

"The spire."

He nodded. "Silica, in that particular form, is rare. It requires immense heat to create it. Or immense energy of some kind which rarely happens in nature. Not with that kind of clarity."

"And?"

Townsend continued. "It's so rare that I only know about its existence in one location in the world. This canyon of yours would officially be the second."

"Where's the first?"

"In the desert of glass."

31

They were 250 miles south of Cairo, 400 kilometers, and were no longer following the mighty and meandering Nile River where most of the country's north and south traffic was concentrated.

Instead, Egypt's Highway 60 was much more remote— a generous term of the word, Mona was thinking.

Barren was more like it.

Kharga was halfway between Cairo and the border of Sudan along a two-lane black asphalt road so dark and straight, it looked like it could have been paved yesterday. Over a hundred miles, perfectly preserved by the country's hot and bone-dry desert conditions. It was one of the driest on the planet, where all things took longer to break down in what could be considered a more modern version of mummification.

Another car appeared on the horizon before them and gradually drew near until finally zipping past Omar's speeding dark blue BMW X2.

All around them, the desolation was astonishing. Dry, barren desert in every direction. Vast stretches of the waist-high brush as far as they could see from the road, interrupted periodically by kilometer-length streaks of bright hot sand, like a lifeless ocean leaving nothing of note, even in the distance, except a few subtle ridges rising from the shimmering horizon, covered by the same endless baking landscape.

All of which made the cool air-conditioning of the BMW even more surreal, at least to Omar, who continued peering through the front windshield as he drove, with Mona quietly turning pages next to him, flipping through the thick folder on her lap.

"Find anything else?"

She shook her head without looking up. "No."

Over the last several days, she had slowly been piecing the papers together into some semblance of organization—or at least in some vague chronological order, trying to connect one dot at a time.

If the original order of the folder had made sense to the old Egyptian pilot, it certainly didn't to her.

With some pieces of the puzzle now identified, she found her attention frequently shifting to the papers at the back of the folder. The copies of newspaper articles.

There were over two dozen, all black and white, copied over the years from what appeared to be newspapers from different countries, judging from the differing languages. But the pictures were more than enough for her to understand what they were.

And they were harrowing.

Article after article, and picture after picture, of significant events–catastrophes–all over the planet spanning the last fifty years.

Omar glanced over from behind the wheel, noting one of the pictures. "What do you think those mean?"

"I haven't the slightest idea."

Mona paged through them again, looking closely for something that might stand out. But each time she came up empty.

There were no marks. No references. No circles or arrows on the papers pointing to a particular image or mention of the story. Just dozens of old copies. More dots that, for some reason, she couldn't seem to connect.

All she knew was that the articles were the *only* pages in the folder Hamed, the retired pilot, had sorted by date. That was all—the one and only consistency.

Mona's quiet contemplation was interrupted when her phone rang from inside the brown leather purse at her feet.

She pulled it out and answered with a standard Arabic

greeting before falling silent. After a moment, she quickly closed the folder and flipped it over, searching for her pen. When she found it she immediately began scribbling on the back cover.

She paused periodically to ask *when, where, or how many* before scribbling furiously again while the two sped down the open road.

Omar glanced over after she'd ended the call.

"Your sister-in-law?"

She nodded. "At the Ministry of Labor."

"Sounds like she found something."

"A few things," answered Mona, rereading her scribbling. She then flipped the folder back over and pulled out the small stack of financial records. "She said the first company they have with Mido Saad's name on it was called Bahgat Construction, established in January of 1970."

"Construction?"

"Uh-huh." Mona studied what she'd written before shifting her attention to the spreadsheets. "It's an international company that doesn't exist anymore—and one for which we don't have any financials."

"What happened to it?"

"She didn't know. But she did still have copies of the employment records, just like you said."

"And?"

"You were right. There was a large and sudden increase in the number of Bahgat employees. They went from three to over a hundred in just a few months."

He glanced at her with surprise. "Really? The company comes into being, and its headcount immediately explodes?"

"Yep. Four months later, in May."

"Now that's some growth."

"That's what she said."

Omar thought it over. "Any chance your sister-in-law made a mistake?"

"What do you mean?"

"You know, got the dates or years mixed up. Or the employee numbers?"

Mona scoffed. "I doubt it. If you knew my sister-in-law, you'd know she's not the kind to make mistakes. At least not many."

"What does that mean?"

"Let's just say she's very detail-oriented. To an extreme. It's probably the reason my brother travels so much."

Omar grinned. "Okay, I was just being objective. So we assume she's right and this company suddenly hires a bunch of people overnight."

"It isn't the only one," said Mona. "It's just the first of several. She said the other companies did the same thing after they were set up. And they grew into the thousands."

"Did she say anything else about this Bahgat company?"

"She said it was international."

"And the employees?"

"Mostly foreign."

"Foreign?"

"From other countries."

"I know what foreign means. I meant *from where*?"

"Oh." She glanced back down at her files. "Peru."

Omar blinked straight ahead. "Peru?"

"Yes."

"He establishes a company here and then hires a bunch of people from Peru?"

"Not *from* Peru," corrected Mona. "*In* Peru."

"These employees were *in* Peru? They didn't come here?"

"Not according to her records."

"So, Mido Saad had some business in Peru and suddenly hires a hundred people?"

"More than a hundred. My sister-in-law says those records show Saad no longer had those employees just two years later. Bahgat was back down to single digits before the headcount spiked again in 1973 to over *two* hundred."

"What?"

"And it stayed that way until 1975, when the company's records were no longer filed. Which she said usually means the company closed."

"Just like that?"

Mona nodded.

"In 1970, his workers in another country surge to over a hundred and then they all disappear. *Then* the number surges again, higher, before the company promptly goes out of business?"

"Strange, right?"

Omar thought it over. "Maybe," he said. "But maybe not. A construction company hiring a bunch of local people for a short-term project isn't all that unusual."

"And they just let them go afterward?"

"A lot of times, yes, depending on the project and when it's completed. Unless there's another project waiting in the wings, without work, most companies have to shrink to survive until they find something else. You said the second surge was a few years later and somewhere else?"

"In Bangladesh."

"Bangladesh," he murmured. After a minute, he frowned. "I hate to say it, but this could just be normal construction company turnover, moving from place to place when it landed another project."

"So, that's it?"

He shrugged, both hands still on the wheel. "Hiring a bunch of people in March of 1970 isn't a lot to go on."

"May," corrected Mona.

"What?"

"I said May. The month was May."

"Whatever. What else did your sister say?"

Mona sighed and went back to her scribbling, reading… until her eyes stopped moving. Slowly, they moved back to the Bahgat name and then stopped again, and then she absently raised her gaze to the car's black dashboard directly in front of her.

From the corner of his eye, Omar noticed a change in her demeanor. "What?"

She didn't answer. Instead, she began paging through the clippings again.

"What's going on?"

She continued examining each piece of paper as she went through them. "May," she said. "1970!"

"What?"

"I know I've seen that date before. In this folder." She withdrew a single sheet. One of the newspaper articles.

Studying it again, Mona held it up for Omar to glance at. When he did, briefly, he immediately checked his rearview mirror and rapidly slowed the car, almost causing the BMW to slide as he pulled off the road into a wide patch of empty sand.

With her right hand bracing herself against the dash, Mona's left was still holding the paper up in front of her. When he'd stopped, Omar plucked it away and examined it closer. The article was written in Spanish and was unreadable to him, but the calendar date at the top was easy. *31st May 1970.*

It took them two minutes to find an app and translate the headline using Mona's phone, but they could already tell what it said, judging from the large black-and-white photo in the center of the page displaying a gruesome scene of incredible destruction.

The word in giant letters was TERRAMOTO—the Spanish word for earthquake.

32

"Now *that*... is weird."

Two sentences at a time, Mona continued translating the article with her phone, listening as the sentences were read back to her in Arabic while staring at Omar.

"Saad creates a construction company and then goes to Peru just a few months before a major earthquake?"

"And hires over a hundred people right before it," said Omar.

He stared at her while she continued typing the text into her phone. Together, sentence by sentence, they both sat listening as the article described a horrific geological event off the coast of Peru, one that caused a mountain in the Yungay province to destabilize, triggering a massive avalanche cascading down the range in a slide of rock, ice and snow, destroying and burying two towns at over a hundred miles per hour under an estimated 80 million cubic meters of matter and debris.

The cataclysm killed over 60,000 people and injured 150,000 others in mere minutes—on May 31, 1970. And the single Xeroxed picture they continued to stare at portrayed an entire field of destruction extending for miles into the distance.

When the last mechanical word sounded from Mona's phone, the two finally looked back up at each other.

"How did Saad know?" whispered Mona.

All Omar could do was shake his head.

"You don't think he–"

"What?"

"Had something to do with it."

He frowned. "You mean as in caused it? How in the

world do you cause an earthquake?"

"I didn't mean *cause* it," she snapped. "I meant in some other way."

"What other way?"

"I don't know! I'm just asking."

Omar eased back in his seat and stared through the windshield at the empty road before them. "How else *could* you know?"

"Maybe someone else knew it was coming. Maybe a group of people."

"Like scientists?"

"Maybe. Maybe there was some instrumentation, and they saw it building up?"

"Maybe. But a month in advance? You can't predict the timing of something like that. Especially back then."

"So, then Saad was just lucky with his timing?"

"And location."

"Then if it couldn't be caused, what about triggered?"

"Triggered how?"

"I don't know. Maybe by a drilling company. Isn't fracking supposed to weaken things in the ground? The substructure or something."

Omar shook. "Fracking is new. And that article said the epicenter was off the coast, in the ocean."

"Fine, then you tell me. How did Mido Saad know?"

He shook his head helplessly. "I don't know."

Mona looked out the window with him before remembering something and returning to the back of her folder. "My sister said he did this with other companies, too." She raised the small stack of newspaper articles and began going through them again.

The rest of the articles dispelled both possibilities. Mido Saad was neither lucky nor a conspirator because each of the events was different both in type and location. In Bangladesh, it was a tornado killing 681. Then another earthquake in Tehran followed years later by a volcanic eruption in Colombia.

Yet each time, Saad was there. Each time he had a new company, and it would turn around less than two years later and shutter its doors—undoubtedly, when its government contract had paid.

The notes Mona had taken from her sister-in-law were nowhere near complete. Still, there was enough ancillary evidence, either through labor reports or in some cases financial records, that showed an odd and repeating pattern, one that seemed to grow larger and more sophisticated with each event, until no company was reused, but instead quickly established just before a catastrophe, run-up into the thousands and then erased from public record.

It was utterly inexplicable.

"I've never seen anything like this before."

"Neither have I."

"I've never even *heard* of something like this."

"I think this is what Hamed was trying to tell me," Mona stammered, "in his hospital room. With the imam."

Gradually, she arranged the papers on her lap and slid them back into the folder. "What do we do?"

Omar absently shook his head. In his rearview mirror, he saw nothing but empty road. "Do you want to keep going?"

"Yes!"

33

The world's orphan epidemic was far worse than most people knew, particularly in Africa, where over thirty percent of the orphans in the world were found, leaving swaths of tent-based encampments scattered throughout dozens of large cities.

This made their trip to the tiny town outside of Kharga all the more puzzling.

When they arrived, Omar pulled the car to a stop, not in front of a group of tents, but rather a small, well-kept and relatively new building. It looked as though it had been built only a handful of years before. Long and two-storied with stucco painted soft white, it stood alone in a vast open lot. The entire setting seemed oddly out of place in such a poverty-ridden countryside.

Several young children were playing in the distance in the dirt beneath a tall marula tree, dressed in matching light-colored clothing.

On the opposite side of the building sat two old and dust-covered vehicles parked side by side, each with a film of dirt almost thick enough to obscure makes and models. It was an odd contrast to the tidiness of the building and the children.

Quietly, they both exited the BMW and stood, feeling the dry, hot desert breeze instantly envelop them.

Still wearing her hair in a bun, Mona reached back into the car to retrieve a khimar and wrapped the light scarf over her head. Together, they strode forward and around the nearest corner of the building until they spotted an open front door. Once inside, the wind disappeared and the temperature dropped in exchange for cooler air that smelled slightly damp.

Mona glanced at Omar, leading him to clear his throat and call out down an open hallway stretching the length of the building. To their left was a large available room hosting several pieces of attractive wooden furniture, and to their right, an open eating area, sparsely decorated with tables and chairs, but clean and functional. The dining room.

A few moments after Omar's call, a figure appeared in the hallway and promptly moved toward them, a woman wearing a dark, loose-fitting robe and colorful green hijab around her head and neck with a face that was young, pleasant and respectful.

"As-Salaam-Alaikum," she said softly, greeting them. *Peace be unto you.*

"Peace be unto you," replied Omar, glancing past the woman as he briefly noticed another figure in the hallway before it disappeared.

"How may I help you?" the young woman asked politely.

"I am Omar Maher, and this is my fiancée, Mona Baraka. We phoned yesterday."

The woman nodded obligingly. "Yes. Of course. We've been expecting you. You asked for some information about our school."

"We did. We're writing a story on the children of Kharga and would appreciate learning about your institution and perhaps meeting some of your children."

"Of course," said the woman, smiling and bowing. "We are happy to help." She extended her smile to Mona and back to Omar. "You are both journalists?"

"We are."

"Wonderful," she replied, gesturing to the house behind her. "I am Rehema. It is my honor to show you around."

The second half of the dining room appeared as expected: simple, practical and clean, with all chairs neatly arranged around each table.

On the far wall, a door led into a large and equally simple kitchen.

"Our Rainbow of Hope house has been here for several years now helping children from nearly fifty kilometers away."

"How many children do you have?" asked Omar.

"Twenty-nine. Sometimes more, sometimes less." She slowly led them through the sitting or sizeable living area before heading back into the hallway and toward the rear of the house. "But we have helped hundreds since we began."

The two nodded while continuing to follow.

"It seems like a very…" Omar said, "*constructive* place for them."

The young woman briefly turned to face them before cracking a door open to another large room. This one was a classroom filled with perhaps two dozen children of varying ages. Nearly all of them silently glanced up before resuming their work.

"Excellent manners."

"Yes," she said with a proud smile. "At Rainbow, we have strong values to ensure our children become healthy, responsible adults someday."

Omar and Mona nodded in unison and smiled back as Rehema finished closing the door and moved on. "You have done stories on other orphanages?" she asked.

"Yes," fibbed Mona. "But we are more interested in the smaller, more personal schools."

"Yes, of course. We have much fewer problems with our children than the larger institutions."

"What kinds of problems?"

"Nothing I'm sure you have not seen. Behavioral issues and difficulties adjusting. Abusiveness between children. Familied children…"

Mona stopped. "Familied children?"

Rehema's expression was matter-of-fact. "Yes."

"I don't… can you explain?"

The younger woman shrugged. "Most orphans in Africa are not parentless," she said.

Omar and Mona shared a surprised glance.

Rehema peered back in a look of confused curiosity. "Most children in orphanages have families."

"Families? You mean a single parent."

There was a slight pause before Rehema shook her head. "Occasionally, yes. But in many cases, the children have both parents. Most children are not orphans due to loss of parents, as many are told. They are orphaned because of poverty."

"You're saying most of these children have parents? Both parents?"

"Not our children. Ours are true orphans. Again, I am speaking of the other institutions. The larger ones." Continuing forward, she passed another classroom door with the number 2 painted on it, leaving them uninterrupted and moving to the end of the building and up to an open screened door. Outside, they could see the younger children playing under the tree perhaps thirty meters away.

"And the abusiveness between the children?"

Rehema peered through the screen, briefly checking on the young ones. "It is very common in those places. When damaged children live amongst one another, they have many problems."

"But not here?"

Rehema shrugged. "Here only occasionally. As I said, we are strong here at Rainbow, and we have very strong values and policies."

"What kind of policies?"

"Who we are to accept," replied Rehema.

Mona stared, momentarily confused. "I thought orphanages accepted any child who needed help."

"Yes. The larger organizations do, those run by UNICEF and similar organizations. But we are a private and very particular house."

"It's a nice place," Omar stated, looking up and around the hallway and then back toward the front. "Do you have enough funding?"

"Oh yes," said the woman. "We have much support.

More than enough."

"From whom?"

"Our foundation." Rehema noticed a small scrap of paper on the floor and moved past them to pick it up. "Lead by Beih Saad."

Omar and Mona both paused but quickly nodded in approval.

Saad. As in Mido Saad. Formally addressed as Beih?

"He runs the foundation?"

"Along with many others. But he once visited us here."

Mona raised her eyebrows, attempting to appear impressed. "And when was that?"

"A few years ago." Rehema displayed another proud smile. "During an exchange. He spoke with me for several minutes. He is a very important man. Wonderful and gentle. We were honored that he took time from his very busy schedule to come visit us."

Mona returned an enthusiastic smile and reached out to squeeze the younger woman's hand. "You are very fortunate."

"That was the exchange?" asked Omar.

"Excuse me?"

"You said *during an exchange*. That was talking with Beih Saad?"

"No, no." The woman shook her head. "An exchange for the children."

They both nodded and began to ask another question when Mona stopped. "I'm sorry?"

"Rehema!"

Someone suddenly called the younger woman from the darkened hallway behind them. It was the second woman Omar had spotted earlier.

The image of the woman disappeared again, inside a doorway, while Rehema excused herself and hurried away.

Gone for only a few minutes, she reemerged and returned apologizing as she approached. "I am sorry. I have work to attend to. Do you have any further questions?"

"Uh," Mona turned to Omar with a frown. "Yes, actually. We had several more."

"I'm sorry. I wish I had more time. You may examine the house and even take pictures if you like. Perhaps of the bedrooms upstairs."

"What about the children?"

"I'm sorry. They will not be out of class for some time."

Omar glanced back to the end of the hall and through the screen door. "Perhaps the younger ones, then."

"I am afraid they wouldn't be able to tell you much. They are very young."

"How many houses like Rainbow does Beih Saad's foundation support?"

"I'm sorry. That I do not know."

"How many *do* you know of?"

Rehema paused again, this time appearing uncomfortable. "I know of only seven or eight others very far from here. Perhaps the foundation can provide you more information if you wish to contact them."

"But if we can just—"

"I am sorry," the woman repeated, cutting Mona off. "Thank you for your interest, but I really must go. May I see you out?"

Outside, both Omar and Mona found themselves standing dumbfounded beneath a bright afternoon sun.

"What... in the world... was that?" she breathed.

"That," replied Omar, "was a first-class brush-off."

"But why?"

"I guess you don't ask too many questions about *Beih* Saad."

She turned back to him and lowered her voice. "So it wasn't just me?"

"Uh, no. It's a very strange way to address him. Almost... patrician."

"They obviously hold him in high regard."

"Wouldn't you? Look at this place. And the kids. Something tells me there isn't an unruly one in the group."

"Yes. Very obedient," Mona said, walking back to the car.

"Not at all like what I've seen of other orphanages."

"You've seen others?"

"I meant on TV."

"Well, I guess we know how they keep the abuse and fighting to a minimum."

When they reached the car, Mona abruptly halted while opening her door. She stared up at the building.

Omar was already inside the vehicle when he noticed she was still standing outside. Rolling down the window, he leaned across. "You coming?"

When there was no answer, he climbed back out and peered at her over the dark, simmering roof of the car. "Mona?"

"She said we could take pictures."

"I don't think they would tell us much more."

She turned and glared at him blithely. "How do we know?"

With that, he watched Mona close her door and begin walking back toward the front entrance. "Mona?"

Trudging forward, she raised her phone and set it to camera mode.

Better yet, video.

Reentering the building, she was again greeted by Rehema, who'd clearly been watching them. "Please. I told you I must work now."

"You said we could take pictures," insisted Mona and held up her phone.

The younger woman suddenly looked nervous, realizing she had inadvertently invited them through the house.

Mona slowly waved her phone, recording both large rooms near the entrance and then heading for the stairs, making it only a few steps before the second, older woman emerged from the hallway yelling.

Covered in robe and niqab, revealing only her eyes, she shouted profoundly from under the fabric.

Undeterred, Mona turned and bolted up the stairs, reaching another wide hallway at the top with doors lining each side. She rushed forward, briefly pushing each of them open and recording each room as the doors swung open.

Below, Omar stepped to the side and glanced down the same hallway in which they'd just been, where he spotted a distant figure, a male, through the screen door, appearing from nowhere and approaching the back of the house.

"Mona!" he yelled.

Above him, she was still pushing doors open and scanning with her phone.

"MONA!"

"What?"

The other man was now running toward the house.

"We have to leave!"

She suddenly appeared at the top of the stairs and looked down, with both women yelling angrily at her.

"NOW!"

By the time the unknown man had made it through the house and out the front door, Omar had started the engine and was pulling the gear shift into reverse, spitting dirt and gravel forward in a cloud as he stomped the accelerator even before his door was shut. Causing the door to swing open wider before suddenly slamming shut when he found the brake.

He then slammed the shift back into drive and stomped on the accelerator again, peeling out in a half donut until bouncing up and over the asphalt.

34

Mido Saad, or *Beih Saad*, was calmly resting in a plush leather chair, quietly peering out through a thick glass window at the giant, expansive estate before him. The sheer vastness of it all, situated on the western outskirts of Cairo and extending into the endless desert beneath a fading sun.

At the moment, however, Saad's aged face was strangely detached from the grandeur before him, both from the view as well as the opulent air-conditioned room in which he was occupying. Decorated throughout in fine red leather, expensive lead glass, and exquisite gold trim around the entire room, all were as far from his thoughts as the immense villa, magnificent and baking outside under the intense afternoon sun.

Instead, Saad simply stared absently and apathetically forward as the nurse quietly flitted around him, silent in her work while administering the treatment.

Saad never looked at his chest, nor at the thin tube running up from it, or even at the machine carefully distributing the liquid directly into his bloodstream through the length of clear tube.

There was almost no acknowledgment of his situation at all. Just acceptance.

The cancer was spreading swiftly, too fast to stop even with ever-increasing doses of chemotherapy. He was not far from the point in which the drug would be doing him more harm than good.

Very few knew he was this sick. Only a handful. Which is how it had to be. He was still a public figure and didn't want to suddenly become susceptible to a never-ending stream of tabloids and overblown stories about his health—about his demise and eventually his wealth. How much did he have? And who would get it? Questions that were so very futile and meaningless.

In the end, money was what everyone worried about, like vultures fighting over a carcass. Who would get the meat, and who would not?

Everything eventually came back to money.

For Saad, it was more than that. Something much more important. The world itself. And the meaning of it all.

Why we were here, and for how long? And what one person could do in a single life span.

And of course, how long Saad's life would turn out to be?

No one knew, not even his doctor and nurse. But he didn't have long.

It was all coming down to this—the last weeks and months of a long and astonishing life.

Counting down the last desperate days like the clock of fate. Slowly decrementing in secrecy, robbing him of knowing just how long was left.

Just like the clocks of countless others who had long since reached that final tock.

Was it desperation he was feeling? Or despair? He could no longer be sure.

Because he was so close.

So astonishingly close.

The door opened behind him, and Saad listened as someone entered the room. He was unable to detect the person's scent as they moved close, thanks to the chemotherapy.

Instead, he was left to wait until the person closed the door and appeared from the side, continuing forward to one of the leather chairs and lowering himself down to wait.

The man's name was Khoury, Saad's Chief of Security. With short black hair, he sat patiently in the chair watching both Saad and his nurse. She continued with her work, pressing buttons on the device to turn it off before reaching down and disconnecting the tube, then winding it carefully, she hung the tubing on a small hoop and returned to close off his chest port.

Khoury continued observing in silence, wordless, as the nurse gathered her things and gingerly buttoned Saad's shirt back up. Moments later, she wheeled the chrome pole and its instrumentation, along with her bag, to the door and exited.

Khoury remained quiet, waiting for Saad to speak first.

"What is it?" Saad finally said, returning to the present.

"We are ready for the next arrival," announced Khoury.

"Good. And the next?"

"And the next." He nodded.

Followed by another, and another, and another—even though they could only use one child per night.

His security chief studied the old man with hidden fascination. Outwardly, there was little indication of the sickness at all. Even with the higher doses of chemo, Saad appeared to the observer to be able and robust. In fact, he seemed far stronger than others Khoury had known in the same stage and condition, making the illness seem especially insidious.

"There is something else," he added, causing Saad to look back at him. "An incident at one of the orphanages. In Kharga."

"What sort of incident?"

"Two journalists asking questions. When asked to leave, they apparently ran upstairs to take pictures."

The old man's expression registered little more than annoyance. It was hardly the first time a journalist had attempted to create a story at his expense.

Even with all the work he had done, there was still an unlimited supply of antagonists.

"I mention it," said Khoury, "because of the timeline."

Saad shrugged. "Ignore it."

"Ignore it?"

"Yes."

"You are sure?"

"It doesn't matter anymore."

Khoury nodded and stood up, facing the old man, who, after additional contemplation, lifted his hand. Without a word, his chief took Saad's hand in his and pulled him smoothly from the chair and onto his feet.

Without speaking, Khoury led his weakened boss across the room and through a glass door into a large office. Decorated in the same taste and lavishness as the rest of the mansion, the room's centerpiece was a giant desk made from solid polished Calcutta marble. Unique and distinctive in its streaks of whites and golds, it was elegant and perfectly polished, the most expensive and rare marble on the planet originating from a single Italian quarry.

On the desk stood several large monitors controlled by a single computer keyboard and mouse in front of them. Otherwise, the giant desk remained utterly empty.

In front of the marble desk was an equally expensive red leather chair into which Saad carefully eased himself.

"Thank you," he sighed.

"Anything else?"

"No, I'm fine. Tell Senura to come in an hour."

Khoury nodded.

The first few hours were always the worst, leaving Saad to seek a stationary, upright position after his treatment, the office and desk where he would relax and watch Khoury leave, easing the large lead glass door closed behind him.

When Saad heard the door to the larger room close half a minute later, he inhaled deeply, fighting through the first wave of nausea. It slowly passed, and he touched a random key on the keyboard, waiting for the monitors to flicker to life.

A single line and field appeared on the middle screen. He typed his password and abruptly paused once again to ensure he was alone before hitting the enter key.

All the screens suddenly beamed to life in unison, displaying deep blue backgrounds with several open computer windows on each. Some had scrolling lines of text, some with bouncing graphs, and the entire center screen displayed various pictures in a rapid process of comparing them side by side, with tiny square blocks simultaneously appearing around various sections of both images.

Saad didn't understand precisely how artificial intelligence worked, but he was familiar with the underlying approach—computers programmed to examine and measure based on mathematical algorithms of complex patterning. *Logical patterning* which emulated human thought on a set of predefined criteria and values.

In other words, looking for items of relational similarities at speeds and levels of granularity that humans could not. *Relational connections* was the term one of the engineers had used.

He remained motionless in his chair, watching the continuous activity across his screens. The tiny squares moved from pixel to pixel, searching for unseen connections, from one hand-drawn picture to another.

He didn't know exactly what they were looking for or what a computer would ultimately decide was connected, but at this point, he had nothing to lose. He needed to use every tool available to him if he would have any chance of succeeding.

The original of each picture was still safely preserved in his concrete-lined *thinking room* located sixty feet below the massive villa. All of them had long since been digitized in ultrahigh definition imagery—millions of pixels per page, down to the tiniest speck of hand-drawn color, scrutinized pixel by pixel. Some of these pictures had been drawn nearly fifty years before.

***

As the Nextant 400's powerful twin engines spun up, Dr. Layla Abo's eyes moved from face to face, searching for signs of anxiety or anything else she may have missed. But she found nothing. Each child sat quietly and obediently in their seat, looking straight ahead or down at the dark carpeted flooring.

Only one was looking back at her—a small girl from a village in western Zambia with short hair and dark brown eyes. She curiously watched the psychiatrist, as the woman moved back down the aisle.

She was bright and intelligent, as were the others. She had no family and was already conditioned to being alone, which was ideal. Quiet, introverted and thoughtful, she spoke only when spoken to and was surprisingly articulate when she did.

The small group had been carefully chosen after undergoing numerous tests and psychological evaluations, ensuring both she and Mido Saad were getting the cream of the crop. At least as much as one could be certain, given their options.

Eight-year-old Eshe glanced down when the woman neared her seat, only looking up again when she had passed. Her eyes then moved to the man standing at the front of the airplane wearing no expression and dressed in dark clothing, patiently waiting for the woman to finish examining the children.

Dr. Abo turned and nodded over the seats to the man, who nodded in response and tapped twice on the cockpit's door. He then reached outside to pull the cabin's main door closed and locked it before moving to his own seat.

Abo brushed back past the children and returned to the front, settling in beside the man whose unreadable face watched her sit silent and unmoving.

And very strong.

Eshe didn't stare out her window like the other children did as the plane moved forward, accelerating moderately as its giant metal body calmly turned to the left, causing the bright sun outside to pour through the dozen or so windows on the plane's starboard side and disappearing as quickly as it had come once the aircraft had completed its turn.

Eshe had never been in something so expensive before, prompting her to turn and study two other children across the aisle. One boy and one girl. Both were sitting along the right side of the narrow cabin with faces glued to their windows and bouncing along with the plane as it reached its runway.

Moments later the plane came to a stop, its engines still roaring outside. Suddenly, the aircraft jerked forward and began to rapidly accelerate.

Eshe felt a wave of nausea pass over her, causing her to swallow repeatedly to avoid getting sick. Finally, the plane and everyone aboard tilted back and left the ground, and the shaking fell away.

Dr. Abo continued watching the children from the front of the cabin. Airsickness was another sign of possible equilibrium issues. This would be quickly addressed on the plane but was something that could present a severe problem later. Cairo was merely the first destination, a layover of sorts before a much more critical second leg.

Fortunately, none of the children showed signs of sickness that she could see. If any did, it could warrant the removal of a child—both from the flight and the program, even with their accelerated timeline.

It would take several hours to reach Cairo, where the good doctor would help situate and settle the children before leaving again, headed for another school and another group of children who were already being prepared.

35

Joe Rickards pensively watched from his seat as a passenger carefully navigated down the wide-body's dark and much longer aisle to one of the multiple restrooms located at the rear of the larger Boeing 787.

"Can't sleep?"

He turned to find Angela beside him, her head pressed gently into a small rectangular pillow.

"I thought you were asleep."

He shrugged and looked back around the darkened cabin. "At least they have movies now."

Angela frowned and glanced at the screen directly in front of him, which was turned off.

"Otherwise, you just sit here all night and think?"

"More or less."

She acquiesced and twisted forward in her seat, glancing now at a sleeping Townsend. Again, he was angled uncomfortably against the window, just as he had been on their previous flight. "If only you had his problem."

"I'd rather see what's going on."

"You're an interesting man, Joe Rickards."

"Believe me," he said with a smirk. "I'm not."

Angela studied the cabin with him for a few moments before turning and leaning back against the headrest. "Surprised to be on yet another flight rather than headed home?"

"I would say yes," he replied, "but this seems to happen a lot when I'm with you."

"I'll take that as a compliment."

He gave her a humorous frown.

"I'm teasing." She reached down and straightened the thin blanket around her legs. "Well, at least I'm *not* going to mention anything about you having nothing better to do."

"Than fly halfway around the world? Thanks."

"You're welcome."

Rickards turned. "I would have thought you'd be the one to say no."

"Why?" she asked. "Because of my traveling phobia?"

He knew it was less about her reluctance to fly and more about the event that caused it, a terrible experience she'd had in South America just out of college.

"Maybe I'm getting better," she said thoughtfully. "Or maybe it's just because I've always wanted to visit Egypt."

"The archeologist in you."

"Egypt *is* at the top of the list for most archeologists. And anthropologists."

"Two for the price of one, then."

She grinned. "There's still a lot of mystery in Egypt. A lot left to be discovered."

"Well, I'm not buying a shovel and digging around with you if that's what you're getting at."

Angela laughed. "That's not what I mean. Archeologically speaking, yes, there is still much left to unearth. But in this case, I was speaking anthropologically."

"You mean culturally?"

"Right. Not just what was there before, but how it all ties together. Take the great pyramids, for example. Archeologically, they have been examined from practically every possible angle by thousands of researchers. But anthropologically, we're only beginning to scratch the surface. I mean, just the sheer effort involved in constructing them from a human standpoint is mind-boggling. Ten thousand people over the span of fifty years or more." She shook her head. "Imagine the sheer scale of human and social sacrifice just to bring one pyramid to fruition."

"I'm guessing the slave labor made things easier."

"Ah, but that's just it. Most people think that. But they weren't slaves."

Rickards turned to look at her.

"For years, decades really, it was assumed the great pyramids were built with slave labor. But recent evidence tells us that's not true."

"No?"

"Skilled laborers built the pyramids. Not slaves. Every block is so well crafted and arranged, not to mention that the structures were so well designed and planned out that the pharaohs would have had to use artisans—and a lot of them. People who knew what they were doing as a trade.

"On top of that, their living quarters have also recently been discovered not far away. Remnants of small communities have been found with evidence of *families*, suggesting more of a regular job than a slave project."

"A regular job?" said Rickards. "As in, 'Bye, honey, I'm off to the pyramid.'"

Angela had to cover her mouth to keep from laughing again. "Yes. Something like that."

"Maybe the Flintstones weren't all that far off the mark then."

"Stop it," she said, punching his arm. After her smile faded, she tilted her head. "Anyway, I guess the excitement is just overwhelming my fear of traveling this time. Besides, no one knows we're coming. Unlike last time."

"Let's hope so."

"What about you?"

He looked at her. "What about me what?"

"What are you afraid of?" she asked.

He shook his head. "Not a lot these days."

"What about in Mexico?"

The question caught him off guard. "Excuse me?"

"You heard me."

"I don't... I'm not *afraid* of Mexico."

"I didn't say you were. I said something *in* Mexico."

Rickards remained staring at her, with a cynical expression but said nothing.

"If not fear, then something else."

"I don't know what you're talking about."

"You're not going to tell me?"

"Tell you what?"

"Seriously? Multiple secret trips to Mexico after your wife died? You're telling me there's not a deeper reason there?"

He turned forward, glaring at the seat in front of him.

"Fine," she relented. "Don't tell me."

They fell quiet again for a long time before Angela changed the subject. "Did you know that Egyptian culture may not have a beginning?"

Rickards didn't answer at first until her words finally sank in. "What was that?"

"I said the history of Egypt may not have a beginning."

He squinted. "I thought it was one of the oldest civilizations on the planet. Aren't their pyramids a couple thousand years old or something?"

Angela gave a wry grin. "4,500 years."

"Sounds pretty old to me."

"That's not what I said," she replied. "I said it may not have a *beginning*."

"What does that mean?"

"It's called the Hypothetical Third Party theory, an idea put forth by a group of leading Egyptologists. Because the archeological evidence of Egypt's early history suggests that rather than develop slowly over time like most other civilizations, Ancient Egypt appears to have emerged all at once and fully formed."

Rickards stared at her as she continued. "Many of humans' earliest languages developed as a series of drawings or simplified pictograms, something that can be seen evolving over hundreds or thousands of years and gradually becoming more detailed and sophisticated—just like everything does, from language to agriculture, to cars and even computers. Everything evolves over time in small, incremental steps. But that doesn't seem to have happened in Egypt. Instead an observable history where their culture and language steadily grew more advanced, their hieroglyphics seem to have appeared suddenly and with a level of complexity and structure many historians cannot explain."

"Is that true?"

"Yes. Even the earliest hieroglyphics were unusually stylized and conventional. The same is true with their mathematics, medicine, astronomy and their architecture— the same understanding of architecture used to build the Great Pyramids."

"How is that possible?"

"No one knows. Most Egyptologists today tend to avoid the subject."

"Why is that?"

"The same reason many others are ignored. The implications. How many revolutionary ideas have been ignored by the establishment throughout history? Many of which ended up being right. Magellan, Copernicus, Einstein." She motioned to the sleeping Townsend. "Even Dr. Townsend said it still happens all the time. A lot of Egyptologists have built their careers on conventional theory, and convention doesn't like radical ideas."

"I thought you said leading Egyptologists were the ones who'd brought up the discrepancy."

"Some. Not all. And when they did, it was often done in papers that pondered or asked questions about it, not necessarily claiming a new theory. It's a much safer way to examine it. But yes, people like John Anthony West or Walter Emery have made multiple mentions of the lack of apparent history in Egypt."

"So, what do they think happened?"

"They don't know. But they do offer some possibilities. Such as the *hypothetical third party.*"

"Someone else was involved?"

"Possibly. Egypt and Mesopotamia both appear to have some similarities, but not nearly enough to prove one came from the other. Only a few cultural fragments, really.

Which means…"

"A third party?"

Angela nodded. "But no one has any idea who that would be. So, either there is a much older and sophisticated culture that existed before any records were kept, or Ancient Egypt suddenly sprang into existence some other way."

"How else could it?"

She shook her head. "I have no idea. But you can see what got me past my fear of traveling—at least this time."

"Excitement, I guess."

"And the possibility that there could be a connection with Egypt and the spire we found in Bolivia."

"You don't think that's tied to Egypt somehow missing a beginning?"

"No. It's just another incentive to go there. The place truly is the land of mystery."

"I suppose so," acknowledged Rickards. "But don't get too excited. Like I said, I'm not digging."

Angela chuckled. "Then I'm not going to tell you the rest."

"Rest of what?"

She stared at him as if considering whether to finish. "Egypt and Mesopotamia are not the only cultures to lack evidence of an evolutionary beginning. The third was the Olmecs."

"And where were the Olmecs located?"

"In Mexico."

He suddenly turned and peered at her.

"Maybe that's what you were doing in Mexico," she joked, prompting Rickards to turn away.

No, he thought to himself. *His reason was entirely different, and having to do with something much more recent.*

A mistake.

One Joe Rickards had made almost twenty years before.

Devastating and unforgiving, it had taught him a terrible and unrelenting lesson—that there are some mistakes a person simply never stopped paying for.

36

It was more than three hours later when the first glimpses of the impending sunrise could be seen over the curve of the Earth's surface. From altitude, the dark midnight sky gradually gave way to soft shifting colors in faint streaks of yellows and oranges.

A steady transition was visible through the window next to a still sleeping Leonard Townsend. And next to him, Angela Reed dozed quietly into the fabric of her small, crooked pillow.

Rickards' eyes felt stiff and tired as they moved back and forth every few minutes, from the heavenly scene through the window back to the cabin, where some of the sleeping passengers were finally beginning to stir.

In the aisle next to him, a man in his early thirties passed and lightly grazed Rickards' sleeve on the way to the restroom, making Rickards wonder if children were designing our modern aircraft these days, given the spatial limitations of not only the aisles but the seats themselves, which seemed to be growing narrower with each new model. Right in lockstep with the overhead baggage compartments.

He glanced across the aisle and watched an elderly couple awaken together, almost at the same time. The wife retrieved a small pill box and flipped the lid open for her husband. In the seat in front of them, a child of perhaps seven or eight years old lounged sprawled over the arm of her own seat like a pretzel and dead to the world around her as though nothing could wake her.

Rickards' eyes moved back to the window to gaze again at the vibrant colors methodically crawling over the distant horizon. When he looked back up, he was again brushed by the same man returning to his seat.

Rickards' tired eyes started to glance away but peered back at the young man as he approached his seat row, where he briefly looked over the heads of several passengers to another person along the cabin's opposite aisle.

Almost without hesitation, the second man rose and headed toward the restrooms.

Rickards blinked, continuing to watch more random passengers rise and make their way back to the head following hours of sleep.

His gaze followed an older Bolivian woman wearing a beautiful green and blue shawl as she too gracefully made her way to the rear of the plane to wait in line. It was then that Joe noticed something.

On the opposite side of the cabin, those at the rear were easier to see, at least without him having to completely twist around in his seat. Which was precisely what he did when Rickards realized he couldn't see the man who had just gotten up. Instead, he was on Joe's side of the cabin and aisle waiting for a lavatory before a door opened and he stepped inside.

It wasn't until the second man finished and returned to his row on the other side of the plane that Rickards' interest picked up. Particularly when the second man nodded to a third before lowering himself back down into his seat.

Now the third man rose, walking to the rear of the plane and making his way through several people, positioning himself in a short but growing line for the same lavatory.

Rickards' eyes returned to the first two men sitting over ten seats apart. Both were now still with heads down, reading.

Without a word, Rickards slid down in his seat and angled his head until he could see the back of his aisle directly behind him in the reflection of his video screen. He watched quietly... when something else peculiar happened.

Patiently waiting in line for the same lavatory, the third man was given the opportunity by a fellow passenger to take another when one of the other restrooms was vacated sooner, at which point, the young man, well-dressed and smiling, shook his head and remained where he was.

Several minutes later, when he too finally emerged and returned to his seat, Rickards noticed once again that another passenger was signaled.

In a calm motion, Joe reached up over his head to push the attendant call button, then slunk back down in his seat, watching the fourth man repeat the same routine.

The attendant arrived promptly and smiled, simultaneously deactivating the light while she lowered her head and greeted him in accented English.

"I need to speak with your air marshal," said Rickards.

The attendant cocked her head with a look of confusion.

"I am sorry?"

"Law enforcement," whispered Rickards. "Your officer on board."

"I'm sorry, sir. We do not have—"

"I know you do," Rickards said, cutting her off. "Now get him. Wake him up if you have to. Now."

The attendant stared at him with her mouth open and stumbled back a step before whirling and quickly walking away.

When the fourth man finally returned to his seat, he, in turn, nodded to a fifth, who rose just as the others had and headed for the rear of the plane, again waiting in line for the same restroom and after a few minutes, disappearing inside, securely locking the door behind him.

His was the final step, requiring slightly more time as he smoothly raised each hand and removed two cufflinks, each composed of small lead balls plated with a thin layer of silver.

He broke off the post and toggle of each cufflink in a

perfectly rehearsed routine, leaving only the two balls, each dome-shaped on one side.

Next, he removed his watch, a Rolex, and turned it over, revealing a narrow tube extending a mere sixteenth of an inch from the watch's metal casing. He gripped the tube with his fingertips and gently pulled it free, carefully setting it on a dry section of the lavatory's sink.

Finally came two pieces from his belt, which appeared to be two decorative metal brads. But upon pulling them from the thick leather, the shapes became clear. Two short, wide metal *casings*.

Carefully, delicately, he retrieved the tube from his watch and bit into one end, puncturing it. Then he cautiously poured its contents, a tiny stream of dark gunpowder, into one of the casings where he then placed one of the lead balls, or bulletheads, atop to keep it from spilling.

Next, the man turned the tube over and punctured the opposite end, again delicately pouring the powder into the second casing and topping it off with the second metal ball.

Meticulously, he slid the tiny tube back into the hole within his watch and retrieved what resembled an elongated thimble from his front pocket. With careful pressure, he used it to gently press each bullethead down, securing it onto the metal casing.

When finished, he dropped the small tool back into his pocket and reached down and around the back of the lavatory sink, looking for the small access panel. When he found it, he pulled it open with a powerful tug and pushed his hand deep inside, searching.

The plastic object didn't look much like a handgun. Instead, it looked like a blaster from a cheap science fiction movie. Or a toy. Because it had to. Each of the four individual pieces had to look entirely different, at least to airport security. Anything but components to a plastic handgun. It was small and blocklike, with only two separate holes, one for each bullet, not unlike a much smaller version of an old-style double-barrel shotgun.

Inserting and then locking a thick clasp in place over both rounds, the man finally raised the gun in his right hand to examine it.

They only needed two bullets—one to kill the senior pilot and another for the air marshal on board, if there was one. If not, one of the flight attendants. This would squash any ideas of resistance from the rest of the passengers. Especially without knowing how many more rounds were left in the gun.

The man twisted his arm and checked the time on his wristwatch.

Practice made perfect.

Double-checking the small restroom for anything he'd missed, he slid the bulky firearm under his shirt and unlatched the lavatory door with his opposite hand.

Outside, a female passenger stood, clearly irritated over the long wait. She stepped to the side and immediately pushed in through the narrow opening when he was out of the way.

But the man in his early forties barely noticed. His heartbeat was rapidly increasing, and his vision beginning to tunnel as he wrapped around the thin wall and crossed through the rear section of the plane, stopping at the corner and gazing up the long starboard aisle, looking for the heads of his compatriots, all of whom were patient and still. Waiting for his signal.

With a deep breath, the man smiled and leaned forward, pulling the makeshift gun from his shirt and lowering it to his side–when he suddenly felt something press into the base of his skull.

He froze without a word before slowly beginning to turn.

"No," the voice stopped him with a whisper. "You turn, and you die."

It took only a moment of contemplation. Mission failure was a contingency for which they had planned, but not like this, leaving the man momentarily stunned until he regained his composure.

There was no going back. It was now or never. Even if he died, he might still get the makeshift gun to one of the others.

In one sudden movement, he would throw his weapon forward and whirl around with the hope of knocking the gun away from his own head. If he saw anything at all, he would know he was still alive.

Instinctively he inhaled, readying himself.

In that instant, there was a loud *thunk*, and his entire body slumped, immediately limp. He was quickly grabbed under each armpit and hauled back around the corner.

It took only three seconds before someone screamed. A woman waiting for one of the lavatories, and she was seized and almost instantaneously muffled by a male flight attendant behind her.

But what she did get out, the four men heard. And in a flash, they were out of their seats, running for the rear of the cabin, knocking passengers to the side as they charged through, reaching the back area of the plane, which appeared oddly quiet.

The first of the four rounded the corner and was immediately clubbed by Rickards, with the air marshal standing behind at a safe distance, his gun raised.

As soon as the first fell, another rounded the corner from the second aisle in perfect timing to receive Joe's second swing, collapsing like a rag doll at their feet. Together, the last two appeared behind him from the same direction, freezing when they came face-to-face with the black barrel of the marshal's gun. Behind him, Joe Rickards scrambled to his feet and aimed their self-made plastic gun directly at them.

37

It should not have gone that smoothly.

Rickards had studied hundreds of hijacking scenarios during his career, from planes to ships to virtually any form of public transportation—exactly as every other investigator in the NTSB had.

But it was never that cut and dried. Or almost never.

Usually, the situation devolved into chaos when the action began, especially in tight quarters where hundreds of variables could change the outcome.

For Rickards' part, he knew the blows from the heavy, oversized bottle would have to be single strikes, hard and fast, enough to neutralize an attacker in one fell swoop. There would simply not be time for another swing—not before the others reached the back of the plane.

And he did make each hit count. All three, in fact, starting with the gunman and then followed by the next two.

Enough, in the end, to even the odds.

However, the greatest asset without question was the marshal, who was not just aboard the plane, but who also had a great deal of training and instinct. Immediate and sure, he acted without hesitation, especially after watching two of the hijackers himself.

Things just didn't go that smoothly.

Even more to Rickards' surprise was the lack of hesitation exercised by the marshal in knocking the last two men unconscious. None whatsoever. He clubbed them both with the bottle and enabled all five to be bound and gagged with zero resistance.

And with the help of the male flight attendant, all five were quickly and individually hauled up the secret flight of stairs to the aft crew rest compartment or CRC, which was sleeping quarters for the plane's crew during unusually long flights. These were compartments most flying passengers never knew about.

In the CRC, all five assailants were laid out on narrow beds with both hands and feet firmly secured. Rags were stuffed in each of their mouths. The marshal, watching over them, left Rickards with the distinct impression that he would lose no sleep at all if some of the men accidentally suffocated.

And yet, the true miracle was that only a few passengers witnessed the event, at least before being immediately silenced by the crew, two of whom were given Valium and strict instructions before being guided back to their seats several minutes later.

There was, of course, a stirring amongst the passengers until a flight attendant explained over the loudspeaker that someone had fainted at the rear of the plane, requiring brief medical attention. But fortunately all was well, and the passenger was in good condition. There was no mention of just who the passenger was, of course, and in the distraction, few remembered to notice the five seats remaining empty until touchdown.

For his part, Joe Rickards returned to find both Angela and Townsend awake, looking around along with many of the others.

"Did you see what happened?" Angela asked.

"What? Oh, yeah. Someone at the back of the plane fell down and had trouble breathing. They were fine after one of the attendants found their medication."

Angela stared at him as he sat. "Really?"

He nodded. "A little excitement, but everything's fine."

She turned to a slightly bewildered Townsend and then back to Rickards. "Why were you back there?"

Joe smiled and held up a fist filled with tiny bags of

pretzels.

"You're kidding."

"What?"

"You stole those while someone was having a heart attack?"

"Not a heart attack," he corrected. "Fell down."

***

Angela and Townsend were still staring at Joe as he ate his pretzels, silently shaking their heads when he offered them some.

"Did you sleep?"

He shook his head. "Unfortunately, not."

"You've just been sitting here the whole time?"

"Mmm-hmm." He chewed and swallowed, then looked over while opening another miniature bag. "And thinking about this desert of glass thing."

Angela blinked and followed his gaze to Townsend.

"Ready to give us the full story, Professor? You conked out pretty quickly."

The older Townsend reached beneath his glasses and wiped at one of his eyes. "Uh, sure." He paused a moment, gathering his thoughts. "But to explain this, I'm afraid we need to delve back into quantum mechanics a bit more."

Rickards smirked. "Maybe I'll get some sleep after all."

***

"What you have to understand is that the fundamentals of the world we live in rest entirely upon a smaller world that truly makes no sense."

"We remember," said Angela, who glanced back at Joe's loud chewing.

"Niels Bohr once stated, 'Anyone who hasn't been shocked by quantum theory, hasn't understood it.' Because it truly was Einstein's nightmare."

"Einstein's nightmare?"

"Everyone's nightmare, really," corrected Townsend. "To this very day."

"Not a single person has figured it out?"

The older man grinned almost condescendingly. "Figured it out? My dear, no one even understands it. Quantum mechanics is so strange that most of it was completely ignored for much of the twentieth century."

"Ignored? By who?"

"Everyone."

"Why was it ignored?" asked Rickards. "I thought you scientist guys lived for this kind of stuff."

"We do," Townsend replied. "Normally. But figuring out the quantum world is not like solving any old puzzle. It would be more akin to solving *the* puzzle. Of everything."

"It's that big?"

He nodded. "It's that big. Imagine everything you believed you knew, and I don't mean just you—I mean everyone. Imagine everything all of us thought we knew about how the world worked suddenly made no sense. Nothing. Not gravity. Not oxygen. Not even the sun rising every morning. Because while they all *appear* to work day in and day out, imagine just peering at everything in the world a little closer to reveal that it was all broken. That water travels uphill rather than downhill. That things were never where you left them. That's how weird it is. Protons, photons and electrons. No one would believe it if it hadn't been proven time and time again to be utterly bizarre."

They both remained still in their seats, letting his words sink in. "So… how is this related to the tower in Bolivia or glass in the desert?"

"I'll tell you how. Because just twenty years ago, there was no way I would have believed something like that glass spire could be real. Not a chance. But in the world of quantum, it's no longer possible to claim *anything* isn't real."

Townsend reached into his seatback and pulled out a magazine. "This magazine," he said, flipping through it, "is

176

as real as anything else in the world, right? Pages made from paper and ink, all bound together with pictures taken by cameras we *know* exist. And yet none of it does. Because while this object, this magazine, is real, every square inch of it is based on building blocks we cannot call real."

"None of the building blocks are real? How is that even possible?"

"No one knows," answered Townsend. "No one. Which is the ultimate conundrum. Not just for me but for every living person on this planet who understands even the smallest modicum of quantum theory."

"Which now includes us."

He nodded. "Which now includes you."

"But... this is all still theory. After all, it is called *Quantum Theory*, right."

"It's called a theory. But it's not. It is extraordinarily and disturbingly real."

"Then," Joe said, looking around, "you're saying this entire plane, the metal, the circuitry, the fuel, even the passengers... none of us are real."

"I'm not saying. I'm asking the same thing Niels Bohr and Albert Einstein asked—how can we consider any of our world real when the constituent parts themselves cannot be real?"

"Wow. That's heavy."

"And it's not all," said Townsend, briefly pausing as a passenger strolled by. "The very definition of *weird* takes on a whole new meaning when it comes to quantum entanglement."

Angela nodded. "Now *that* I've heard of. I don't understand it, but I've heard of it."

"Quantum particles are strange enough, but entanglement of those particles truly puts weirdness in the rearview mirror."

"Entanglement has to do with them being connected, right?"

"That's right. In ways that should be, for all practical

purposes, impossible, but aren't."

"And this has to do with the spire in Bolivia?"

"I believe so," said Townsend. "And the desert glass in Egypt."

They continued listening.

"You want to hear it?" he asked, surprised.

"Why not?" answered Rickards. "We have another two hours."

Townsend nodded and adjusted himself in his seat. "Let me begin by saying I believe the spire is real."

"Yeah, so do we."

"No, what I mean is I think I know *why* it's real. Maybe not how, but why."

"Because of quantum mechanics?"

"More or less. And entanglement." He stopped to think before taking a deep breath and holding both hands up in front of him. "Hear me out on this."

38

"What I'm about to explain to you is going to sound very strange. Even fantastical. But the longer I talk, the more sense it's going to make. Because these are all provable facts. You can look them up."

"Let us have it."

Again, Townsend nodded, gazing at them through his glasses. "The quantum world is truly and utterly bizarre," he stated. "That is a fact. Particles like electrons make up most of the world we see around us. Fact. And electrons, like other particles, are completely unpredictable in their quantum state."

He suddenly pointed to Angela, who grinned and said, "If you say so." When Townsend frowned, she corrected herself. "Sorry... *Fact.*"

"Quantum entanglement is when these particles are created together, interact with each other or exist in proximity such that their quantum states become linked and indistinguishable from one another. Another fact."

"When you say proximity, how far are we talking about?"

"We don't know," answered Townsend. "But we know that particles can be bound together in different ways, either when created or sometime afterward. In fact, the greatest distance these entanglement connections have been demonstrated to date is over eleven miles. But we're sure they can and do exist over much longer distances. Nevertheless, electron entanglement is a fact. However, the big question here is just how many or how often electrons, the energy particles of the universe, become entangled?"

Angela shrugged. "How often?"

"It's not a riddle," he said. "No one knows. But it may

be a lot. It may even be a common occurrence among particles. And if electrons are a building block of nearly everything, do those entangled connections continue to exist within larger objects?"

"I'm not sure I follow."

"What I'm saying is that we are now finding entanglements everywhere we look." He held up the magazine again. "There are probably millions of electrons in this single magazine. What does that mean for the magazine if a large portion of the electrons within it are currently entangled?"

"Oh," breathed Angela. "I see."

"Electrons are in *everything*. Even us. Including our neurons, otherwise known as brain cells. So, what would it mean if those electrons in our brain cells were also in a state of entanglement?"

"Connected to what?"

With a shrug, Townsend said, "Other electrons."

Rickards raised an eyebrow. "You mean other electrons in our body or somewhere else?"

Townsend stared back. "You tell me."

Joe turned to Angela.

"Now, back to your spire in Bolivia, found by Mike Morton as a location where, for whatever reason, different forms of energy engage and merge from the Earth's atmosphere."

"Reaching the surface."

Townsend stopped and held up a finger. "Not reaching the surface," he said. "Reaching through it."

"*Through* the surface?"

"I very much doubt energy that powerful and that concentrated would simply stop at the Earth's crust."

"You think it goes through?"

"Other forms of energy certainly do. For example, our magnetic field. It constantly moves through our entire planet in both directions. And I think this coalescence of different forms of energies is similar. If it moved even remotely similar to our magnetic field, it would stand to reason the energy enters in one place and exits another, like a pin traveling through a cushion."

"In one side and out the other," repeated Rickards.

"Presumably."

"Are you saying the crystal spire is one end... and the desert glass is the other?"

"I think so. They are on opposite sides of the planet, though not precisely. I did a little research before we left, and Egypt is not the exact geographic opposite of Bolivia, which is called an antipode point. Bolivia's antipode point is closer to India. But on a global scale, it is still not all that far off. And frankly, some level of deviation traveling through dense matter is to be expected."

"Wow," breathed Angela.

"So that's the connection between the two."

Townsend nodded at Rickards. "It wasn't just the similarity in the silica glass and the suggested antipodes. The most intriguing piece is the spire itself. Or at least what happens there. What you saw. And later, what *I* saw." He went on. "Remember when I told you that energy never disappears?"

"You said it either goes somewhere else or turns into another form."

"Precisely. And do you recall my explanation in the hotel room, with the bed? About a universal framework that still holds remnants of what used to be?"

"And that nothing is ever truly gone."

"Yes," said Townsend. "I think *that* is what is happening at the spire. And believable or not, it's all still rooted in physics."

Angela stared at the professor dubiously. "I saw my dead mother."

"A mother whose existence, or energy, was never completely gone," he replied, lowering his voice. "Tell me, if connections and entanglements are real and our bodies are packed with electrons... what do you suppose happens if some of these are connected to someone or something… that dies?"

Rickards' face was as white as Angela's, reeling from the suggestion. Thinking back to what happened to him at the spire. What and who he had seen.

Neither spoke, leaving the older man with one final statement.

"Niels Bohr, who argued with Einstein over quantum theory for years and was eventually proven right, once described the separation between our world and the quantum world as a giant curtain standing between the two. Something tells me that the spire in Bolivia… *is* the curtain."

39

The UNICEF office in Cairo was three blocks from Egypt's famed Nile River, near Abrag AlShaheed, with a bright ambient waiting room glowing from the patchwork of lightly colored flooring and large windows. A sizeable Egyptian rug lay neatly between several antique-styled coffee tables and chairs, all arranged and facing a chest-high reception desk approximately thirty feet away attended by two young women who remained quiet with their heads down.

Mona Baraka finally turned her eyes to Omar from one of the chairs and raised both eyebrows impatiently, receiving only a shrug in response.

They had been waiting over thirty minutes.

"What is taking so long?" she mouthed.

"We didn't exactly have an appointment," answered Omar in a whisper.

Mona leaned into her chair without replying, trying to glimpse a piece of the office around a corner of the wall. She was about to speak again when a woman in a light-gray pantsuit with long, light-brown hair finally appeared and approached them.

She smiled graciously and held out a hand, shaking Mona's as she rose to meet her.

"I'm sorry for the delay," she apologized. "We're all terribly busy this afternoon. I was told you wished to speak with someone."

"Yes, we do. Thank you."

"My name is Shani Darwish. How may I help you?"

"What is your role here, Ms. Darwish?"

"I work in the Public Relations department of Egypt UNICEF. I was told you wanted to speak about one of our orphanages."

"In a manner of speaking. Is there a quiet place we can talk?"

"Of course." The young woman motioned behind her. "Follow me, please."

Together they rounded the corner revealing a large open layout with working chairs and tables in the middle, several occupied, and lined on each side with wooden walls and office doors.

Turning again, the three approached a series of glassed conference rooms and entered the only one that was empty.

"Please, sit down," the woman offered. "May I get you something to drink?"

"No. We're fine," replied Mona, sitting in one of six black leather chairs at the end of the table and directly across from Omar.

When the door was closed, Darwish moved to another chair and sat facing them. "I understand you are both journalists."

"Yes," she lied. "Thank you for seeing us on short notice."

Shani Darwish smiled politely.

How about no notice.

"We wanted to speak to you about some of your children."

"Of course."

"We just came from an orphanage outside Kharga."

Darwish wrinkled her nose slightly. "I don't believe we have any homes in Kharga."

"It was a Rainbow of Hope house."

The woman's expression changed to a disappointing frown. "I'm sorry, the Rainbow houses are not owned or operated by UNICEF. They are managed by another organization."

"Yes, we know," said Mona. "By Mido Saad."

"One of his charitable organizations, yes."

"It's not the organization per se that we're interested in.

It's more about the children there."

"I'm sorry, we don't have any oversight of Beih Saad's affairs."

Mona glanced at Omar, who was quietly listening.

There it was again, the term Beih.

"We understand that you don't oversee those particular houses. But we were hoping you had some insight on the children, or how they are–"

"I'm sorry," repeated Darwish. "Multiple organizations are trying to help the children in these countries. Some we work with and some we don't. Beih Saad's Rainbow Foundation is completely independent of ours. I'm happy to speak of our own efforts or those of our partnering charities."

Mona paused, deciding to change tack. "I'm sorry. We are very aware of UNICEF's role in helping so many children, especially here in Africa. I guess what we're trying to understand is some of the differences in doing so."

"I'm afraid I don't understand."

"Well, the difference between UNICEF's practices versus other charities and orphanages. I mean, UNICEF is the largest and most well-known charity for this mission with more funding and political support than anyone."

Darwish's face didn't change. She continued with her eyes fixed on Mona, nodding. "Yes. We are charged with the greatest global campaign efforts and responsibilities, but I'm not sure exactly what you're asking."

"What we're asking," explained Mona, "is why are most of the housing projects supplied by UNICEF and even your partners made up of tents, when housing provided by private organizations such as Mr. Saad's, appear much more... able?"

From the end of the table, Shani Darwish's face grew defensive. "We have far more children to care for," she said with a stiff grin.

"Yes. I understand that. But the conditions are so vastly different. Even the children themselves. We stopped by one of your assistance locations on the way here where you are housing thousands of children and their families. But Mr. Saad's houses hold far less with what appears to be far more afforded per child."

"Again," said the other woman, "I'm not sure what you are asking."

Finally, Omar spoke up. "We are not insinuating anything, Ms. Darwish. We are not suggesting UNICEF is doing anything less than it could. We are simply trying to understand why Mr. Saad's organization can do so much more. Or conversely, why are they not helping more children?"

Somewhat surprising, the woman didn't appear fazed in the least. "As I stated," she repeated calmly, "we do not have any control over Beih Saad's organizations or decisions."

Mona retrieved her phone and began playing the video, pushing it forward across the table. "We took this of the rooms at one of Mr. Saad's Rainbow houses."

Darwish peered at the video as it played until it ended with shakiness of the picture and someone yelling in the background. She looked back at them. "I cannot speak for anything the other homes are doing."

"At least at your locations, the children are *playing*," said Mona. "At Rainbow, they look… I don't know, militant."

"The Rainbow of Hope houses have very high standards," offered Darwish. "And more resources to apply them."

"But why?" asked Mona. "If someone were really trying to help as many children as they could and had access to more resources, why wouldn't they be trying to help UNICEF or partner with them? Why only help a few children here and there in very remote places?"

"There are children everywhere that need help, Ms. Baraka."

"Yes, but UNICEF has camps literally everywhere, while Mr. Saad has houses almost nowhere. Does that seem odd to you?"

Again, Shani Darwish smiled politely. "I am truly sorry, Ms. Baraka. And Mr. Maher," she added, turning to Omar. "We just do not have any insight into Mr. Saad's affairs. Their houses are independently owned and managed. I'm afraid we simply have more than enough of our own issues to worry about. I wish I could give you more of what you seek."

With that, Darwish gently rose from the chair. "I would recommend you reach out directly to the Rainbow Foundation. I'm sure they can answer your questions."

Back through the reception area, Mona stared at Omar, stunned, as they exited through the office's large double doors.

"Are you kidding?!"

"That was not helpful."

"Not helpful?! That was *more* than not helpful. That was weird!" She turned around, looking along the open street.

"She was hiding something."

"Something? How about everything? There is no way an organization as large and powerful as UNICEF would not know everything about Saad's supposed charity."

"Well, he is awfully good at keeping out of public view. Maybe he's just—"

"No," retorted Mona. "If we can walk into one of Saad's places that easily, then so can they—unless they don't want to."

"Why would they not want to know what he's doing with those children?"

"That's my point! They would. UNICEF, probably more than any other organization, isn't merely about housing kids. They're trying to save lives in any way they can!"

"Maybe she's right, then," said Omar. "Maybe they just have too much on their plates to worry about. If they know about the Rainbow houses but don't think it poses any serious problems, maybe they just let it go."

Frustrated, Mona glared at him. "Then why wouldn't she just say that?"

He thought about it while turning and quietly walking back to the car. When they reached the vehicle, they climbed in and closed both doors.

"That woman is hiding something," said Mona. "I know it."

Omar was still thinking. "Maybe we should try to talk to someone else."

"Maybe. Unless they're all hiding something."

"What would they be hiding?"

"What if–"

Suddenly someone frantically pounded on the car's side window, causing them both to jump in their seats and Mona to emit a brief scream.

Outside, another woman was standing beside the car, one hand still pounding on the window and the other raised over her brow, trying to see through the bright reflective glass.

When she had their attention, the woman, older and dressed in similar attire, motioned for Omar to lower his window.

When he did, she stared in, examining both of them before speaking. "You were asking about Mido Saad."

Omar nodded, looking back at Mona. "Yes."

The woman tried the handle of the rear door and Omar unlocked it from the inside. After a hasty scan around the parking lot, she immediately climbed in and pulled the door closed behind her.

"Go!"

40

Back out on the main road, the woman, looking to be in her fifties, pointed forward toward a row of eucalyptus trees lining the boulevard. "Over there, under the trees."

Omar crossed and turned with the traffic, finding an open spot in the shade. When he stopped, the woman behind him stared through the windows, studying both sides of the street.

"Who are you?!"

"I work for UNICEF, like the woman you just spoke with. That is all you need to know."

"I think we're going to need–"

"Quiet!" she snapped, still scanning. "Do you want your questions answered or not?"

Mona twisted in her seat but the woman reached forward and pushed her forward again. "Sit normally," she said. "And speak forward. Tell me why you were asking about Saad."

A sudden fear washed over Mona at the thought of the woman being aligned with Saad. But it passed quickly.

If that were true, she wouldn't be acting paranoid.

"What were you asking about?" the woman demanded.

"We... were asking about his charity houses. The Rainbow houses."

The woman studied Omar's eyes through the rearview mirror. "And what did Shani Darwish tell you?"

"That UNICEF doesn't have any insight to Mr. Saad's organizations."

The woman in the back seat almost snorted. "Of course she did. What else?"

"She said Saad's foundation is privatized and well run," said Mona. "And that UNICEF has its hands full and has no time to spend on Saad's affairs."

"She called him Beih Saad," added Omar.

He thought he caught a hint of disgust in the woman's eyes. "They all do."

"Do you know something?" asked Mona.

There was a pause as the woman contemplated from the back seat before she finally answered. "Several of us do. More than anyone is willing to say."

"Like what?"

The woman eyed them both. "Tell me who you are first."

"My name is Mona Baraka. I'm a journalist here in Cairo. He is Omar Maher, a financial analyst. And my fiancé."

"Why are you asking about Saad?"

"I was given information by someone before he passed indicating Mido Saad may be involved in something odious."

The woman snickered. "That's an understatement. How much do you know about him?"

"Not much. We have financial records for some of his old companies. Employment information. Pictures…"

"You have enough, then to know something is not right. And enough for Saad to know about *you*."

"What does that mean?"

The woman lowered her voice. "He has ears everywhere. Even in UNICEF. If he did not know who you were before, he will soon."

"From Darwish?"

"Yes, from Darwish! Do you really believe an organization as large and powerful as UNICEF doesn't know about Saad?"

Mona angled her eyes toward Omar and mouthed the words: *I told you.*

"Saad is not who you think he is," the woman continued. "He remains in the shadows using things like bribery and coercion. Even murder."

"What?!"

"I have worked for UNICEF for eight years. Long enough to see two others make the mistake of trying to find out more about him. They dug too deeply into his businesses and his past."

"What happened?"

"They disappeared," she said. "Never seen again by their friends or their family."

"For investigating Saad?"

"For digging too deep! Deep enough to draw Saad's attention. Like the shaitan."

Omar and Mona glanced at each other. *Islamic demons.*

"Did they tell you what they found?"

The woman didn't answer. Instead, she peered forward in a momentary trance. "It cannot go on," she breathed. "It must end. It must all end."

"What must end?"

"What he is doing. What Saad is doing."

"What? What is he doing?"

The woman continued blankly staring. "Saad is a master of deceit, of deception and falsehood. He portrays himself as a patron of Allah while secretly praying on the weak and fearful, both in children and adults."

Using her peripheral vision, Mona tried to study the woman. "Everything we've read about Saad says he is a philanthropist and gives most of his money to help children."

The woman narrowed her eyes and stared at Mona. "If you believed that, you wouldn't be here asking questions. Why do you think the children he helps are so far away—in barren regions or cities?"

"That's what we asked Darwish."

"And what did she say?"

"Basically, that he targets remote areas where children are neglected."

The woman sneered. "Neglected. All of that wealth focused on the smallest, poorest areas. Areas where it costs nothing to help them. Where food and water can be attained with only a few qirshes and a building erected with little more, all on the backs of the destitute."

"Then what is he doing?" asked Omar. "Where does the money go?"

"Some goes to the children, but not as much as people think. More goes to the people."

"What people?"

"His agents. For their allegiance," she said, leaning forward. "And their silence."

"Silence?"

"To look away. So no one looks too closely at his charities. At what his *houses* are doing. While he harvests."

Mona felt the hairs rise on the back of her neck. "Did you say *harvests*?"

"Yes."

"The children?"

"Yes."

Mona felt a churn in her stomach. "What is he using them for?"

"I don't know. No one does."

Omar stared at the woman through his mirror. "Is he... selling them?"

"No." The woman shook her head of dark hair. "He is *rotating* them."

Mona finally turned and looked at the woman. "What?"

"Rotating them," she repeated. "And giving them back to us."

Mona stared at the woman, blinking as though not hearing correctly. "Giving them back to who?"

"UNICEF. And our partners."

"He's giving them *back*?"

She nodded.

Mona looked at Omar, who had the same perplexed expression. "We don't understand."

"And neither do we," responded the woman

sarcastically.

"But–"

"In poor countries, it is not uncommon for children to be returned after adoption, if they are not strong enough or intelligent enough. Or worse, if there is something wrong with them. If they are mentally or physically broken."

"You mean disabled?"

"Yes. Some families do not want that. They do not want the burden of dealing with a broken child."

"So they bring them back?"

The woman nodded. "It does not happen often. But yes."

"How often?"

"Perhaps one out of twenty."

"And this is what Mido Saad is doing?"

She nodded again. "He gives his broken children to UNICEF and pays us to take them. Not our charity. Our administrators."

"He pays the people who run UNICEF to take these broken children in and look the other way?"

"That's right. And he pays them a lot, as well as families to take them."

"So that's where the money goes," murmured Omar.

"How often does he give a child– *put* a child back in the system?"

"All the time."

Mona looked back again. "What does that mean—*all the time*?"

"Every time." The woman looked suspiciously back and forth at Mona and Omar. "All of Saad's children are broken. All of them."

41

Deep in his bunker, his thinking room, Mido Saad stood motionless, once again quietly staring at the patchwork of pictures, a colorful mosaic of papers covering two entire walls and most of another. They were arranged and perfectly hung like a giant hand-drawn puzzle but with pieces that did not match.

He gazed at them for several minutes before finally reaching forward and pressing a hidden button behind one of the pages, causing a door to click and swing slowly inward, still obscured beneath the checkerboard of paper drawings.

Saad turned to verify the main door to his bunker was locked from the inside before stepping through the smaller doorway and into another, narrower space.

Perhaps eight feet wide and twelve long, the hidden room appeared distinctly different from the bunker, adorned with nothing on its walls and containing only a single table and chair beneath three bright overhead lights affixed to the concrete ceiling.

On the table, beneath a rectangular pane of glass, rested a solitary object. A book. Ancient and brittle and splayed open, revealing two of its hundreds of pages.

Saad approached the table, staring down, mesmerized, with his eyes intently focused. He absently pulled the chair toward him and lowered himself into it.

Raising the protective glass, he pushed it up until it remained propped open, allowing him to lower his fingers upon the delicate, frail papyrus pages.

He still needed to touch it.

Having done so thousands of times, Mido Saad simply could not keep from caressing the fragile paper, pages so thin and frail they were beginning to crumble at their darkened edges. He knew full well that the oil and residue from his fingertips only added to the object's gradual demise.

He didn't care.

Unlike the pictures on his walls, the book had never been digitized. Memorialized, yes, but not digitized. He could not risk the possibility of a copy of the book's contents being discovered by someone else.

Even accidentally.

No, he had gone to extraordinary lengths to ensure no one else had ever laid eyes on it.

At least no one alive.

No one on the planet was aware of its existence, what it said or who had written it.

His fingertips softly traced the outside edges of one of the pages of papyrus, causing tiny pieces to crumble and fall away, though he was careful not to get too close to the lettering. It was written in Sumerian, the oldest language on Earth.

The book's only copy had been created by Saad's own hand, translated into modern Arabic and encoded, then hidden in a place that would appear little more than gibberish if discovered.

It had been stowed and hidden as a precaution in the unlikely event that something happened to the original. Damage, deterioration or theft. As impossible as it seemed, it had been hidden below ground in Saad's bunker for the last half-century.

There was perhaps an even more uncomfortable possibility of damage—intentional destruction. By Saad himself, should another person become aware of it.

Over his right shoulder, in the corner of the tiny space, were the only other objects in the room—a five-gallon metal can of gasoline and a box of matches.

He was so close now. So very close. He had seen what the book told him he would when the miracle was near. Just as the others had, whose secret writings filled the entirety of the ancient pages. Other people who had lived long before him, telling him what he would need to do—and, of course, *how* he would need to do it.

An ancient, mysterious tome passed from one hand to another, known by perhaps only a dozen living souls in all of human history before disappearing from all existence for eons, locked away in the tomb of one of Egypt's most remarkable and misunderstood figures.

42

January 1907

With one last heave, the heavy limestone block finally gave way and fell backward, disappearing into blackness, revealing a hole in the thick wall of rocks and boulders.

Breathing heavily, the man reached up and adjusted the cloth back over his nose while pressing himself against the rocky wall, allowing a second man to step forward and assist.

Both were struggling for air, not just because of the tunnel but also the ravaging sandstorm outside, ready to pelt them like a giant sandblaster the moment they stepped back into the open. The narrow tunnel sheltered them from the stinging winds, but the tradeoff wasn't much better—complete envelopment inside the tunnel as they struggled for oxygen through the smokey clouds of their oil-wick lamps.

The lamps were frustratingly dim, requiring the men to hold their faces mere inches from whatever it was they were trying to see, which was now the rock wall directly in front of them displaying a pitch-black hole in its center.

On the verge of hyperventilating, the man named Ayrton raised his lamp in front of the opening and attempted to peer inside. But he could see nothing, leaving both men striving to get all four hands around the edges for a hold.

Together, they worked the next boulder back and forth, over and over until pebbles began to fall from its edges.

"Careful," warned Ayrton under his cloth mask. "This one probably weighs three or four hundred kilos. Don't let it land on your foot!"

Several minutes later, the second square stone finally gave way and tumbled forward, missing the tips of their dirty boots by inches and providing a much larger hole through which to peer.

The entrance had been discovered only three days earlier when Ayrton had noticed an odd ledge along one of the larger stones they were in the process of unearthing, leading them to the ground and outline of a stone step. It was the beginning of a long-forgotten passageway filled with collapsed sand and rocky debris.

Now, with enough removed by their crew, both men were able to crawl through the tight opening on hands and knees, sliding clumsily over the tops of boulders until reaching what appeared to be the final wall, or door, to the tomb.

Even after the second stone had been pulled free, it would take several more hours to move enough debris to create a hole large enough to squeeze through, carefully stacking each piece to avoid blocking their exit.

With a groan, Ayrton scrambled over a stone too large to move and extended his leg through the opening until he could feel the cool, dry air on his exposed calf. Then, awkwardly, he folded his body at the waist and used his backside to push through, immediately losing his footing in the darkness and falling inside with a sudden yell.

The sound of a crack was heard, followed by two heavy thuds.

"Are you all right?!"

The question was followed by a long silence, with only the cloud of fine dust swirling between them before Ayrton's voice was heard.

"I think so," he groaned. "My lamp went out. Can't see a blasted thing. Pass me yours."

The second lamp was passed through the hole, its flame flickering feebly in the darkness, grasped by Ayrton's dirty hand.

When the flame disappeared from view, scuffling sounds were all the second man, Mahid, could make out until they ended and were followed by complete and utter silence.

"Blimey," Ayrton finally whispered as he stared in awe at the dim images before him.

"What is it?"

Ayrton regained his bearings and turned back around, looking for his own lamp and spotting it amongst the rocks. He retrieved it, then relit it with the second.

He scrambled carefully back to the wall and extended Mahid's lamp through the opening. "Mind that first step— it's a doozy."

Once both men were inside, they spread apart, using their oil lamps to maximize the illumination over dozens of objects.

Not far from the entrance were parts of a dismantled, gilded shrine related to what appeared to be the tomb's original door. Against the southern wall and lying atop the decayed remains of a lion-headed bier was a sarcophagus with its lid appearing slightly ajar.

Above the coffin rested four Canopic jars made from Egyptian alabaster. And in the far corner were remnants of what remained of several wooden boxes and their contents.

Completing his scan, Ayrton turned back to the shrine and bent down, studying several different seal impressions, and next to them, four bricks with hieroglyphic etchings still visible on two.

The men's eyes returned to each other's with expressions of incredulity, stunned at what they had found entirely by accident in a mere three days.

The tomb looked unlike any they had seen before, even in pictures, with walls that appeared unfinished, plastered only on two sides, and poorly at that.

A family of lower status, he thought. *Or perhaps simply prepared in a rush.*

Ayrton moved to the sarcophagus and lowered his lamp, peering through the narrow gap. Inside, he could see a sliver of the mummy and a glimmer from the vulture pectoral wrapped around it.

"A pharaoh," he said, looking up at Mahid.

The Egyptian turned and looked around again, this time with confusion. "A pharaoh? In a place like this?"

There would be decades of speculation using dozens of clues left behind hinting at several possible occupants, from the condition of the unfinished room to signs of a second coffin having been removed from the tomb, likely sometime during Egypt's Ancient Twentieth Dynasty.

But it wouldn't be until 2010, a full hundred years later, that genetic testing would reveal the man entombed to be the one and only Akhenaten, King Tut's enigmatic and mysterious father.

43

Several months later, Robert Ayrton stood alone in the quiet, empty tomb. Its contents had been removed and meticulously cataloged, along with thousands of black-and-white photographs, creating a visual map of every square inch of the room.

Now with several waist-high lamps brightly burning in the tomb, every section could be clearly seen. Chunks of plaster fell away from two of the walls. The other two, along with the ceiling, were marvelously chiseled within giant sections of solid bedrock, along with dozens of conflicting markings on each that would take archeologists many years to puzzle out.

Even the corridor was clear of rocks or boulders, leaving the long walkway free with its twenty perfectly cut stone steps leading up to its opening; Ayrton mused humorously at the memory of his maiden entry. He fell clumsily through the opening, eager with anticipation to see what lay within, completely unaware that another, even more spectacular find would be unearthed nearby in the not-too-distant future and take the world by storm.

Tutankhamen himself.

Ayrton took in one last look at his mysterious KV55 tomb before beginning his long trip back to England.

Satisfied, he turned and started to exit when his boot caught something on the floor; a tiny corner of stone slab sticking up and jutting a mere quarter inch above the rest, no doubt from thousands of years of deep geological shifting below Egypt's famed Valley of the Kings.

Ayrton playfully tapped the corner of the stone with his boot and had just resumed his turn when he felt something strange.

Pausing, he turned back around, again staring down at the corner of flooring and touching it with the toe of his boot. When nothing happened, he leaned forward and added more weight—and felt it again.

Curious, he stepped back and studied the floor, bending down into a crouched position. Examining the corner more closely, he placed two fingers then the palm of his hand on it and pushed.

Nothing.

With a modest frown, he touched his fingertips to the corner's edge and found several grains of loose sand. Silently, Ayrton rose again and returned his body weight to the small rise. Once again, he felt something; the faintest sensation of movement.

He stepped back and continued staring for a moment, then gradually turned his head to look for a tool and spotted a large rectangular wooden box near the tomb's entrance.

Striding back to the opening, Ayrton retrieved a rusted iron pry bar from the box and marched back down the passageway.

He now noticed the stone slab was one of the smaller pieces in the floor, though still large and heavy, taking him several tries to attain a grip with the bar's open claw. When he had purchase, he leaned against the tool with his entire body.

The slab moved.

It took several more tools before he could raise the thick stone enough to glimpse a large opening beneath, a deep cavity with what appeared to be a box approximately four square feet in size and at just over a foot and a half deep. The wooden container appeared to be in notably better condition than the other items removed from the tomb.

Lifting it out and reaching for another, smaller bar, Ayrton gripped one edge of the wood and pried it up with a screech and a small burst of shattered wooden pieces.

Removing the lid revealed a bundled square object carefully wrapped in familiar gray fabric exposing a thick leatherbound book with hundreds of papyrus-inked pages when unraveled.

44

Dr. Layla Abo was sitting quietly in her seat with her dark head lowered, slowly scrolling through pages of evaluation data on her phone, completely tuning out the roaring sound of the aircraft.

In front of her, filling the rest of the private cabin, sat all six children—three boys and three girls. Together, they averaged eight-and-a-half years old. They were respectful and obedient, either peering out through their windows or directly at the seatbacks in front of them.

Except for Eshe.

She could see the man sitting at the front of the cabin, but not the woman, unless she leaned into the aisle where she could then glimpse the doctor's dark hair as she looked down and read.

The young girl didn't know what to make of the female doctor or the man next to her, whose face didn't seem to be capable of any expression at all.

In the beginning, the female doctor had seemed kind and caring, but throughout the tests, she'd gradually become less and less talkative and less interested in asking Eshe questions until the whole experience began to feel like a well-rehearsed drill, almost mechanical. It made Eshe wonder with a hidden grin if the woman doctor was secretly a robot.

The Rainbow of Hope House wasn't the first orphanage she'd been in. Not the others either. But it was the nicest and cleanest. And the strictest.

Most of the other children didn't care and said it was worth the plentiful food and clean beds. So, they did whatever was asked of them to ensure they wouldn't have to leave.

Whatever the adults asked, the children did, including Eshe.

Because for all of its rules and punishments, Rainbow was nothing like the other places she'd lived, where the beds were dirty, as well as the people, and bad things happened to the older kids at nighttime, causing them to want to stay in their beds for days and days.

Rainbow was different. Rainbow was safe.

And that was the reason why no one wanted to leave. They even had doctors, who came to look at them a lot, checking for problems or sores, even in their mouths and ears.

The adults and teachers who ran the house weren't as friendly, but they didn't hurt you unless you did something wrong, and even then, the doctors would come to check you again right away.

It was hard living there. But it was still better.

Eshe continued watching the expressionless man in his seat, wondering who he was. She didn't remember seeing him before, or even the woman doctor. Not until the examinations had started. Suddenly, she'd appeared and began asking all sorts of questions, like whether Eshe could remember her family. How she liked the house. Whether anyone had hurt her before, and if so, where?

It was more than the other doctors asked, at least all at once. But whatever she'd said to the woman doctor must have been good because she'd been chosen with the others and was now aboard a fancy airplane.

Eshe didn't understand most of the testing, which had lasted for days, or what, exactly, they were being tested for. She'd tried to ask, but the woman doctor had never answered her. She'd simply tell her *not to worry* before continuing with the examination.

They were strange questions, too. How well did Eshe sleep? What kinds of dreams did she have? Did she like music? Or art? Did she get nervous? What things was she afraid of? Did she like to play? Could she draw?

So many questions. And then there were the tests. Then more questions. Eshe had been convinced the woman liked her and enjoyed talking to her.

Now she wasn't so sure.

The woman barely spoke to any of them except for simple things or to give instructions.

But Eshe wasn't worried. She must be important to them. Otherwise, the woman wouldn't have picked her.

In her seat, Dr. Abo was already scrolling through the information on the next group of children currently at their Rainbow school in Northern Tanzania. Things had never been this hectic before, and it was introducing problems in an otherwise perfect routine which had been developed over dozens of years to identify and select the right children for their needs.

For Saad's needs.

His health was now rapidly declining, causing everything to be accelerated. Not just for Abo but for everyone, leaving her utterly exhausted.

Of course, he paid her extraordinarily well both for her service and her discretion. For her ability to tune things out—whether jet engines or particular ethical dilemmas.

The money had done that for a long while, until Abo couldn't help but start piecing things together. The pictures. The children. The charities. The schools. And their unusual disciplinary practices.

Mido Saad was an extremely private person, keeping important details very close to the chest. But over the years, through slight hints and innuendos, Abo had assembled enough information to become more than intrigued with the man. With each shipment of children, she'd gleaned more and more—like dumping children off to the UNICEF camps after something detrimental had happened to them. All of which she had been about to blow the whistle on.

Until she'd glimpsed something else.

Through helping him interpret the hundreds of hand-drawn pictures, Abo was slowly developing a sense of what Saad was doing—and more importantly, what he was truly after.

His clock was counting down ever faster with the cancer, leaving Saad not just eager but downright desperate.

Even as careful as the man had been and as paranoid, he still occasionally slipped up. A word here and there that might seem irrelevant to the average person but not a psychiatrist, and certainly not one who'd spent over a decade helping him round up children no one would ever miss. Perhaps *harvest* was a more appropriate term—all for a particular reason that only Saad knew.

He did not have much time now. And she could now feel the desperation in his voice every time they spoke. It was the kind of anxiety and despair a person felt when an impending crisis was visible on the horizon.

Whatever Saad was trying to accomplish, he was very close. Or he believed he was. He no longer focused on anything else. Not on any of his businesses, several of which were still operational. Not on any ventures of any kind.

Only this.

Relentlessly pushing Dr. Abo and dozens of others in Saad's employ to deliver as many viable candidates as possible.

But after all this time, she still didn't know why. Or what. What was the man seeking in the children's pictures? What was he searching for?

And what was he hiding in that underground bunker of his?

45

"I need to speak with you at once."

It was the voice of Khoury again, Saad's head of security and a man who rarely sounded ruffled or excited, prompting Saad to immediately walk to the intercom speaker in the bunker's main room.

Pressing the large button, he responded. "What is it?"

"Your instruction was not to allow any interference, but one problem is growing uncomfortably more serious."

Saad stared at the device on the wall, thinking for a moment before finally nodding. "I'll be right up."

Saad's residence, or compound, was nothing short of palatial, evident from the giant study Khoury was waiting in when the old man appeared from a side hall.

Like the living room, a wall of glass filled one entire length of the study, but the shades were drawn to reduce the sun's thermal heat.

He came to a stop on the moondust-colored carpet and placed both hands behind his back. "What is it?"

"The woman," replied Khoury. "The reporter."

"Yes?"

"She just showed up at the UNICEF office in Cairo, asking questions."

"About?"

"About you. And the Rainbow houses."

Saad still didn't sense alarm. "That's hardly a first."

"Someone at the Ministry of Labor is also digging—a woman related to the journalist."

"Related?"

"The woman's sister-in-law."

Saad finally frowned. "Is that so?"

"I doubt they are looking up your birthday."

Saad blinked at the sarcasm and continued reasoning. The alarm was not in the digging. It was the *unpredictability* of it. It would take the woman months, probably years, to glean anything truly useful. Over the years, dozens of others had tried, many with far greater resources.

What was unpredictable, however, was in what the woman may know. A piece of information, no matter how remote or minor, had a way of morphing into something much more significant—possibly attracting attention from someone who may have resources or clout enough to hamper Saad's plans.

"She wasted no time going to UNICEF."

Khoury shook his head.

Saad turned to the giant window, pondering. "What could they know?"

Khoury didn't answer.

"What could they know," he repeated, this time to himself.

Why would the Labor department be involved? What could they be looking at? And why now? What could they know?

No, he decided. *It was impossible. He'd spent the better half of seventy years making sure no one could unravel it.*

It had to be something else. Something small and inconsequential.

But sometimes, even the inconsequential was still worth eliminating.

What Saad failed to consider at that moment was that some revelations–some history-changing events–happened simply by accident.

46

Landing in the early afternoon, Angela Reed, Leonard Townsend and Joe Rickards all shuffled through the giant aircraft's interior cabin in a huddled mass of people before narrowing into a single file out and up the ramp, eventually pouring into one of Cairo International Airport's air-conditioned waiting areas.

Together, they followed more than two hundred accompanying passengers over a quarter mile of marble flooring before descending one floor by escalator to the baggage claim area, where over a thousand other people were packed amongst dozens of baggage carousels.

Finding their corresponding carousel, the three patiently waited for it to come to life. Angela studied Rickards with a wary expression until he finally turned to her.

"What?"

"What happened on that plane?" she asked.

"What do you mean?"

"There were emergency vehicles waiting for us and the flight attendant hugged you when we deplaned."

Rickards watched as Townsend also turned to peer at him.

"I don't know."

"You don't know?!"

He raised both hands. "What?"

Angela turned to the older Townsend for help. "Have you ever seen a flight attendant hug someone when leaving the plane?"

Townsend shook his head.

"I helped her when that sick passenger fell down in the back of the plane."

"Right," replied Angela, producing a twisted frown,

leaving Rickards the opening he needed to change the subject.

"So, Professor, what's our plan for getting to this glass desert of yours?"

Townsend shrugged. "You don't look as if you've slept much. I thought we could all get a good night's sleep and start fresh in the morning."

Angela nodded, observing with frustration the crowd around them. "Sounds good to me."

"We'll need to call around from the hotel and find a pilot."

Rickards looked away when the carousel lurched to life, then turned back. "What?"

"A pilot."

"A pilot for what?"

"To see the desert."

"We need a pilot?"

Townsend squinted, bemused, then peered at him earnestly. "The glass desert is very large, but the land is privately owned."

"Privately owned?"

"At least it was before, about ten years ago, when I was here with my wife on a group tour. That's when we learned about it. We wanted to go see it, but our guide said it wasn't allowed."

Rickards wore a bleak stare. "We just flew halfway around the world, and we can't even go there?"

"Sure we can, just not on the ground. The good news is we'll be able to see a lot more from the air."

Rickards glanced at Angela. "Wow, that is good news."

"I'm fine with it."

He looked away and sighed. "Democracy prevails."

"Don't worry," said Townsend. "This is a better way to see it. It's over a hundred square miles. If there's something there, we'll have a much better chance of spotting it from higher up."

"If what is there?"

"Anything that stands out." He shrugged.

Angela raised an eyebrow. "You mean like a spire?"

"Doubtful. Unlike the spire, where the glass is all one piece, here it's dispersed all over the surface in many pieces, which would actually make sense."

"Why?"

"If this is the exit point of that energy, it would. Exit points are always dispersed by passing through something no matter what the medium."

"So, then," said Rickards, "the energy is more concentrated going in than coming out."

Townsend frowned. "That's what I just said."

"Are you saying that's what created all the desert glass?"

"That's my suspicion," answered the professor. "Normal formation of glass silica typically requires high concentrations of energy and heat. But it's possible this form of silica was somehow made with less intensity over a much longer period."

"How many people know about this glass?" Angela asked.

"Almost everyone, I'd imagine."

Rickards continued listening while watching the crowd around them. "But if we're the only ones who know about this flow through the planet, how does everyone else think the glass got here?"

"Most scientists think it was a meteor."

"A meteor?"

Townsend nodded. "That's been the prevailing opinion for a long time. An explosion in the air close enough to the ground and with enough heat to form glass. We've seen small examples like that around other impact sites but nothing like this."

"I see."

"But..." Townsend continued, "there's just a tiny problem with that theory."

"What sort of problem?"

"For starters, if the glass was created quickly, say in a

212

meteor explosion, particularly over such a large area, there would be evidence. Like a crater."

"Even if it exploded in the air?"

"Yes. The great glass, the explosion, would have had to have been close to the surface—close enough to leave at least a shallow crater behind. But there isn't one."

"None at all?"

He shook his head. "None at all. Which is the proverbial thorn in their theory's side."

"So, all this time," said Angela, "no one *knew* where the glass came from?"

"Not for sure."

Rickards turned back to Angela. "Sounds a little like your Egyptian history problem."

Townsend paused and looked at the taller Rickards. "Come again?"

Instead of answering, he grinned at Angela. "Go head. Tell him."

Angela shook her head dismissively. "It's nothing."

"It doesn't sound like nothing."

"Apparently," offered Rickards, "Egyptian history doesn't have a history."

Angela rolled her eyes. "That's not what I said."

"I was paraphrasing."

"Try *butchering*."

"Fine." He shrugged, turning to watch the bags as they finally began appearing in the carousel. "You explain it."

With a sigh, Angela returned her attention to Townsend. "What I said was that a number of people, experts, are coming to a shared conclusion—that Egypt's early developmental history is missing some pieces."

"What do you mean *missing*?"

"Just that with most civilizations, their early development can be easily observed and mapped over long periods of time through things like early drawings and rudimentary writings, providing details of a naturally evolving culture."

"But not Egypt?"

"Not really."

"I thought Egypt had one of the oldest cultures. Look at the pyramids."

"That's what *I* said," quipped Rickards.

"Egypt *does* have a very old culture," she corrected. "That's not the timeline to which I'm referring. What I'm talking about is *before* that. Believe it or not, most of Egypt's recorded history is quite sophisticated in language, architecture and mathematics, leaving very little archeological evidence in the way of *how* it got to that level of sophistication. It's as if Egyptian culture just kind of sprang onto the scene shortly before the pyramids."

"Maybe they just didn't talk much in those days," offered Joe, prompting even a tired Angela to laugh.

"Maybe. But doubtful."

"Maybe they were embarrassed by their early penmanship."

"Will you stop?"

In front of her, Townsend crossed his arms. "I've never heard of this theory before."

"Most people haven't. A lot of experts in Egyptology don't like to talk about it."

"Why is that?"

"How much of a historical expert can you be if most of the timeline is missing?"

"Maybe their shorter lifespans back then made it more difficult to track their cultural evolution?"

"It would be just the opposite," Angela replied. "In other ancient cultures, shorter lifespans resulted in *more* evidence, as things had to be passed on to many more generations. Take something like stone-working," she said. "Or basic medicinal knowledge. With an average lifespan of thirty or so years, there's only so much a person can learn and master before they have to pass those skills onto the next generation, dramatically slowing cultural development. A lot of that communication was verbal, but not all of it.

Other ways were through writings or drawings. Very unsophisticated, granted, but there would have been a lot of it for us to find. But we haven't—at least not like other very old cultures.

"Long lifespans would have the opposite effect," she continued. "The longer you live, the more you learn and the more valuable and effective your personal experience becomes, resulting in a deeper cultural knowledge base. Take any topic and think about how much more a person can know about it with a lifespan like ours versus the early civilizations. Today we live almost triple the number of years compared to back then. A significantly longer lifespan provides an almost unimaginable advantage when it comes to life experience—not just knowledge, but wisdom."

"Aren't those two the same thing?"

"Anthropologically speaking, knowledge would be the details of how to do something. Wisdom is more about why. Not just *what* we do, but *why*. Or perhaps whether we should. Think," she said, "about how different our view of the world is when we're old as opposed to when we're young. For example, what would we do differently if we had to relive our lives?"

Both men stared at her, thinking.

"Believe it or not, most of the changes we'd make would have less to do with knowledge than wisdom, lessons we've learned surviving through this world. Lessons and experiences that have shaped who we are over a long period of time. Personal experience that is deeply individual and something no one can pass on no matter how long we live. Knowledge yes, experience no.

"Thousands of generations, maybe tens of thousands from the dawn of time trying to pass on what they could, even as limited as they were. Many of them had to make the same mistakes over and over."

Townsend smiled. "Wisdom is non-transferable."

"Exactly. Even the transfer of basic knowledge has its problems, which is why early civilizations evolved so much slower over time, with great difficulty and struggle just to survive."

"Egypt survived."

She nodded at Townsend.

"But you can't find any of its evolution."

"Not like we should have."

"That is puzzling indeed."

"Which is also why experts unable to find Egypt's early beginnings are now beginning to ask another, bigger question—which is if Egypt's cultural sophistication *did* manage to spring forth somehow faster than any of the others... where exactly did it come from?"

47

The glass doors were pushed open in a rush, allowing Omar and Mona into the dimly lit reception of Omar's office. He stormed forward, briskly passing through a short hallway and into a broad open office area where dozens of half-height cubicles sat empty and silent, barely illuminated by a handful of overhead florescent tubes.

Through the windows, the outside sky had grown dark and projected the city's lights several stories below, stretching out to form the rest of Cairo's immense cityscape.

Mona walked as fast as she could, sometimes trotting to keep up while simultaneously talking into her phone.

"We're here," she breathed heavily, increasing her pace once again to catch Omar, who'd turned another corner and was heading for his office. The rest of the suite appeared empty except for the one office on the far side of the open floor plan.

Once they reached Omar's door, he unlocked it with a key and strode in, barely breaking stride. He circled the desk and sat down while Mona pulled a chair up next to him.

"She said she just sent them," she said, momentarily dropping the phone from her mouth and simultaneously watching as Omar logged into his computer system and pulled up his emails. Displayed on three different lines were messages from Mona's sister-in-law Dalilah.

Clicking on each one revealed its contents—a short sentence with dozens of attached documents. One had close to eighty.

"Wow."

"We got them," confirmed Mona. "Which should we start with?"

She paused, listening to her sister-in-law speak before

raising her eyebrows. "Really? Which one is that?" she asked, leaning in to examine the screen. She pointed, instructing Omar to reopen the second email.

Scanning, she found the attached file to which Dalilah was directing her, titled *Elsewedey Enterprise*.

"Open it," she whispered.

Once open, her sister-in-law began walking her through dozens and dozens of smaller companies listed within.

"These are all real estate holdings?"

Another pause while Mona glanced down and eased herself into the seat. Still listening, she leaned forward and swatted Omar's hand away from the mouse, taking control and scrolling down several pages.

She stopped on a digitized copy of a deed, slightly crooked on the screen with dark printed lines.

Mona listened while Omar tried to read it, but without warning, she jumped from the computer window and back to the email, selecting another file. Again, she scrolled down while Dalilah spoke.

"Hmm."

Once again, she stopped, and Omar began to read, this time bumping her hand from the peripheral and steadying the screen.

"I've never heard of that before." More listening and then a nod. "Okay. Thanks. Call me back when you have it."

Mona pulled the phone from her ear and hung up, intently staring at Omar's screen.

"How in the world did your sister-in-law get all this?"

"From contacts in different departments. All these attachments represent a different holding company, most of them with ties back to Saad."

Omar scrolled and kept reading. "This goes deep."

"Yeah, but the two she pointed out are different."

"In what way?"

"Scroll down farther," she instructed. "To the bottom of the page."

He complied and reached the bottom of the document. It took a minute, but he eventually spotted it.

"Is this what I think it is?"

Mona nodded. "Supposedly. One of only a few assets directly owned by Saad instead of one of his holdings."

Omar jumped back to the second file and scrolled to the bottom. "Both of them, it seems."

"Dalilah said these are the only ones she found not owned by other companies or trusts. Just him."

Omar finished reading. "And why not these?"

Mona shrugged. "She has no idea. Neither does the person from whom she got it. The point is, Saad owns a lot of assets, including a lot of real estate."

"Not a surprise. Most rich people do."

"Right. But judging from my sister's tone, he may be richer than anyone knows."

"Huge amounts of wealth, all buried beneath layers and layers of corporate shelters. Except these. Why?"

"There may be more. She doesn't know. She thinks they might be some of the first properties Saad ever bought— before he had his shelters in place. She also said something else—that most systems this complicated are created for avoiding taxes. Something you mentioned, too. Loophole after loophole allowing rich individuals to pay paltry amounts in taxes. But with Saad, it's different. He doesn't avoid paying taxes. She said he actually pays more than necessary."

This time, Omar stopped reading and turned with a look of genuine surprise. "Excuse me?"

"That's what she said. Evidently, Saad has been paying more taxes than required. His corporate structures are complicated, but not his taxes. He pays a lot more than necessary, even without loopholes. It's been that way for a long time."

"That... doesn't make any sense."

"That's what I was thinking." There was a long silence before she spoke again. "Or does it?"

"What?"

Mona continued thinking it through. "Saad," she said slowly, "is a very private person, right?"

"Right."

"And a very thorough person."

"Clearly."

"Someone who doesn't want anyone looking too closely at his activities," she continued. "Or his actions. Or his money."

"Correct."

"And the best way to prevent that…"

"Is to bury everything so deeply that no one can figure it out."

Mona looked at him. "But then again, maybe he didn't stop there."

"What do you mean?"

"Think about it. If he's really that thorough, would he also have taken *additional* steps… than just burying everything in a bunch of legal documentation?"

"I'm afraid I'm not following."

"What's another way," she said, "of keeping people away? From looking too closely?"

Omar blinked. "Bribe them."

"Exactly. Which we already know he's doing with people at UNICEF. But the government itself may be too big, especially multiple governments in multiple countries. So, what's the next best thing?"

"Than bribing?

"Yes! What is it that gets governments to investigate 'high worth' individuals more than anything else?"

"Taxes."

"Taxes," she nodded. "Or more importantly, lack of paying taxes."

"But your sister just said—"

"She said he pays more than his share."

Omar finally saw where she was going. "Egyptian Taxing Authority focuses on people who pay very little taxes, not people who pay too much."

"Why would they," Mona said. "What government is going to complain that you gave them too much money?"

Omar turned back around in his chair, impressed. "He can't bribe everyone, so instead he pays so much in taxes that he removes himself as a target."

"Exactly."

He thought it through before nodding his head. "That's brilliant."

"It's not a mistake. Or some magnanimous gesture. It's a strategy."

"To keep from being investigated."

"Financially or politically, I'm guessing. All the while, he's being labeled the great philanthropist."

"The great *Beih* Saad," said Omar.

It was all coming together. One enormous, mind-numbingly complex puzzle whose pieces initially didn't seem to fit at all was finally beginning to do just that.

Until Omar broke the silence with a shrug and a question.

"But why?"

"Why what?"

"Why... all of this?" he said, motioning back to the screen. "Why spend so much time creating a system so vast and extraordinarily complicated and then pay a huge amount of money every year to keep people from looking at you?"

"To hide something, obviously."

"Like the children."

Mona nodded. "Like the children."

He continued staring. Thinking. "But we don't even know what that is."

It was true. The woman who'd jumped into the back of Omar's car had never given her name—intentionally. But she'd provided a lot of information on how the children were secretly being handed off. Swapped, as she called it, with UNICEF children who would be rotated back into

Saad's Rainbow houses in some strange, repeating cycle.

And yet, one of the things the strange woman had been sure about when it came to Saad's bizarre operation was that the children weren't being used for sexual reasons.

Which made a strange kind of sense. At least to Omar. Child trafficking operations had been successfully run for years in circles far less complicated than Saad's. And in trafficking, you didn't purposely damage your product, physically or mentally, as deeply uncomfortable a term as it was to think of children as a *product*.

He knew enough to know that the people in charge of such rings were business-minded, unlike the predators eagerly waiting on the other end of the transaction.

There was something different in play here. What it was, he couldn't say. But a vastly overcomplex system seemed odd, unless Saad was going to extreme lengths to ensure he was never caught.

But he had more than enough money to buy himself out of any serious problem, so none of it still seemed to make sense. Which brought them back to the same question—*why?*

As if reading his mind, Mona spoke up. "If he had all that money, what would he need that much protection from?"

"He can't bribe everyone."

"What do you mean?"

"Bribing so many influential people in numerous countries would have to be hugely complicated and very risky. Political landscapes and people constantly change. It would take a tremendous amount of money and time to stay on top of it all, all the while trying to keep out of view. It just seems... nonsensical."

"Then where does that leave us?"

"In the same place," said Omar. "For some reason, the man just wants to remain completely out of sight. Invisible. But why? What could he possibly be trying to hide from everyone that would justify so much effort and cost over several decades?"

Mona sat quietly next to him, thinking.

"What could it be that we haven't seen a thousand times before? Some giant political scandal? Corruption? A love child? Coming out of the closet? What?"

She almost grinned but gradually became serious again. "Whatever it is, it must pale in comparison to hurting children."

"How is that even possible?"

"I don't know."

"Which means that it *has* to be the children, then. We just don't know how."

"Or *why*?"

"Or why," he acknowledged. "Bringing us back to the beginning. If it's not some kind of sexual exploitation, then what is it? And why are the kids coming back, like the woman said, mentally broken?"

48

Eshe's small hands suddenly grasped the arms of her chair when the Nextant 400 jet descended through a layer of unexpected turbulence, immediately followed by another jolt that caused the young girl's eyes to widen with fear as she glanced at the other children directly across the narrow aisle. All were just as frightened as she, clutching their seats with hands like vices.

Another giant shudder gave a sensation of sway in the plane's tail, causing two of the children to emit an audible whine.

Panicked, Eshe leaned out and stared forward, spotting both the doctor and the man next to her, both with heads down and seemingly unconcerned at the plane's sudden movements that felt to Eshe as if it were going to crash.

The man's name was Badawi. Middle-aged, bald and muscular, he calmly swayed back and forth with the aircraft before finally opening his eyes when his phone vibrated inside the pocket of his black pants.

Smoothly and barely moving, he reached down, ripping open the Velcro strap to retrieve it and reading the message on the small screen.

How long?

Badawi instinctively glanced at his watch, then out through a nearby window, seeing a vast stretch of Cairo's city lights passing slowly below them.

He typed back.

10 minutes.

It took only a moment for his phone to buzz again.

Report immediately. Job waiting.

With no reaction, Badawi tilted the phone and pressed a side button, darkening the screen before sliding the device back into his pocket.

Next to him, the doctor was still reading through pages of typewritten data on her screen. She was completely unaware of the turbulence from the jet's giant turbofan engines audibly winding down. Nor did she seem to notice the children worriedly staring at her from their facing seats.

There was nothing she could do. The landing was always frightening for them. If not the turbulence, then the abrupt impact of the runway until the aircraft's braking came to an end and the shaking gave way, allowing the craft to roll smoothly forward. Years of experience had taught her the best thing she could do was to remain calm and simply let them experience it. In the end, it was constructive conditioning for them and would make what was coming next a little easier.

Approaching the private gate, Dr. Abo finally unbuckled her seat belt and rose to her feet scanning the children, whose eyes were still wide but borne by faces that were quickly calming, relieved at the brevity of the plane's harrowing gyrations and landing. Their faces were now beginning to return traces of their previous smiles and excitement over their journey.

When the plane came to a stop, Abo spoke loudly to them and signaled them all forward. "Please unfasten your buckles, children, and come to the front of the plane."

Behind Abo, the larger Badawi opened the door from the inside with his two powerful arms and waited for the built-in metal stairway to be lowered.

When everything was in place, the doctor motioned the children to follow her and exited through the hatch and down the stairs.

One by one, each child paused at the sight from the doorway before stepping out, gazing eagerly at the blanket of dark sky overhead and miles of city lights in all directions.

They descended the metal steps with soft echoes beneath their feet until reaching the black asphalt and falling in behind Abo, who had now been joined by another man and woman waiting on the tarmac.

Multiple women present always kept the children calm.

Abo waited patiently, studying each child for any last signs of anxiety or ill reactions before turning back to the two adults and following them to a pair of silver SUVs parked nearby. Together, in the darkness, they opened the rear doors of both vehicles and ushered the children inside.

Each child was thrilled as they slid across the soft seats and into position, pulling seat belts down and clicking them into place as if trained to do so. They then examined the luxurious interior softly illuminated beneath a series of tiny overhead lights.

Five of the six children sported grins from ear to ear. It was unlike anything they had ever experienced except in pictures or stories. Expensive cars and airplanes immaculately adorned with leather upholstery and doors, and awash in cool and refreshing conditioned air.

In all of their excitement, none of the children except Eshe noticed the man Badawi exit the plane behind them and turn in the opposite direction, toward the rear of the aircraft, where another vehicle, a white Land Rover, sat idling.

In one smooth motion, Badawi opened the passenger side door and slid into the black leather seat, not giving the children so much as a second glance.

49

Less than two kilometers from downtown Cairo, Dalilah Baraka's gaze remained fixed upon her glowing laptop monitor, her eyes scanning document after document looking for more connections.

The only two assets specifically registered under Mido Saad's name seemed odd, prompting her to dig deeper.

Why would Saad protect all of his other assets under offshore corporations except just two—his residential estate and a large expanse of empty desert near the Libyan border?

At first, she believed it to be a matter of simple timing, those properties being some of the first real estate purchased by Saad in the early 1960s, long before his corporate entities had come into existence, but she dismissed that idea once she discovered several other real estate holdings purchased around the same time. Those had been rolled beneath the umbrella of Saad's empire several years later.

So why not the others?

Upstairs, Dalilah's two young children screamed playfully and ran up and down the hallway in what sounded like a herd of thundering animals.

"Get ready for bed!" she yelled, angling her head toward the stairs.

A few documents later, she was again interrupted by more laughs and then a muffled crash, immediately followed by a burgeoning cry.

She was up from the table in an instant, rushing for the stairs and reaching the top in half a dozen steps. At the end of the hall, she found her twin boys on the floor of their bedroom, one crying and holding a cheek while the second stared sheepishly up at his mother.

"What happened?"

"We... just fell."

With an irritated sigh, Dalilah knelt and pulled her crying son's hand from his face, searching for blood and relieved to find none, just redness and tears.

She pulled him firmly to his feet before grabbing the second boy with her free hand. "What did I tell you about playing before bed?"

Both were smart enough to say nothing. Each received a light swat before she ushered them back down the hall.

"Brush your teeth!" she barked, hovering over them while they scrambled for their toothbrushes.

When the younger of the two displayed a set of sad eyes, she frowned. "You do not get immunity just because you're the one that fell."

The boy obediently inserted the toothbrush into his mouth and began brushing. He looked away as he did and missed the sudden change of expression on his mother's face.

Immunity.

Diplomatic immunity.

"Go to bed when you're done. I'll be right there."

With that, Dalilah Baraka disappeared from the bathroom and raced back downstairs, jumping through files she had open on her computer.

It was the last window she checked, and she immediately sat down to read.

It wasn't diplomatic immunity, per se. That was for foreign diplomats who were exempted from specific laws or restrictions by the countries in which they were working. Mido Saad wasn't a foreign national or a diplomat. But there were similar provisions in various Egyptian laws regarding its citizens.

The Emergency Law was enacted in Egypt in 1958

during the Arab-Israeli War. Known also as *Law No. 162 of 1958*, the act created numerous restrictions upon its citizens. Eventually, this catalyzed the great rise of the Egyptian Revolution of 2011, political desperation in which police powers had been extended for decades along with numerous forms of censorship, all legalized by the Arab Republic of Egypt.

But there was one specific apportionment amongst the censorship laws that Dalilah remembered reading about years before while still in college. It was a statute that had stood out to her as feeling particularly egregious, highlighting the chasm of inequality between the people and their government.

Dalilah found it and reread it, quickly remembering why it had stuck out—a provision in Article 43, allowing *regions or territories owned by political leaders, religious leaders, dignitaries or those deemed consubstantial.*

Her breathing slowed as she read.

... protections of leaders, dignitaries and consubstantial from all threats and in all forms, be it land, sea or air.

There it was. The answer she had been searching for. An explanation of why Mido Saad had not incorporated those two properties. Because if they were still held in his name as a person or a consubstantial, no one could come near him. In other words, both areas were officially recognized by Egyptian law as protected and sovereign and therefore illegal to encroach, duly enforced by the Arab Republic of Egypt. Sovereign land which would also be considered *no-fly zones.*

Dalilah Baraka had just stepped back from her kitchen table in silence, staring at the screen when she heard a loud knock.

Her first glance was upstairs until she realized the sound had come from the front of the house. Her brow slowly furrowed, and she checked her watch, walking gingerly from her kitchen into the family room.

She continued until slowing to a stop just a few meters from the front door.

It came again. This time several louder knocks.

Baffled, her brow grew tighter.

Who would be knocking at this hour?

Dalilah inched forward, now within two meters of the door, standing and waiting in silence.

Nervously, she moved forward within reach of the front window and peeled one edge of the heavy curtain away, revealing a small sliver of darkened window.

Leaning forward, she peered out through the glass and spotted something on the street in front—a large white vehicle.

She stared for a moment before moving, still puzzled and raising a hand to shield the interior glare upon the glass.

The vehicle's headlights were on, facing away from the house, and she thought she could see wisps of exhaust at the rear indicating the truck's engine was running.

The knocking came again. Dalilah quickly checked the door to ensure the lock was engaged.

"Who… is it?" she called.

Someone spoke faintly from the other side, but the words were unintelligible.

"Who?" she repeated louder.

Again came a response she could not quite make out.

***

Mona Baraka awoke on a stiff vinyl surface and squinted as she looked around. She pushed herself up, trying to recollect where she was.

It was the couch in Omar's office, and she'd been startled awake by something outside his office door, like someone moving around.

Her watch read just before 6:00 a.m., prompting her to

rise from the firm couch and move to the door, where she turned the chrome handle and eased it open.

The sounds continued until the image of a figure flashed by at the end of the hallway as they walked past. A woman in a black full-length dress disappeared, only to reappear again moments later moving in the opposite direction and carrying something in her arms. Office supplies.

Mona sighed and gently eased the door closed, then turned around to face the room, spotting something on the desk in front of her—a large piece of paper on the surface with a handwritten message.

Get some rest. Went to get some things from my place.

She nodded and absently pushed the paper away with a fingertip, then turned to search for her bag. Finding it at the base of the couch, she was picking through it searching for a brush when her phone rang and lit up inside.

"Mona?"

"Yes."

"It's Mawra. Thank Allah I found you."

Mona raised an eyebrow. "What is it?"

"It's Omar."

She found the brush and pulled it out, setting the bag down. "He's not here at the moment." She glanced again at her watch. "Wait, why are you—"

"Mona, he's been in an accident."

Her eyes froze. "What?!"

"He's been in a car accident," the woman repeated. "I just found out and ran down here."

"What are you talking about? When?!"

"They think about an hour ago. They're loading him into the ambulance right now."

Mona's heart quickly turned to panic. "Where?!"

"Near the Arabian Mall. They said they're taking him to

Coptic Hospital."

"What happened?!" she said, nearly shouting. "Is he okay?!"

The woman's voice was calm. "Just get to the hospital."

***

It took forty minutes in morning traffic. Forty long and agonizing minutes before Mona's car roared into the parking lot and screeched to a halt in an open space reserved for hospital staff.

She leaped out and sprinted toward the emergency entrance, darting past a team of medical technicians on their way out. Glancing around, she immediately spotted her long-time friend and fellow journalist Mawra standing in the corner on her phone.

Upon seeing Mona, Mawra abruptly ended the call and rushed to meet her.

"How is he?!" Mona asked.

"He's hurt. They're taking him into surgery right now."

"Surgery?!"

"Easy. Easy," said Mawra in a calm voice. "An expert just came in, and another is on his way. They think he's going to be okay, but they need to go in right away to stop the bleeding."

Mona's face became ashen. She was completely stunned and disbelieving.

She'd just been with him. What could have possibly happened?

Her mouth trembled as she fought to get the words out. "I... was just with him."

"Where?"

"At... his office. Last night."

Mawra's expression grew serious, and she looked around the room, dropping her voice. "Quiet. Don't say that too loudly."

Mona shook her head. "It wasn't like that. He was...helping me. With research."

232

"Okay, good. Don't say anything but that."

"It's true."

"I believe you," the woman whispered. "But others may not."

"I don't care what they think," she growled, pushing angrily past to the large desk where a nurse was seated behind a computer screen.

"Omar Maher. I need to know how he is!"

The nurse looked up. "The doctors are conferring right now."

"Conferring?! For how long?!"

Instead of irritation, the nurse beamed up at Mona with empathetic eyes. "We're doing all we can. They're preparing to take him into surgery."

"What are they going to do?" Mona stammered. "What happened to him?"

Behind her, Mawra gripped Mona's arm and gently turned her around. "Mona, let her work. She can't answer your questions."

"Well, somebody can!"

"They're working on him," reassured her friend. "Right now. Bothering the doctors will only delay them." She held up her phone. "I was talking to one of the officers when you came in. They think Omar may have lost control of his car and hit a wall. How late were you with him?"

She blinked. "What?"

"I said, how late were you with him? At his office."

She tried to think. "Uh, maybe 2:00 a.m. I fell asleep on the couch in his office. He left a note saying he was getting some things from his apartment."

"Like what?"

"I don't know."

Mawra frowned. "Was he drinking?"

"What? No. He wasn't drinking!"

"Are you sure?"

"Yes, I'm sure."

The other woman nodded. "Was he still up when you

fell asleep?"

"Of course, he was. How else would he have written a note?"

Mawra touched her arm again. "Mona, do you think it's possible he fell asleep—you know, while driving?"

"What? No! Of course not!"

"I'm not judging. I'm only asking. Trying to understand what happened. The officer I spoke with was asking the same questions."

"He would *not* have fallen asleep."

"You're sure?"

Mona opened her mouth to reply and stopped, reflecting. "Was anyone else involved?"

"It doesn't look like it."

"Were there any witnesses?"

"They're looking."

Mona's demeanor slowly began to change.

Was this her fault? He already told her he'd been working long hours. And she'd more or less hijacked him from what he was doing. Was it possible she'd pushed him to exhaustion?

She stepped back with a look of mounting fear.

"Mona, are you okay?"

"I don't know," she murmured, backing up and lowering herself into a chair, letting her purse slide to the floor in front of her.

Mona stared at the blue-and-gray carpet, worried at what she might have done.

Had Omar crashed because he was too tired to drive? And what was so important for him to get from his apartment?

Her gaze fixed on the carpet, Mona began to straighten in her chair when she finally noticed her large, suede purse lying at a slant just below her knees.

She glanced at the opening at some of the items inside. It took a minute to realize what had caught her attention. Something was missing.

The folder.

All the information she'd been carrying around on Saad.

The entire folder was gone.

Mona suddenly widened her legs and yanked her bag from the floor, pulling it open and frantically digging through it. Everything else was there except the folder.

She raised her head in a look of dread, staring straight ahead.

"Is everything okay?"

Mona didn't hear her friend. She was already searching through her memory at the image of Omar's office before she'd received Mawra's call.

Was the folder still there?

She saw the desk... then the couch... then the chair. One by one, she recalled the images at each spot in the room, every object she could remember. But she couldn't recall seeing the folder.

"Mona?"

It was too late. She was already on her feet, racing back to the nurse.

"Where are his things?"

"Excuse me?"

"Omar Maher. Where are his things?"

"I don't..."

"His things!" she yelled. "His clothes! Everything he came in here with!"

The nurse appeared briefly confused. "Who are you?"

"I'm his fiancé," she lied.

The nurse stared back for a moment then rose from her chair. "Let me see."

"I'm sorry," the woman said upon returning. "Your fiancé's only belongings were his clothes. Would you like me to bring them to you?"

Mona shook her head. "No. Keep them here." She then turned to Mawra. "You said the accident was near the Mall of Arabia?"

"Yes. Along the 26th of July Corridor."

It was a rhetorical question. She remembered what

Mawra had said. But that mall was nowhere near Omar's apartment. Nor was it close to his office or even in the same direction.

"Something's wrong," Mona whispered to herself.

"What?"

Again, she didn't answer. The Mall of Arabia was on the west side of the city. Omar's apartment was north and his office east, making the location a mystery as much as the accident itself. It was something she should have caught earlier when she'd learned he'd been taken to Coptic Hospital.

"Mona?"

Blankly, she turned back to her friend.

"Are you all right?"

Mona turned to peer back at the nurse, then at the wide double doors leading into the trauma unit. Finally, she twisted around and looked outside. "Something's not right."

"What is not right?"

"I'm not sure," she answered numbly, running through the night in Omar's office again.

Where was the folder?

Mawra's phone rang, but she continued watching Mona as she accepted the call and raised the phone to her ear. "This is Mawra."

The exchange was brief. "It's the officer. He's asking if there are any requests for where to tow the car."

Mona rose from the chair, facing the double doors as she fought to keep her mind from the image of Omar on the other side, being wheeled into surgery.

"Tell them I'll be right there."

50

Viewed by many as a living presence, Cairo's street names reflected a unique and deep sense of the city's history and memories, a veritable kaleidoscope of events for both the ancient capital and its millions of inhabitants. Surprisingly, many streets were named by the people of the city, not the authorities, including the *26th of July Corridor*, where Mona eased her car to a stop less than a hundred feet from the accident site.

Pushing the gearshift into park, she stared despondently through the windshield at the scene, watching Omar's dark blue BMW being slowly dragged up onto the flatbed of a large tow vehicle. Her stomach roiled as though she were going to vomit.

The entire front of the car was demolished, mangled beyond recognition up until the driver's door, which appeared to have been cut into multiple pieces, likely to extricate Omar as quickly as possible.

Glass and debris were scattered over the street and the giant sidewalk next to it, and one of the rescue crew was in the process of sweeping it up.

She couldn't move.

Inside her own car, Mona struggled even to move so much as her hand forward to the door latch. Instead, she sat frozen, caught in a moment in time, unable to keep her mind from replaying the event as it must have happened. The impact, followed by the slow-motion destruction of the first half of the car, with Omar trapped inside like a crash test dummy.

By pure instinct, her trembling fingertips finally found the latch and pulled, her grip shaky as she pushed the door wide open and fumbled for the seat belt.

When she stepped out, the scent of oil mixed with gasoline assaulted her nostrils, causing her to fight back another, more substantial wave of nausea.

Determined, she strode forward, unbalanced and leaning, unable to look away from the vehicle on the ramp as it gradually pitched forward with a loud mechanical whine.

She forced her eyes closed and turned to the side before reopening her lids, forcing herself to look somewhere else— at the building or the sidewalk, where dozens of people were gathered gawking at the remnants of Omar's vehicle with several already beginning to stroll away.

Next to the crowd stood an officer of the Egyptian National Police. Resolute and dressed in a dark short-sleeve uniform with his head down, he wrote on a clipboard, ignoring Mona as she approached until she made a loud noise, clearing her throat.

The man, perhaps in his thirties, turned and looked at her without speaking.

"Where is this being taken?"

He looked her over. "Who are you?"

Mona replied with a quivering voice. "I'm his fiancé."

The officer's face softened. Not much, but enough to see a change in his disposition. "I'm sorry. You've just come from Coptic?"

"Yes."

"The car is on its way to a tow yard. Unless you have another location you'd prefer."

Mona shook her head. "No. I just... wanted to get some things from inside."

The man stared at her and glanced at his partner, who was speaking with someone in the shadow of a palm tree. He then waved to the truck operator and motioned to Mona. "She needs to get inside."

The man nodded, waiting and watching as Mona stepped forward and studied the flatbed, trying to discern a way up.

Awkwardly, she scrambled up onto the bed of the truck and shuffled along the side of the car until reaching the passenger side window.

Grasping the handle for balance, she closed her eyes and took a deep breath.

The scene inside was petrifying.

The entire steering column and dashboard were mangled and bent, making room for part of the engine, which had been pushed back into the interior of the car. The front windshield was shattered and sagging inward, littering the two front seats with a blanket of glass fragments, along with the driver's side window, which was completely gone. But worst of all was seeing the crimson blood on Omar's seat.

Her convulsions returned almost immediately, forcing Mona to turn away, fighting to keep her stomach from erupting.

"Be quick," said the tow truck driver, who was still watching while unwinding a thick strap. Mona nodded and looked again, her gaze avoiding the blood-soaked seat.

She searched the front but found no trace of the brown folder, then carefully reached in to push the button on the passenger's dash to release the glove compartment door.

Reaching in, she retrieved several pieces of paper and the driver's manual but nothing else.

Mona then straightened and shuffled two steps back to the rear doors, both of which still had windows.

One more step allowed her to grip the door handle and pull the door open to her side, revealing more scattered glass in the back.

Still no folder.

Then her eye caught something on the floor.

Protruding beneath the passenger seat was a small corner of white paper. She adjusted her stance and bent down, reaching for it and pulling it out to reveal a full-sized page along with a few others. All were lying on top of one another.

When Mona examined the contents, her heart leaped. They were pages from the missing folder. Four separate pieces from the dying pilot. Random, but definitely from his folder.

From *her* folder.

The rest was gone.

She turned them over, examining both sides and finding three to be part of the dozens of financial statements she'd collected, with the last being one of the aerial maps.

Glancing over her shoulder, Mona quickly tucked the papers into her purse, and then with a final check below both seats, she rose back up and closed the car door.

Both men were now watching her.

"Was there anything else in here?" she asked.

"No."

"Can you open the trunk?"

"It's empty. I checked."

"Completely?"

"Completely."

"We had some important documents—"

"I said it's empty. No papers."

Nervously, Mona nodded and moved back to the corner of the flatbed, where she began climbing back down. Suddenly, she noticed a large indentation in the BMW's rear passenger fender, badly scraped and crumpled with thick lines of white paint.

"What is this?"

"We think where he hit the wall."

Mona looked around, finding a chest-high wall traveling the length of the nearby sidewalk. "Where?"

The officer pointed to a section of painted wall reflecting minimal damage and no skid marks, causing Mona to reexamine the back fender. "How exactly did he do that?"

The officer didn't respond. Instead, he approached and handed her a piece of paper. "This is where the car will be taken, assuming you want it back."

Mona thanked the officer and hurried back to her own car.

She started the engine and checked the rearview mirror before pulling her bag onto her lap to retrieve the pages.

Where were the rest? And why were these under the seat? Could they have fallen during the crash?

She turned around in her seat, examining the buildings behind her and then the sky, trying to get her bearings. She grabbed her phone and opened its map application, then expanded the screen with her fingers, highlighting her location.

Again, she studied the buildings around her and continued zooming in until she spotted the road labeled *26th of July Corridor.* She then found what she was looking for.

Based on the lane Omar's car had been in at the time of the accident, his direction was evident.

West.

Away both from his apartment and his office, where he had left Mona sleeping.

51

"Good morning."

Appearing tired, Joe Rickards nodded as he entered the room. "Morning."

Leonard Townsend was seated at a round table in the hotel's dining room eating a breakfast of bread, cheese and fried eggs. "Did you get some sleep?"

He blinked slowly, spotting the counter on the far side of the room which contained the food. "Some. Until about 3:00 a.m."

"Jet lag."

Rickards nodded before continuing past the professor. He retrieved a few items and returned to relax in the wooden chair opposite Townsend. "Let me guess—you slept like a baby."

"Not a baby. A log."

"Wonderful."

The older man grinned while chewing. "You're being facetious again."

"Not facetious. Jealous."

"Well, if it's any consolation, I was also up before dawn. I think I got too much sleep on the plane."

Joe rolled his eyes and lifted a coffee cup to his mouth. "Seen Angela?"

"She went to see the concierge to arrange a ride for us."

"Where to?"

"A local airstrip."

When Rickards raised an eyebrow, Townsend added, "I found a pilot."

"You did?"

"Yes. Although not a lot of charter pilots here speak English, so I've either chartered a plane or possibly a camel."

"Fifty-fifty chance," said Rickards, lowering his cup back to the table. He then asked, "You said you'd been here before?"

"The last time was about ten years or so. My wife loves to travel. She especially loves Egypt."

Rickards nodded and took a bite of egg. "I've never been."

"To Egypt?"

"Anywhere."

"Not a big travel bug, I take it?"

He shrugged as he ate. "Used to travel a lot domestically for work, so I've spent more than my share of time on airplanes."

"And your wife?"

"Wasn't big on traveling either. So, does our pilot know where we're headed?"

"Yes. Sounds like most of the area is private airspace, but he insists he can get us close enough for a look."

"Assuming it's not on a camel."

Townsend laughed.

"Then what?"

"What do you mean?"

"Then what?" repeated Rickards. "After that."

"You mean, 'What do we do?'"

"Yes."

"Depends on how close we can get, I guess. We're looking for something that might point to an epicenter of sorts. Satellite pictures of the area aren't very detailed. And hopefully we can also retrieve a sample."

"A sample?"

"Of the glass. I took some close-up photos of the spire and want to measure the silica composition. See how similar they are."

"And if they match?"

"Then we get our hands on another isotropic probe and find a way to get access to that area."

"What about—"

They were interrupted by Angela, who approached and sat down at the table with them. "Taxi will be ready in thirty minutes, which should get us there right on time. What did I miss?"

Rickards picked up his coffee. "We were just discussing how wonderful Leonard's sleep was last night."

She chuckled but stopped when she looked closer at Joe. "You look awful. Are you sure you're up for this?"

He stared across the table at Townsend. "That's my kind of compliment."

"Sorry. That came out wrong."

"I can't wait to hear how it was supposed to come out."

Angela grinned. "I meant... that you look pretty tired. That's all. Are you sure you don't want to get some more sleep?"

Rickards grasped his coffee cup and held it up. "This is all the sleep I need."

Their trip to the airport was uneventful except for the traffic, which, not surprisingly, was considerably worse during late morning. It took almost an hour for them to reach the small private airfield west of Cairo called Ahlan Airport, which consisted of little more than a long row of commercial hangars positioned alongside a clean, dark black 1,500-foot runway.

The seventh hangar in line, average in size and painted dark gray, had its large door fully open and a Daher Kodiak turboprop parked outside waiting, gleaming white under a broiling morning sun.

Inside the hangar, the three were promptly met by a man in his late sixties sporting a thick gray mustache and thinning hair. He was lean, with a modest belly protruding from under his short-sleeve tan shirt. When he spoke, it was both abrupt and impatient from behind a set of dark aviation glasses.

"We are ready. You must fill out paperwork quickly."

He ushered them into a small office cooled by a single vibrating fan and called out to someone in the back.

Moments later, an overweight woman appeared, dressed in a bright-colored niqab. Approaching the desk in much less of a hurry than the pilot seemed to be, she pulled her chair forward to sit down and arranged a set of papers, placing them neatly on the countertop.

She spoke in Arabic in a friendly tone, leaving all three looking back and forth at each other.

"Fill out," said the pilot. "We then leave. Just name and passport numbers. No address."

Rickards pulled the form toward him and stared at it. The text was utterly unrecognizable except the header citing the name and address of Egypt's Ministry of Interior Travel.

He peered at Angela. "We're signing this?"

"Um."

"Quickly," said the pilot. "Name and passports."

"Where?"

The pilot stepped forward and tapped his finger on the section of lines near the top. "Here. Names. Passports."

"Don't we need to say where we're going?" asked Rickards.

"No! No necessary. Just say sightsee."

"Is there a flight plan?"

"No flight plan. No necessary."

Rickards stared at the form, quietly contemplating.

No flight plan meant no one would know where they were going. Or, more importantly, where to look if they didn't return.

"Believe it or not, this is normal with tours," said Townsend from behind them. When they both turned around, he nodded. "They cut a lot of corners here."

Rickards turned to Angela, who shrugged helplessly. "As long as it flies, I guess."

He put his pen down and held up a hand to the pilot, leaving the office and walking back to the Kodiak. When he reached it, he slowly circled the aircraft, carefully examining it and paying special attention to the condition of both the engine and propeller. It had dents and dings along its body but nothing to indicate excessive mechanical or metal fatigue where it mattered.

When he turned, he found the pilot watching him, impatient but seemingly unworried. Without speaking, the man held up his hands in a familiar gesture.

Do you want to go or not?

The Quest Kodiak was a STOL utility aircraft which stood for Short Takeoff and Landing. With increased lift requiring less runway, its tradeoff was speed, particularly given its design that was also commonly used as a seaplane. In this instance, however, their version was built for hard landings. Anything from runways to dirt roads. Even sandy terrain. And it was significantly more comfortable than they were expecting, given its limit of only ten passengers. One by one, they climbed in and sat down, with Rickards, the largest, shoulder to shoulder with the pilot.

The plane's engine and prop started smoothly, providing Rickards a hint of solace in light of their rash decision—but not enough to keep him from watching the pilot very closely.

Once onto the runway, they turned south and into a non-existent breeze and idled up while the pilot spoke unintelligibly into his headset's microphone.

Finally, the engine grew louder and began pulling them forward, gaining traction and then speed before leaving the ground with a short thundering roar.

Once airborne, much of the vibration subsided, allowing Angela and Townsend an enjoyable, distracting view through their side windows as the ground fell away.

In the distance, less than ten miles away, the shapes of the giant pyramids were easily visible above the mass of city streets and buildings surrounding them.

Angela couldn't look away. Instead, she gazed at the giant monuments in pure awe. She heard Townsend's voice from inside her headset. He sat next to her and was peering over her shoulder.

"Magnificent, aren't they? They never get less amazing no matter how many times you see them."

She nodded with a wide grin. "All that remains of the Ancient Seven Wonders."

"Something tells me they will remain for a long time to come." He turned and glanced out his window before returning to hers. "I can see why Tesla was so fascinated."

Angela peered at him over her shoulder. "What?"

"Nikola Tesla. The great inventor."

"I know who he is. I didn't know he was interested in the Pyramids."

Townsend nodded as the plane leveled off and headed northeast. "Obsessed is more like it. He was convinced they were built for a completely different reason—to harness and transmit energy. Huge amounts of it."

"Really?"

"Yep. He even designed his famous Tesla towers after them, using their pyramid design and locating them in a similar distance and alignment from the Earth's equator."

"I had no idea."

"Most people don't," replied Townsend loudly. "But the man was one smart cookie."

When the pyramids were finally lost from view, together they both turned to face forward, listening as Rickards spoke to the pilot.

"So, you know where we're going?"

"Yes, yes." The pilot nodded. "To the glass."

"How close do you think you can get us?"

"Very close," he said, scanning the horizon. "But no for long time. It is restricted."

"Restricted by who?"

The pilot shrugged. "The government. Too long and they send jets."

"What kind of jets?"

"Fighter jets."

Due to its slower speed, it took a full hour to reach the beginnings of what they were looking for. It was visible first as a glimmer across the barren horizon and stretching as far as any of them could see in both directions.

Soon the glimmering line thickened and deepened as they approached, surrounded by the deafening roar of the Kodiak's powerful Pratt & Whitney Canada single engine.

At about ten miles out, the pilot banked the aircraft, gently turning to align with the edge of the strange desert spectacle.

"What can you tell us about it?"

The pilot motioned toward the vast sea of glimmering desert beneath them. "It is old. Older than Egypt. Or pharaohs. Created by giant meteorite many thousand years ago."

Behind them, Townsend glanced at Angela and frowned, shaking his head.

"Makes the desert glow. Even night."

Rickards squinted. "It glows at night?"

"Sometime."

"Can we get a sample?" asked Townsend.

The pilot nodded. "In Cairo. Some people sneak out. Then sell glass to tourists. But be careful. Tourists get in trouble trying to take glass out of Egypt."

"It's illegal."

"Illegal to sell? No. Illegal to take? Yes."

Townsend held up his phone and began video recording as they passed along the glass desert's perimeter. After a few minutes, he stopped and lowered it again, peering into the distance.

Glancing over his right shoulder, the pilot motioned to their seats. "Glasses in your seats."

"What?"

"Glasses." He paused, searching for the word. "Binocolers."

Together they searched and found a set tucked inside

each of their seat pouches.

Retrieving his, while Angela handed a third pair to Rickards, Townsend peered out at the distant, shining landscape and adjusted the focus.

"Incredible."

"You see anything?"

He waited to respond, still adjusting his view. "I think so."

"Really? Where?"

He lowered his binoculars and pointed a few degrees northwest. "Out there. Looks like a small structure, maybe."

Angela leaned across in front of him and raised her own set, searching. "What kind of structure?"

"I'm guessing an old house. Or a building."

"I see it. Looks as if it may be abandoned."

Townsend tapped the pilot on the shoulder. "Do you know what that is?"

The pilot shook his head.

"Hmm." The professor turned again to the window as Angela stood up and circled to the empty seat behind him.

"It looks like the whole desert is shining."

"The sun's directly overhead, so the surface is experiencing maximum reflectivity."

"Maximum reflectivity?" teased Angela.

"Too nerdy?"

She laughed. "Yeah. Way too nerdy."

In front, Rickards peered down at the ground ahead of them, noting a trail snaking through the terrain below them. "What's that?"

The pilot looked out over the plane's nose and shrugged. "Old road."

"How often do you bring people out here?" asked Angela.

"Only you in one year. Most tourists want to see Pyramids." He turned and smiled broadly at Rickards. "And tip very well."

Without missing a beat, Rickards turned backward. "Hear that, Professor?"

"What?"

"Sounds like you're a great tipper."

52

From her vantage point, Mona Baraka could see clearly through her own set of binoculars, a set of much lower quality she'd purchased from a gift store on her way to the edge of town. It was still strong enough to reveal some of the detail of what she was looking at.

Positioned on Cairo's western outskirts near an area called West Somid, she stood motionless on the edge of a newly developed and empty road, staring into the distance through the twin magnified tubes across miles of wavering white sands at something that looked downright *palatial*.

It was one of the two locations sent by her sister-in-law the night before which were registered under Mido Saad's actual name, unlike everything else he owned. This was a vast estate that looked from a distance like its own massive, secluded oasis, miles outside any developed area, surrounded by a dense line of thick green trees and probably hundreds of square feddans in size. It was significantly larger than stated on the original deed.

She continued gazing, trying to peer through the distant waves of heat at a large object on the edge of Saad's massive estate and nestled in the middle of nothing but open desert. The object she was studying was tall and angled, jutting just past the edge of the distant trees. It was blurry but still familiar, looking very much like the tail fin of an airplane.

Mona's phone rang behind her, causing her to lower the binoculars and rush to her purse.

"Mawra! How is he?!"

Her friend spoke encouragingly. "He's doing better. The doctors say he's out of immediate danger, but he's going to be in critical care for a while."

"Okay. I'm coming back!"

"You have a little time, Mona. Stop and get some things together. Clothes and anything else you need. It may be a while before he regains consciousness."

"Right. I will. Thank you!"

Mona hung up and exhaled, somewhat relieved. She dropped the phone back into her open purse, sitting idly atop the hood of her car for a moment before grabbing the bag and binoculars and rounding the front of her car to open the passenger side door.

Suddenly, something interrupted her—a distant sound overhead.

She looked up and searched the pale azure sky before spotting a small, slow-flying aircraft a few miles to the west headed back toward the city.

She looked away, preparing to leave, but paused, thinking a moment before peering up again.

The plane had a distinctly different shape than a passenger jet, even a small one. And it was moving much slower in the sky.

She glanced down at her bag and reached in, searching for the papers and pulling out one of the pages she'd found, or rescued, from Omar's BMW.

It was the map—one of several old man Hamed had included in his folder. The map was covered in graphs, waypoints and topographical items and measurements, better known as an aeronautical chart, with a prominent red *X* near the upper left-hand corner.

She remembered having seen the map amongst all the other papers before, but she'd failed to notice the geographic section it covered—the southwest edge of Cairo.

Now studying it closer, she could see it also covered much of the desert region beyond, including an extensive area of desert not far from where the second of Saad's land deeds was supposed to be.

Curiously, Mona held the paper out in front of her, flat

and angled by almost 45 degrees to match the direction she was facing. She then looked back up at the plane.

According to Hamed's chart, the airplane overhead appeared to be flying a very similar direction to the red X on her paper and a waypoint located in the middle of the desert.

Is that where it happened? Where Hamed had shot down the private jet all those years ago?

It was a startling thought. And one that felt more than just coincidental.

Saad owning a giant stretch of private desert, a dead pilot's map and now an airplane traveling back from the same direction?

Then there was Saad's enormous estate, still within eyesight, which appeared to have its own airstrip drawing yet another veritable line between the estate and the mysterious red X. Mona Baraka stood on the road perplexed and wondering exactly who was on board the small aircraft overhead.

She quickly dug into her purse for a pen and paper, then held the binoculars back up with her opposite hand, readjusting the tiny dial for focus. The plane was a good mile away and flying away from her.

But with a bit of luck, she might just be able to make out the identification numbers on the aircraft's fuselage.

53

With its tail rising high in the air, Saad's private jet remained at rest at the end of the estate's private airstrip and well out of sight from the narrow window in Eshe's room.

At that moment, the girl was staring north, studying the deep blue of the overhead sky painted with faint wisps of white cloud above a horizon not far from the shores of the great Mediterranean Sea.

But to Eshe, there was no beauty to be seen in the boundless sky outside or the lush green trees surrounding the rest of the giant estate.

There was something wrong.

Something very, very wrong.

Unlike the other children, she was no longer filled with a sense of joy or adventure, but rather a gradual and terrible feeling deep inside her stomach telling her that things were not as they seemed.

After landing the night before, all six children had been escorted over the giant estate's grounds to a row of buildings, stopping at one that housed several private rooms. They were clean and empty, well-decorated—and sterile, with the unmistakable feeling that hers had been cleaned very recently.

Just for her.

There was a bed, a dresser, a lamp and an empty closet, even a desk with paper and more colored pens. The furniture was nice but somehow portrayed a sense that not only was Eshe and the others *not* the first to stay here, but that none of the previous inhabitants had stayed very long.

Her deep feeling of dread only added to the sickening fear she'd had since getting off the plane.

It was the change in the doctor's demeanor. The

withdrawal of all communication outside of simple instructions and commands while being shown to their rooms.

Now very worried, she gently tiptoed across the room without making a sound to try the door handle.

It was still locked.

She jumped when someone suddenly began screaming outside from the hallway. There was a shrill, terrifying scream followed by a loud scuffle.

It sounded like a boy screaming in fear of something that was happening.

Immediately, Eshe ran and jumped up onto her bed, scampering over the covers and into the corner, where she brought both knees to her chest in a ball.

Outside, the screaming continued, the boy's words muffled but recognizable.

No! No! Please! I don't want to!

Eshe knew the other children were sensing something was wrong too, just like she was. She curled tightly into herself as her bottom lip trembled with fear.

It was bad. Whatever it was, it was bad.

The voice she was hearing was from a child who had been in his room long enough to know that none of the children taken ever came back.

***

Outside beneath an early evening sky, Khoury could also hear the young boy's screaming as he was escorted, or instead carried, from his room to a waiting vehicle outside the building. It was one of the silver SUVs that had just brought the new group of children from the plane.

Khoury ignored the struggle and calmly brought a cigarette to his lips, inhaling deeply before letting the smoke back out through a long, slow exhale.

He watched as the SUV drove past, heading toward the

west gate where sunset was nearing the horizon, highlighting the gently rolling desert terrain around the estate in all directions. The scene was secluded and peaceful—if not for the screaming.

Khoury looked up when the figure of Layla Abo appeared, glancing around to ensure they couldn't be seen from the main building.

"Where is Saad?"

"Where else? Underground."

Abo stepped closer. "How is he?"

Khoury shrugged and took another drag. "Close."

"How close?"

"Closer than he admits."

"We have to do something," said the psychiatrist. "Before it's too late."

"Not yet."

"What if he dies?"

Again, Khoury shrugged. "Then he dies."

"But—"

"I told you, it doesn't matter. He either finds what he's looking for, or he doesn't."

"If he finds it, it could be too late."

"I doubt it."

Khoury was far less worried than Abo. The old man was weak, and not just from the disease. Saad was pushing eighty, which meant that he was no match for someone like Khoury even in perfect health.

He didn't know precisely what Saad was hiding in the bunker, but he did know that even if the man found what he was looking for, it would eventually belong to Khoury— one way or another.

"Then what do we do?" asked Abo.

Saad's head of security looked at her, peering into the woman's eyes. Such a beautiful face, with a high level of intelligence to match. But like most women, she still lacked strength. Not just physical strength, but a more substantial kind. That edge. That toughness that only appeared in men, and a small percentage of those, the physical ability and a mental ruthlessness to do whatever was necessary when the time came no matter how grueling or gruesome. To do whatever was necessary to get what one was after.

"We wait," he finally said, inhaling again. "Until the moment is right."

"But if we act now, we can learn what he knows."

"A man this paranoid always has safeguards," he replied. "Best to let him do the work for us. We'll help him find what he's looking for, because he'll need us more than ever if he does."

Layla Abo reluctantly shook her mane of long dark hair but acquiesced. They didn't know what Saad was protecting, but they did know what he was looking for, what he'd been searching for, for a very long time. And now, desperately.

A single child beyond the thousands he had already gone through and who he had already used. Now there was only one left to find— one exceptional child who would complete his life's mission.

Whatever that was.

In the meantime, they would continue with the others.

Khoury didn't know what this final child was for, either. Or what they were supposed to do for Saad. Or tell him. But he did believe that whatever extraordinary benefit Saad was expecting from the children would almost certainly benefit a younger, stronger Khoury even more.

As long as Saad didn't suddenly die on them.

If he did, Khoury would still get into the bunker, even if he had to use Saad's lifeless handprint to do it.

54

Mido Saad never heard the screaming. Even if he had, he would not have noticed. He was still underground, where he was fixated upon his precious treasure as if in a trance.

The book.

The ancient text found hidden in King Akhenaten's tomb and written long before the reign of the Egyptian Pharaohs.

"The needle to reveal the child."

Saad had memorized most of the ancient tome, as millions of others would the Koran or Bible, something that had taken years, first to learn the Sumerian language and then to translate the writings imprinted upon hundreds of frail papyrus sheets of which no other living person on the Earth was aware.

But the most arduous task had been the translation. Deciphering the meanings of words penned thousands of years before and hidden for more than two millennia in deep hibernation beneath the lifeless mummified remains of Akhenaten, a man cloaked deeply in enigmatic legend and prophecy whose reign had been riddled with accusation, abnormality and controversy. Of the King's appearance. His behavior. And most of all, his godlike knowledge.

"The needle to reveal the child.
The mind to survive the binding."

Mido Saad slowly turned each page, brittle and delicate, speaking the words under his breath as he recited sections of the faded text.

The book had taught him everything. Whom to target. Who would be most conducive. The importance of hiding his efforts from the rest of the world, from those who would try to stop him. And, of course, how to read and use the drawn images.

He would have to learn to apply these instructions in a modern world. But apply, he had, creating a web so deep and so vast that no one could discern his true intent.

Many on the outside had tried, but none had succeeded. And only a few on the inside understood much if anything. Yes, the children were being culled. Gleaned. Harvested, even. But still, no one understood why.

Why it had to be children. And why their drawings had led him to know about the disasters.

Saad suddenly coughed—moderate at first, then violently. He covered his mouth with a cloth, but not in time to keep a small drop of blood from hitting and staining the delicate paper.

He leaned back and closed his eyes, suffering through another brief but violent episode before managing to calm his breathing.

Pulling the cloth away, he now saw dozens of red blobs.

It was accelerating. Quickly growing worse. But thankfully, no one knew just how bad he really was.

Saad folded the soiled cloth and tucked it into a breast pocket, retrieving a clean replacement from another before leaning forward to resume reading.

It had taken well over a decade to translate the words, to begin understanding and receiving the knowledge written by dozens of hands over the course of many years. But only by a few different *people*. Of that, Saad was certain.

Just a handful of people… living over and over again.

55

Mona Baraka raced across town, headed for the hospital, weaving in and out of Cairo's evening traffic.

She wanted to be there when Omar woke up, having quickly retrieved some things from her apartment, including a change of clothing.

She had to know he was going to be okay.

Cars in front of her slowed, prompting her to swerve into another lane and look for an open side street, an alternative to the approaching bottleneck leading into the city's most congested arteries.

She turned right onto what resembled an alley more than a street and accelerated past tightly packed parking spots of downtown apartment buildings. She traveled several short blocks before turning back out onto another avenue.

By the time she reached Coptic Hospital, the sky was completely dark, forcing her to slow her car through the narrow two-lane entrance and ease forward in search of a place to park.

Once out of the car, she walked briskly in the warm evening darkness, following a sidewalk out of a small parking lot and toward the hospital's main entrance.

She needed Omar to be okay.

She stopped at a rounded corner while another car passed, entering the grounds from the same direction and passing her before turning right toward the east wing of the towering hospital.

As the vehicle turned, its headlights illuminated a large section of manicured lawn along with several trees as the light washed over them, including a row of cars parked on the opposite side of the street—the first being a white Land Rover.

Something caught Mona's attention. A significant dent in the Rover's front fender, visible when the passing car's headlights briefly swept over it. Even more noteworthy were what looked to be two silhouettes sitting in the Rover's front seats.

Her phone rang from inside her purse.

"Hello?"

"Are you there yet?"

It was Mawra. "I just parked."

"Good. I had to leave and come back to the office. Let me know as soon as he's awake."

"I will. Thank you again, Mawra. I really appreciate it."

"You're welcome. Oh, and by the way. I was sorry to hear about your sister-in-law."

Mona was about to end the call when she stopped in mid-motion. "What?"

"Your sister-in-law. Dalilah."

"What do you mean?"

There was a brief sound of apprehension in Mawra's voice. "You don't know?"

Mona's breathing stopped. "Know *what?*"

"Oh, Mona. I'm sorry. I thought you knew."

"Knew WHAT?"

"Your sister-in-law has been reported missing. Her picture is on the news."

Mona eased back, stunned. "WHAT?!"

"Since late last night. Her children are saying she disappeared from their house while they were upstairs."

Speechless, Mona stared forward without moving, blinking slowly and barely breathing. Her heart felt as though it had just been stabbed as her mind struggled to comprehend the news. "Are... you sure?"

"I recognized her picture," said Mawra, her voice mournful. "I'm so sorry."

Mona remained frozen on the sidewalk, peering across the street at the hospital's brightly lit entrance.

It can't be true, she stammered. *It can't!*

She'd just talked to Dalilah last night when she'd sent the emails to Omar when they were at his office.

"What time?"

"They're saying sometime between 8:30 and 10:00 p.m."

The dagger in her chest sank deeper.

No. There had to be another explanation. A mistake. Or a reason Dalilah had left. But... from her children?

What other explanation could there be—other than the obvious. Dalilah was the only other person who knew about her and Omar digging into Saad's past. And she not only knew—she was helping.

Mona's gaze slowly climbed, rising from the entrance, up the front of the building to the upper floors, many of which shed light in the towering darkness.

It couldn't be. It couldn't be related to Saad. It couldn't be because of HER!

First Omar. Now her sister-in-law?

"Mona? Are you there?"

She gently stepped backward, dropping her eyes back to the street as another car passed. Then, absently, her gaze returned to the white Land Rover parked across the street and again, to the giant dent in its front fender, highlighted by another passing car.

The papers.

Mona had assumed Omar had done something with Hamed's folder and its contents. Hidden them somewhere, perhaps. At his apartment. But now, she wasn't so sure. What if the crash hadn't been an accident? What if it had involved more than one car? And the folder had been with Omar at the scene—until someone else took them?

She lowered the phone, pressing the red button on the screen to hang up as she slowly turned and began walking back toward her car, quickening her pace toward the small parking lot. She briefly glanced back at the Rover, only to see its headlights illuminate and hear its engine start.

Mona broke into a run, rushing to her small sedan and unlocking it as she approached in a sprint. She pulled the door open and threw herself inside, immediately closing the door and locking it again.

The white Land Rover roared away from the curb and turned left, heading for her parking lot, while Mona simultaneously started her car and yanked her seat belt across her body.

Once in reverse, she squealed out of the spot uncontrollably, nearly hitting another car behind her, then pulled the shift back into drive and stomped on the gas, squealing again through a tight turn and toward the narrow exit just as the Rover entered the lot behind her.

Clutching the steering wheel in a death grip, she accelerated through one of the lot's empty intersections, up one side of the curb and down again in a violent bounce.

Behind her, the Rover had no problem with its higher clearance and drove directly over the curb, smashing through a row of decorative bushes.

Heading for the hospital's entrance, Mona continued to accelerate through the gate's narrow passage and out onto the open street, swerving hard to the right and once again mashing the gas pedal against the floor.

The power of her humble sedan was surprising, as though awakening to roar like an angry beast. Shooting forward in and out of traffic, Mona desperately tried to avoid the cars in her path.

She was not a good driver, or an experienced one, leading her to oversteer, swerving wildly back and forth.

"Get out of my way!" she screamed. "Get out of my way!"

The Land Rover was bigger and stronger, accelerating as it tightly wove in and out of traffic, smoothly closing the distance between them.

Frantically, Mona turned at another intersection and panicked upon seeing another mass of red brake lights in front of her. She searched ahead for a clear lane, but there wasn't one. Less than a quarter kilometer in front of her, the sea of red became solid and united.

Mona swerved to the right, cutting off cars and causing one to brake hard and spin while she headed for what little gap there was—the sidewalk, peppered with dark figures walking.

She slammed her hand against the steering wheel, sounding the car's horn in a frantic attempt to clear a path.

And people reacted. Panic-stricken, they scrambled out of the way as she traveled up and over the curb, throwing herself back and forth inside the car while still desperately clutching the wheel, driving through a portion of black gating and glancing off a piece of the stone wall behind it. She smashed through the narrow gap and into the intersection of the street beyond, where she turned again and narrowly avoided a line of cars patiently waiting for their stoplight.

Behind her, the Rover continued forward, avoiding both the fence and the remnants of the damaged wall.

Again, more brake lights appeared, forcing Mona to stomp and skid into a fishtail, searching for another break in the traffic. This time it was a low-lying mound covered in neatly maintained grass and flowers which were utterly destroyed when Mona plowed over them and down the other side into a small parklike setting and past a sculpted fountain, leaving deep grooves in the perfectly maintained sod behind her.

Still, the Rover followed over the mound with little difficulty, briefly scraping the edge of the fountain.

Back onto a broad thoroughfare, Mona again pressed the gas, passing several cars traveling in the same direction.

An opening appeared next to her when an adjacent car slowed to make a right turn, and Mona swerved into it. Then, moments later, another space materialized when another lane began to accelerate, briefly expanding the distance between cars.

One by one, small gaps appeared, allowing Mona to either squeeze or force her way into them, keeping the larger

Rover behind her by several lengths until she reached another intersection and accelerated just in time to make it through the stoplight, which changed from yellow to red, forcing the trapped Rover behind her to slow with the other vehicles.

She turned at the next available street and then sped up and turned again—then again and again, until she was sure her pursuers would have too many options for the direction she'd gone.

Taking a deep breath, she calmly decelerated and turned into a parking garage entrance, where she paused to take a ticket and then continued inside and up two ramps before finding an open spot.

She fumbled for her phone and was starting to dial when she stopped at the third digit.

Was it safe to call the police? Or did Saad have connections with them, too, like at UNICEF or a dozen of other agencies?

Exactly how safe was she?

She jumped when her phone dinged in her hand from a text message.

It was Ammon from her office.

Have information on the airplane ID numbers.

The identification numbers. She'd almost forgotten.

She pressed a button and dialed his phone number.

"Hi, Mona," he said, answering immediately. "I have the information you wanted."

"Yes. Thank you, Ammon."

"The plane charters from a small private airport called Ahlan about five kilometers from Giza."

Mona listened intently, her gaze on the garage's concrete wall in front of her car. "Say that again?"

"I said it's a charter plane not far from Giza."

"Do you have an address?"

"I do. And a phone number, which I already called. A

woman there said that plane was chartered by some Americans today."

Mona blinked. "Americans?"

"That's what she said."

"Did she say where they went?"

"The pilot wouldn't tell her."

"Why not?"

"She didn't say. To be honest, I was surprised anyone answered the phone given the hour. I'm guessing the phone at the airport is set to auto-forward to her cell."

"What else?"

"That's it. I didn't press much. I was just trying to verify the plane and the phone number. I figured you'd want to talk to them yourself."

"Right." She nodded. "Of course. Can you text me their number and address?"

"Sure, will do."

"Great. Thanks, Ammon."

"You're welcome. Hope it helps."

Mona didn't bother looking a few moments after the call when her phone dinged again with the information she was expecting. Instead, she maintained her stare through the car's front windshield.

Americans? Why would Americans be interested in Saad?

266

56

They retired upstairs to Joe's room after dinner, being issued a suite with a modest sitting area and couch which allowed the three to relax and discuss next steps while enjoying a few bottles of *Stella*, Egypt's most popular beer.

"So where exactly do we get an isotropic probe?"

"Hopefully from a nearby university. I have a friend making some calls for me."

Rickards glanced at his watch. "A friend from Hawaii?"

"No," replied Townsend, "an old friend from NASA. I worked with him for years before retiring. He's much younger and very sharp, and he works for the Navy now."

Rickards nodded. "Okay, so if we find another probe, how close do you need to be to detect the energy?"

"It's hard to say. Depends on how concentrated the area is. Like I said before, if the energy enters in Bolivia and exits here, it stands to reason the surface area where it escapes will be wider. Potentially much wider."

"Yeah, we get that. But that doesn't answer the question. How close?"

He shrugged. "A wider range should theoretically make the energy field easier to detect. So, I should be able to pick it up even at its edge."

"Even if it's weaker?"

"These probes can detect very faint energy fields."

"Okay, great. So, we procure ourselves a probe and see if we can get access to the place in the desert."

"Well…" said Townsend, tilting his head.

"What?"

"Or… we could just go."

Rickards raised an eyebrow.

"You know what they say," said the professor with a

grin. "Easier to beg forgiveness than ask permission."

"You're suggesting we go without asking?"

"Something like that."

"Isn't that illegal or something?" asked Angela.

"If it's just government land, how bad could it be?"

"You mean for a group of unknown Americans with no valid reason to be out there?"

Townsend grinned. "I'm just an *old* man who got lost with a couple youngsters."

Rickards looked at Angela. "Are you hearing this?"

She laughed. "I'm all for following rules, but he does have a point."

"And what would *our* excuse be?"

"I don't know, just out taking pictures?"

"This place is a good two hours away. We can't exactly claim to be lost or separated from our tour group."

Now Townsend laughed. "Yes, that would be a stretch."

"Well," said Rickards, "not to be a stick in the mud, but do we even need to get close? The pilot said we could buy pieces of the glass around town. Why don't we just get a sample, and you can test that?"

"That's not how it works. It's the energy, not the glass, and whether the same phenomenon happens here as it does in Bolivia."

"We didn't see a spire."

"There may not be a spire," said Townsend, "but something is clearly occurring here."

"Because we saw an old run-down shack?"

"Because the glass is here. Because it exists here, in one spot, surrounded by the largest desert on the planet. Just the fact that the glass exists shows that something had to create it."

"Like this energy we think is flowing through the planet."

"Correct."

Rickards shook his head and leaned back in his chair. *Had they flown all that way for this? To sneak out into the desert and take some measurements?*

Then what?

The trip was beginning to feel more futile by the hour. What if this area was too spread out for the energy to do much of anything…except to gradually turn sand into pieces of glass over thousands of years—and nothing more.

Rickards' thoughts were interrupted by a knock on the door.

He looked at Angela and Townsend. "Expecting someone?"

Both shook their heads.

He rose from his seat and moved forward, stopping a few feet from the door and listening.

The knock came again.

Rickards glanced back to the other two before scanning the room for something he could use as a weapon. He quickly stepped away, disappearing and returning from the room's closet holding an iron in his right hand.

"Are we planning to press them to death?" asked Townsend.

Rickards glared at Townsend before carefully reaching forward and grasping the door handle. When the third knock sounded, he turned the handle and yanked open the door in one motion, keeping his right hand, the one holding the iron, floating at the ready behind him.

Standing in the empty hallway on the other side of the door was an Arabic woman dressed in pants and a long-sleeved shirt and appearing noticeably disheveled.

57

"Can I help you?"

Mona glanced past the man in the doorway and spotted the two others sitting on a couch, a light-brunette woman next to an older, dark-skinned man with a head of white hair.

The American in front of her was larger, probably in his forties and holding a clothes iron in his opposite hand.

"My name is Mona Baraka," she said cautiously. "I'm a journalist here in Cairo. And I need to speak with you."

Rickards stared at her for a moment, perplexed, before turning to the others. Both wore similar expressions.

"What about?"

"You are Americans, correct?"

"Yes."

Mona looked to the left, back down the long hallway. "May I come in? I'd like to speak with you confidentially."

Her English was surprisingly good, and Rickards stepped back, allowing her inside before gently closing the door behind her.

"I'm sorry to bother you."

"What is this about?" asked Angela.

Mona smiled politely. "It's about your airplane charter today."

Angela immediately glanced nervously at Joe.

"Charter?"

Mona turned to Rickards and nodded. "Your trip to the Desert of Glass."

His face remained calm. "I'm not sure we know what you're referring to."

"You're not in any trouble," reassured Mona. "I just wanted to know more about why you went."

"Young lady," said Townsend, "we're just touring your beautiful country. We don't know anything—"

With a hint of irritation, Mona interrupted. "As I said, you're not in trouble. I just need to know *why*."

"Why what?"

"Why you went," she repeated. "And why now?"

Angela rose from the couch, concerned. "Are you all right?"

"Yes!" exclaimed Mona, growing frustrated. "I'm fine. I just need you to tell me!"

Behind her, Rickards lowered the iron and placed it on top of the room's credenza. "Are you hurt?"

She turned to him, examining him closely before shaking her head. "No. I don't know. I just—I saw your plane earlier today. It was obvious where you were coming from." She looked between the three. "And I talked to the woman at the charter company. She said your trip was a secret."

Rickards glanced at Angela. "It wasn't a secret."

"There was no flight plan logged," said Mona, "and only you three and the pilot knew where you were headed. What would you call it?"

"Listen," explained Rickards, "I don't know what you—"

Without warning, she took a small step backward and interrupted again. "Please tell me you're here for a reason."

Rickards squinted in confusion. "What?"

"Please tell me you're here about him."

"About who?"

"Mido Saad!"

Again, Rickards glanced at the others. "Who the hell is Mido Saad?"

Now a few feet away, Mona studied his face, looking for hints of deception.

"I think you may have the wrong room," he replied. "And maybe the wrong Americans."

"You were on the plane, yes?"

"Yes."

"Are you Rickards or Townsend?"

Joe turned and looked across the room. "Well, as much as I'd like to say Townsend…"

"I'm Townsend," the professor said, rising to his feet. "What is this all about?"

"I told you. I need to know about your flight."

"Why? Did we do something wrong?"

"No. Nothing like that. I need to know why you were there and what you were looking for."

Rickards studied the woman's posture as she spoke, noticing a slight jitter.

Townsend also examined her before extending a hand and gently shaking hers. "Are you sure you're all right?"

"I already told you I am. Are you going to tell me about the plane?"

"Yes," said Angela. "We will. As soon as you sit down and relax. You don't need to be afraid of us."

Mona studied them for a long time before inching toward a chair and cautiously lowering herself into it.

Townsend and Angela returned to the couch while Rickards remained standing.

"Why exactly are you here?" Angela asked.

"Because of Mido Saad."

"We don't know who that is," she said softly. "Is that a friend or someone you know?"

Mona stared at them, almost bewildered. "A friend?"

Rickards shrugged from the wall. "A relative?"

"You really have no idea?"

The three shook their heads. "Should we?"

Gradually, Mona began to relax. "Why exactly are you three here?"

"I'm a physicist," answered Townsend. "We're here to learn more about the desert glass."

"A physicist?"

Mona looked at Angela, who then added, "I'm an anthropologist."

Surprised again, Mona then turned to Rickards, who frowned.

272

"I'm unemployed."

"You're all researchers?" she mumbled.

"In a manner of speaking."

"That's why you chartered the plane?"

"Yes. We're interested in the glass and its surrounding area. And we chartered a plane to get a look at it."

Mona stared at him, unblinking. "So, you don't know anything about Saad."

"I'm afraid we still don't know who that is."

"Mido Saad," she said simply, "is the man who owns the property the desert of glass is on."

A surprised Townsend looked up at Rickards. "We thought the government owned it."

Mona shook her head. "The government protects it for him, but he owns the land."

"For what purpose?"

"I don't know."

Angela leaned forward on the couch. "Is that what you're trying to figure out?"

"I thought you might have information that could help me." She exhaled weakly. "But it sounds like you don't."

"You're investigating Saad?" Rickards asked.

She nodded.

"Because he owns part of the desert?"

"No. For other reasons. But he also owns that."

Rickards moved away from the wall. "Something tells me you don't like this person."

"No."

"Because... of what you've found?"

"That's right."

"Which is what?"

Mona looked up. "Huh?"

"What did you find on him?"

"That he does very bad things."

"Like what?"

She sighed. "Corruption. Exploitation. Murder. Take

your pick."

"He's powerful, then?"

"Very."

Rickards retrieved a second chair from the wall and sat down. "Well, no offense, but you look as if you've been through a rough couple of days. You want to talk about it?"

"Not really."

He nodded, turning to Townsend. "Something tells me our chances of getting a look around out there just dropped by a lot."

"Agreed."

Mona looked at them. "You were planning to go out there?"

"That was the hope—to get close enough to run some tests."

"Tests for what?"

Rickards turned and gave the others an opportunity to answer first before he simply said, "It's a long story."

"So is mine."

"I'm sure it is. But ours may be a little hard to believe."

"So is mine," she repeated.

Rickards grinned.

After a long silence, Mona had a thought. "If you find what you're looking for with your measurements, would it make that land valuable?"

"Yeah."

"How valuable?"

"Very."

"How much is very?"

"Like an international incident."

Mona's eyes widened. "You mean oil?"

"Bigger. Like I said, it's a long story."

"Gold?"

Rickards chuckled. "This is not exactly something you can put in your pocket."

"Or in a barrel," added Angela.

"So what is it, then?"

"Let's just say it's a special type of energy."

"But it would be worth a lot," said Mona.

"Yes."

Could this be it? she thought. *Could this be part of what Saad was hiding? An expanse of desert worth untold riches?*

The excitement lasted only a moment.

Saad was already rich beyond the dreams of most people on the planet. What could he possibly want with more wealth?

"Mona?"

She turned to Angela.

"You did say it was Mona, correct?"

"Yes."

"My name is Angela. This is Leonard and that's Joe."

She smiled politely at them. "I know. I'm sorry for barging in."

"You know our names?"

"From the applications you filled out for the charter plane."

Angela reflected. "How did you know *where* we were staying?"

"One of you wrote down the name of your hotel."

Angela looked at Townsend, who shrugged and then looked at Rickards.

"What do you want me to tell you?" He shrugged. "I'm an investigator. You leave a trail. Especially in a foreign country with no flight plan."

He glanced at Mona to find the woman peering intently at him.

"You are an investigator?"

"I used to be," he said.

Mona Baraka focused her attention on Rickards. "What kind of investigator?"

"Accidents primarily."

All at once, Mona bolted from her seat. "I need your help."

58

Rickards remained quiet, his arms folded, gazing at Mona for a long time.

"Let me get this straight. You think this Saad guy is responsible for your friend's near-fatal car accident and your missing sister-in-law?"

"I do."

"A rich billionaire who runs a bunch of orphanages?"

"Yes. Supposedly."

"What does that mean?"

"He owns and runs them, yes. But not to help children. He does it to *use* them."

Rickards' brow narrowed. "Use them?"

Mona nodded.

"As in trafficking?"

"Yes. But not in the way you may think."

"I *think* there's only one primary reason people traffic children. And it's sickening."

"Yes," agreed Mona. "But I don't believe this is that. Saad wants them for a different purpose."

"What kind of a different purpose?"

"I'm still not sure. But it's not sexual. Maybe something worse."

"What's worse than that?"

"I don't know," she repeated. "Something deeper."

"And you think digging too much into this man's past resulted in your sister-in-law going missing and your friend crashing his car."

"Correct. And they almost got me tonight."

Now it made sense. The woman appeared so disheveled because she'd just had the scare of her life.

"What are you planning to do?" he asked.

"I don't know yet."

"How did you know we were investigating at the glass?"

Mona reached down to retrieve her purse, digging through it and producing the map.

Rickards studied it. "This is an old aeronautical map."

"Yes."

"And you got this from…"

"From the man who passed the folder to me before he died. Abasi Hamed."

"And you said the rest of the papers were taken."

"I believe so."

Rickards inhaled. He studied the sheet of paper from different angles. "And what's this red X?"

"A location a few hundred kilometers from the Desert of Glass. I believe that's where Hamed said he shot down a private jet in 1977, and what eventually drove him to learn the truth."

"About who he shot down?"

Mona nodded. "And why."

Angela moved in next to Rickards, studying the map from the side.

"Where does Saad keep these children who he takes from his orphanages?"

"At his estate, I believe, a large compound outside of Cairo which is also protected space, according to the government."

"So, no one's allowed to get near the desert glass or his estate?"

"Correct."

"But this red X isn't near the glass, at least as far as I can tell."

"I have a theory, but I can't be sure."

"Let's hear it."

"When I spoke with him," began Mona, "Hamed said he was pursuing the jet when he shot it down. So, I don't think the plane was traveling toward the glass or even Saad's estate. I think it may have been traveling away from it."

"Away from the desert? Or away from his estate?"

"I don't know. Either."

Rickards reexamined the map. "That's all?"

"No," Mona continued. "He also said he knew who was on the plane."

"So who was it?"

"He said… Allah."

Joe and Angela both looked at the woman in surprise. "Allah?"

"Yes."

"As in the God of Islam?"

"I don't think he meant it was *actually* Allah. But perhaps something close. Something just as bad."

"What would be just as bad as killing Allah?" asked Rickards.

"Perhaps something Allah cherishes just as much."

Angela's gaze widened, and she laid a hand on Joe's arm. "He shot down *children*."

59

There was no sound. No one was moving except Townsend, who slowly walked forward and leaned in to whisper to both Rickards and Angela. "I need to talk to you two. Privately."

Excusing themselves, the three walked into the bedroom and briefly closed the door.

Inside, Leonard Townsend continued toward the window, where he stopped and peered out.

"You okay?"

The older man didn't answer. Instead, he remained staring through the glass. "Everything we call real is made of things we cannot call real," he murmured.

"Pardon?"

Townsend shook his head and turned around. "Am I still rational?"

"What do you mean?"

Townsend looked at both of them. "I'm asking you if I am still rational?"

"Uh... yes?"

"I'm not so sure anymore."

"What the hell are you talking about?"

Townsend continued staring. "A rational person would not believe this."

"I can't exactly argue with you on that one."

"No rational person would believe..." said Townsend, "what I am about to tell you."

Angela and Joe remained quiet, waiting.

"When we were in Bolivia," said Townsend slowly, "I went in there. Into the canyon. And I saw the spire. But I never told you what happened to me, or what I saw."

Listlessly, the professor turned back toward the window.

"The reason… was because I didn't understand it, even though I knew what I was seeing was real." He reached forward and gently touched the glass with his fingertips. "I just didn't understand it."

"Understand what?"

"Angela," Townsend said, without turning around. "You said you saw your mother."

"That's right," she replied.

"And Joe. You saw your wife and daughter."

"Yes."

"Do you both believe that what you saw was real?"

Hesitantly, they nodded. "Yes."

Townsend nodded too, his fingers still on the pane. "Just as mine was real. But I didn't see a person, or even two."

Again, he rotated away from the window. "I saw *several.*"

Rickards and Angela remained still.

"I saw several," Townsend repeated. "But I didn't know them."

"None at all?"

He shook his head. "Which is why I didn't understand. Until now."

Rickards turned his hands up in a questioning gesture.

"What I saw were children," said Townsend. "Several children, all standing before me with burnt faces and burnt clothing. In the desert. They stared at me but said nothing."

His face looked forlorn. "I saw the children Mona just described—the ones who perished in that accident. Young, innocent children who may as well have been Allah."

Angela and Rickards were both shocked and gaped back at him with their mouths open. Angela abruptly raising a hand to cover hers.

There were no words, only a stunned silence before Townsend slowly stepped forward and reached into his pants pocket, where he withdrew and dropped a small fragment of burnt clothing onto Joe's bed.

60

Sitting at the desk, Eshe heard the door to her room open behind her, leading her to spin around and see a strange woman entering with a food tray.

The woman glanced momentarily at the young girl as she stepped forward and lowered the tray onto the small bed. Then, without looking back at the girl, she straightened and left, pulling the door closed behind her and leaving Eshe staring quietly.

Her eyes returned to the colored pen in her tiny hand and then to the scrawling on her left forearm.

She placed the pen onto the desk before turning back to the door, wondering if she had heard correctly and whether the woman had noticed it, too.

Eshe hadn't heard the door's latch click shut like it had in the past.

Had she missed it?

The young girl stood up and walked to the bed, examining the plate of fruit and cheese and then picking up a date and sniffing it.

Would they do something to the food? She'd heard stories about bad people poisoning food or putting things inside to make people tired.

Eshe lowered her hand and dropped it back onto the plate, then turned and looked up through the room's dark window at the blanket of overhead stars.

The screaming boy from the hallway never came back, leaving Eshe not just frightened, but now sure it would probably happen to her as well. And the other five children.

Suddenly, she remembered something from when she was younger, when she was living in another children's home. One of the older girls had told the group a story about her and her brother, trapped in a giant fire with several other kids, and how the adults were trying to keep them calm while the massive flames consumed everything around them. Everyone had been cornered and screaming for help while telling the children to listen and obey.

But the girl was too scared and hadn't listened. She'd been defiant when they'd screamed after her, and she'd run from room to room, frantically searching for a way out. She finally found one through a small hole in the floor just large enough to squeeze through. Barely making it under the flooring before the roof of the building had collapsed.

The girl told them the help never came, that the others were killed because they'd given up—including her brother, who'd continued to listen and obey.

It was a story Eshe thought about many times. About whether she would have had the courage to keep trying even when she was scared to death.

She peered back at the door, then quietly padded across the tiled floor until she was facing it.

Did it click? Or didn't it?

She was fearful that if the door *was* still ajar, simply bumping it with her hand could be enough to cause it to lock again, so she carefully raised her hand over the metal handle and, with a deep breath, grasped it tightly in one quick motion and yanked it toward her.

She was shocked when it moved.

She only had a moment to make her decision. She didn't stop the motion, but rather continued pulling until the door was wide open, exposing a bright hallway on the other side.

Quickly, Eshe snaked a foot around the base to prop it open before discreetly edging her eyes out past the door frame.

The hallway was empty.

And in that moment, Eshe ran.

***

Once again aboard Saad's private jet, Dr. Layla Abo relaxed in the solitude of utter stillness, reclining in one of the white leather seats within the cabin's muted interior. She closed her eyes as she thought through the next trip. Another six children to last another six days before another trip, and another, continuing until either Saad succumbed to his illness, or Khoury agreed it was time to act.

"The needle would reveal the child," Saad had told her. Which she still didn't understand.

What needle? What did it look like, and how would it reveal the child? And when? Or how?

Most importantly, why?

Each child taken into the desert, to the glass, came away in a profoundly different state.

Damaged. Sometimes deeply.

At times their experience resulted in their minds being wholly wiped clean to that of an infant. But minds were plastic, especially young minds. All had the ability to adapt. To change. And even damaged young minds could remold themselves into a brain that could eventually learn again. Function again. Limited perhaps, but functional.

Their lives would never be what they had been. Or could have been. Abo knew that. But they *could* still lead an adequate existence with the help of a loving family, which was the one thought that still allowed Layla Abo to sleep at night and live with what they were doing.

What *she* was doing.

The truth was that simple minds were usually the happiest.

It was enough psychoanalysis to allow her to look beyond what was happening to the children to the high likelihood that most of those children would have eventually died anyway without her and Saad's help—from disease or starvation or some other terminal malaise, suffering for years through a slow, spiraling decline through a terrible system that would never really change.

Poverty was the greatest destroyer of all—not just of the

body but of the soul.

In a very real sense, Abo was saving the children from that terrible fate, from the certainty of suffering and misery. From their own tortured lives. The only trade-off was a portion of their mental acuity.

Sometimes difficult decisions had to be made for those too young, too naïve or too uneducated to make for themselves, those who could not understand the cruel and immoral long-term consequences of existence on this planet.

The truth was, there would always be those who suffered.

It was this rescuing from that suffering that gave Abo the emotional and mental exoneration she needed, allowing her to assure herself that she was not part of the problem but rather the solution, as difficult as it might sound. Because Allah would only give those difficult decisions to someone who could truly bear them.

It was her frustration over Khoury's reluctance to act that caused her mind to shift and her eyes to finally reopen. She stared at the cabin's polished wooden trim overhead, its gleaming chrome vents pointing down, delivering a gentle flow of crisp, cool air.

As difficult as her moral obligation was, Abo was careful not to allow those thoughts to cross into the unpleasant subject of *personal gain*.

She wanted what Saad had. Both she and Khoury did. Both knew that whatever was in the bunker held enormous value for a man of such sound mind and body to dedicate everything he had—his entire life.

They just had to hold on a little longer, according to Khoury. Saad not only had the resources, but he also had the knowledge, which they did not. Better to let him achieve the goal and *then* steal the trophy.

Taking a deep breath and smoothly letting it out, Abo

tried to relax until she could feel her beating heart just below her breastbone, telling herself things would work out as they were supposed to.

And no sooner but did fate intervene, when she lowered her eyes to the seat directly in front of her, empty and still, before continuing down to the leather seatback pouch—

Where she spotted it.

Abo stared, frozen in a mixture of surprise and curiosity before leaning forward to pick up the piece of paper protruding from the seat's pouch and slowly revealing the rest as she pulled up and out, until the entire page could be seen, and behind it, several others.

The pictures were all the same—hand drawn and in different colors, but all of the same object.

The doctor slowly inhaled as she blankly stared at the image before her.

It took several long seconds to find her breath, and when she did, she leaped from her seat and ran, the paper clutched in her hand, for the cabin's door.

61

The hall stretched over a hundred feet past dozens of narrow locked doors and then four larger double doors on both sides. Eshe's eyes widened as her short legs carried her to the end.

The exit door was made of metal and glass, the dark backdrop from the outside world reflecting her petite frame as she approached. She slowed only briefly in her white cotton shirt and checkered dress before holding her breath and pushing forward.

The outer door opened easily, and she stumbled into the darkness, immediately spotting outlines of two more buildings nearby, all surrounded in lush dark foliage. It was more than she had ever seen in one place.

Rushing forward and directly into a thick row of bushes, Eshe pushed inward and settled to the ground, hiding, panting and peering out through a mass of large dark leaves.

There was nothing but silence and crickets, no movement of any kind—until suddenly she heard a man's voice in the distance.

She crawled forward until she found a line of sight with two men standing near a large vehicle in the distance. Like the one she'd ridden in from the plane, it was silver and gleaming beneath an overhead light. Both men were talking to one another, with one eventually laughing at something the other had said.

There was nowhere she could see to go except one of the other buildings or a different patch of bushes. But there was nothing to suggest she might find help anywhere.

Eshe wondered how long it would take for them to find her room empty and begin searching for her.

***

On the other side of the estate, Mido Saad stared at the object in his hands, turning it over and opening one of the covers before casually fanning through its loose pages.

"This is it."

Khoury, his chief of security, nodded. "Retrieved from the fiancé's vehicle."

Saad stopped and studied one of the pages. Financial statements for some of his old companies. Entities that had long since been liquidated. He then continued, moving to another and then another.

The young woman had more information on him than he'd expected. Much more. And much more harmful than others had in the past.

Yet, it wasn't until he neared the end that his expression changed from curiosity to mild panic.

There were articles—dozens of articles about the catastrophes spanning back to the 60s, each one to which Saad had been connected beginning with Peru.

How had she found this? How did they know about the accidents?

He continued leafing, carefully now, when the articles finally stopped and gave way to the last few sheets of paper.

Maps.

Saad moved and sat down weakly onto a wooden slatted bench nearby beneath the ambient glow of the giant interior windows behind him.

He had completely underestimated them—both the journalist and her fiancé.

Saad returned to the front of the folder and began going through it again, this time slower. There were letters from people connected to some of the original companies. There were financials, along with accompanying labor reports from the government, including copies of real estate deeds.

"These must have been from the woman's friend," Saad said.

"Her sister-in-law."

"And the condition of her sister-in-law now?"

"She's gone," replied Khoury.

"Gone?"

"Permanently."

"And the journalist?"

"We nearly had her at the hospital and are searching again. It won't be long."

Saad nodded as he continued from one page to the next. When he reached the end for the second time, his worry had lessened. What the woman had was damning but still incomplete. Many dots were still unconnected, which meant she was still grasping and likely lacked an answer to the biggest question of all.

Why?

Nevertheless, it was still enough for this woman to get someone else to notice, perhaps someone with enough clout to form an investigation. A low likelihood, but still sufficient to silence her.

Almost on cue, Khoury's phone rang, and he fished it out, answering and listening to someone as they spoke.

Saad could read the look on his chief's face. They had located the woman.

"Get her. Quickly," was all Khoury said.

He ended the call and looked back at Saad. "Our problem is about to be resolved."

Saad nodded again, coughing, before returning to the back of the folder and stopping at one of the maps. This one depicted Eastern Libya and the desert on the far side of the giant glass field, as well as the one behind it highlighting the area to the north. Both were aeronautical maps used by pilots and took Saad a mere second to realize who they must have come from.

62

Layla Abo surprised both Saad and Khoury when she burst into the bright room behind them, scanning before spotting them outside and racing toward the outer door, pushing it open and rushing into the warm evening air.

The two men turned without saying a word, studying the look of shock on the woman's face. It looked as though the doctor had seen a ghost.

In her hand were several folded pieces of paper which she raised and handed to Saad.

His reaction was identical to what hers had been aboard the plane—puzzlement followed by gradual recognition. It was the same recognition one displayed after being hit over the head by the proverbial board.

The needle to reveal the child.

The drawing on the paper, on each of the pages, was of the same object, drawn in different sizes and different colors, but they were unmistakable.

All this time, Saad had mistakenly assumed the image would resemble an actual needle. He realized only now that his interpretation had been far too literal. It was not a needle they had been looking for, but instead, an object that appeared *needle-like*.

Thin and sharp, like a blade or a point. Or, in this case, what looked to be a sharp, twisted spiral crystal.

63

"We need to get you to the police."

Mona Baraka stared at them as Joe, Angela and Leonard Townsend all emerged from the bedroom, Townsend with a phone already to his ear.

"What were you talking about in there?"

"It doesn't matter," said Rickards.

Mona narrowed her brow. "Somehow, I doubt that."

"Fine. It matters, but it would take too long to explain. Let's just say we think you're right. This is about the children."

"I know that already. I just don't know why. Do you?"

"No. But we're trying to find out. In the meantime, we need to get you to the police so you can explain."

"Explain what?"

"Everything."

"Everything? With what? All my evidence is gone. All I have is four pages," she said, looking down at the table, "and some emails."

"You didn't make copies of your files?"

"I took some pictures with my phone, but only a few. No one is going to believe me with that," said Mona. "Besides, I need to find out if my sister-in-law is okay. And Omar."

"Try calling them again."

Rickards watched Mona as she picked up her phone and began to dial. Then, without warning, he reached out and yanked it from her hand.

"What are you—"

"Wait a minute," he interrupted.

"Why?"

He remained still, deliberating. "If you're right," he said, "and this guy Saad is trying to find you, it wouldn't be hard to triangulate your location using your phone." He turned the device over and examined it, searching for the power button before pressing and holding it down. After several seconds, the screen blinked off.

"Okay. Now what?"

Rickards continued thinking. "I'll go with you."

"Where?"

"To the police."

"I told you, they won't believe me. Even if they do, it doesn't mean anyone is going to investigate Saad."

"We have to try."

Behind Rickards, Townsend spoke aloud, thanking someone on the phone before hanging up.

"That was my friend. He's doing some digging." He looked expectantly at the others. "So what's the plan?"

"We're going to the police."

"No, we're not!" exclaimed Mona.

"Yes. We are."

"Then you go!" she said, reaching down to pick up her purse. "I'm going to find Dalilah, and then see to Omar." She grabbed her phone back from Rickards. "I'll keep it off."

"Listen to me. If Saad is as big as you say he is and is embroiled in some kind of child trafficking, you're not going to be safe by yourself. It sounds as if he already got to your sister-in-law and your friend."

Hearing the words from Rickards' mouth made her stop. It was precisely the conclusion she'd been trying to avoid. Instead, she'd tried to think of all the reasons it couldn't be true. That they were not in danger because of her. That the events were somehow still unrelated. But deep down, her gut said otherwise.

Nervously, Mona stared back at him. "It may be a coincidence," she tried.

"There are no coincidences. Trust me."

"Maybe–"

"Listen to me. Our best move is to get the police involved at whatever level we can. At the very least, we can give Saad something else to worry about."

Mona glanced at Angela and Townsend. Both were standing next to Rickards, nodding in agreement.

"What do I tell them?"

Rickards folded his arms. "Let's work on that."

The story took some rehearsal, with as much information as Mona could recite from memory and authoritatively along with her remaining pages and pictures. Not to mention the video she'd taken from the Rainbow of Hope house funded and managed by Saad. She'd also include their visit to the UNICEF office, followed by the mystery woman's revelations in the back of Omar's car. And finally, the details around Omar's accident and her sister-in-law's disappearance.

Her recounting was smooth enough, unemotional and objective yet still alarming. Hopefully, it would be enough to at least get someone talking, though ultimately, Mona was right. If Saad had connections in law enforcement, any interest in the case could be short-lived.

But they had to try something, because if there was one thing Rickards knew, it was that you wanted the police on your side as early as possible.

Especially if things got messy.

"What was the pilot's name again?"

"The one who gave me the folder?"

"Yes."

"Abasi Hamed. Turns out he's somewhat of a war hero."

"Good," said Rickards. "Begin with that."

The two were preparing to leave when Leonard Townsend's phone rang, and he answered it, signaling for them to wait.

He listened intently without interrupting before he

finally pulled the phone down and pressed it against his chest.

"My friend has access to satellite footage, and he says there are indications of traffic between Saad's estate and the glass desert. A lot of it. At night."

"How much is a lot?"

Townsend raised his phone and asked and then looked back at Rickards. "Every night."

"What does that mean?" Mona frowned.

Townsend listened again. "He says it looks like a car, maybe two, traveling out into the desert in the dark with no lights and then coming back before dawn."

Mona was dumbfounded, while Rickards thought for a moment. "If there are no lights, how can your friend see them?"

Townsend asked his friend the question and then replied to Rickards. "Thermal imaging."

With no more questions, Townsend raised his phone once more. "Thanks, Will. I'll call you back."

"Wh-what does that mean?" asked Mona.

The other three were all looking at each other, reluctant to speak. Only they knew about the effects of the energy field.

"My guess," said Angela, "is that Saad is taking these children out into the desert every night, perhaps one at a time."

Mona frowned, confused. "Why on earth would he do that?"

Joe, seated next to her, lowered his head. "Quite possibly as test subjects."

64

Khoury stormed down the hall in a hail of fury, followed immediately by Saad and Dr. Abo. The doctor had no trouble remembering who sat in that particular seat aboard Saad's jet, and therefore who had drawn the pictures of the needle.

The girl's name was Eshe from Zambia—the one who'd always appeared to be watching her from the moment they left.

Together, they reached her room halfway down the hall, unlocking the door from the outside and forcefully swinging it open, sending it slamming against the inside wall. With one step inside, it was clear they had a problem.

The room was empty.

***

In the darkness, Joe Rickards and Mona Baraka descended concrete exterior stairs until they reached the bottom floor outside the hotel's north wing.

Together they rounded the corner and crossed a wide strip of grass toward the parking lot, where multiple rows of cars gleamed beneath the lot's bright overhead lamps. Weaving between them, Mona led the way to her car until slowing to a stop when two men climbed out of a silver SUV and stood next to her sedan. Both wore dark clothing and were clearly waiting for her.

She gasped beneath her breath and stepped back as the two men approached.

"Stop right there," barked Rickards, stepping in front of Mona.

Both men ignored him, remaining focused on her.

"Mona Baraka?"

Rickards took a defensive position and reached one hand behind his back.

It was a bluff. He had no weapon. But the movement, along with the tone in his voice, was enough to slow the men's advance, causing them to finally look at him.

"You're an American," said one of them, almost curiously. "We are here to talk to her."

"Then talk."

The men continued looking him over. "This is not your affair."

"I'm nosey." Rickards shrugged.

"We're not here to hurt anyone," the second man said. "We just need her to come answer some questions. We are ENP."

Mona turned to Rickards and shook her head.

"If you're the police, let's see some identification."

Khouri's man, named Badawi, took a small step forward, smiling at Joe. "In Egypt, we are not required to show it."

"Then I'm not required to believe it."

Badawi, the older of the two men, frowned. "I do not know who you are, but you should know that Americans are not immune from our laws."

"And you should know that I work for the United States government, and Ms. Baraka is currently under diplomatic protection."

A brief look of surprise passed over the men's faces before quickly disappearing. Each man inched another step closer.

"I told you to stay where you are."

Badawi's eyes glanced around the darkened parking lot before returning to him. "Perhaps you should both come with us."

"There's even less chance of that happening."

Suddenly, Rickards noticed something moving in the background behind them, inside the men's SUV.

The men turned, following his gaze inside of the truck's

darkened interior where a strange jumble of movement could be seen. Something white or checkered flashed over the rear seat, until coming to a stop in the middle of the vehicle and peering out through the windshield at all of them.

A young girl.

In a sudden flurry, Badawi barked, yelling for the younger man to grab her. The girl was already pushing the driver's door open and attempting to scramble out.

The man moved like lightning, sprinting back to the vehicle and around the hood, but he was too late to grab the girl, who was already out and running and screaming, snaking between the densely parked cars.

Rickards seized the moment, instantly sprinting forward several steps, and launching himself into Badawi, who'd partially turned to witness the girl's escape. He reacted only a moment before Rickards' airborne figure impacted him.

Badawi recovered quickly, rolling with the hit and scrambling out from under Rickards' weight, pushing himself onto one knee and smashing his left fist into the American's lower back.

Rickards was also moving. He winced at the blow but continued forward, lunging back at Badawi and tightly wrapping both arms around the man's legs. He used his own feet to thrust forward and push Badawi off-balance. They toppled back down onto the hard concrete.

As fast as Saad's man reacted, so did Rickards, immediately pulling Badawi close and slamming an elbow into the side of his jaw, followed by another blow.

"Saa'adinii!"

Behind them, Mona looked up when she heard the girl's scream, and without a moment's hesitation raced after her.

Another hit to Badawi's face, and Rickards was virtually on top of him, spotting the man's hand frantically searching his right side.

With one hand clenched under the man's chin, Rickards forced Badawi's face up and away from him while he looked down and found the weapon the man had been searching for just as Badawi's hand found it. Badawi pulled the gun free and into the open, forcing Rickards to grasp his wrist and drive it back down with all his strength, striking Badawi's hand repeatedly against the pavement.

After another strike to Badawi's face, Rickards was the first to climb back to his feet, pushing off from the man's chest and yanking the gun away as he rose.

There was another scream, this time from Mona. It was in Arabic and sounded more like a battle cry than wailing, allowing Rickards to pinpoint and run after them. He found her on top of the second man's back, pulling and scratching as the man desperately tried to yank the woman off.

At their feet, scurrying beneath the cars was the young girl trying to stay beneath the vehicles and out of reach.

Rickards raised the gun and yelled. "Let her go! Right now!"

The man paused before being bathed in bright light when the SUV swerved out of its space and headed toward them.

Rickards grabbed Mona and jumped back with the gun still raised while the truck skidded to a stop, allowing Badawi's man to scramble back into the vehicle.

With the squealing of tires, the SUV was gone, reaching the end of the lot and careening out of sight and leaving Rickards heaving and looking back at Mona, the gun still in his hand. "You okay?"

She nodded and shrank to the ground, leaning against a nearby fender before remembering the girl and scrambling down to ground level. She scanned the asphalt and found her stuck two cars over.

Back onto her feet, Mona circled and knelt next to the girl's only visible appendage—a thin, exposed right leg, along with short white sock and black shoe.

"We're not going to hurt you," she reassured the little girl in Arabic. "We want to help."

The girl stopped struggling.

"I promise," breathed Mona, falling back again and trying to catch her breath.

Beneath the car, Eshe could see the woman's feet and then her knees, hands, and finally her face and dark hair. A few moments and several breaths passed before a man's feet appeared next to her, following in the same order until she saw his light-skinned face, larger and breathing just as heavily.

65

Saad's face was utterly livid.

They'd lost her! The one thing he needed more than any other...they'd lost!

Next to him, Khoury was on the phone speaking angrily at Badawi.

"Stay where you are and maintain visual contact. Do not let the child from your sight no matter what you have to do. I'm sending reinforcements."

"No weapons around the girl," added Saad, smoldering and leaving Khoury to nod and repeat the order.

He'd finally found her after decades of searching and waiting, studying the pictures and knowing he was growing ever closer to his one chance in a million.

Whether a girl or a boy, it didn't matter, as long as they saw the needle, giving Saad what he ultimately needed. 'The needle to reveal the child. And the mind to survive the binding.'

How many children had he taken to the glass field? Thousands? One at a time, he'd locked each one in the room overnight and allowed the energy to build, rising first through the glass and then through their bodies.

This energy created the visions Saad forced them to draw upon waking, before their minds were slowly wiped clean by the trauma. Over and over again. Thousands of children over fifty long years. Hand-drawn pictures that would ultimately allow him to see what was coming. The great catastrophes before they struck.

And profit from them.

All from rebuilding. Villages, to cities, to portions of countries. Government money was plentiful to those prepared to receive it.

Of course, that was before he'd seen the larger picture. Before he'd finished the ancient book's translation—the book stolen from its previous owner by Saad as a young man.

Momentarily distracted, Saad tried to think back.

What had it taken? A decade to learn Sumerian and decipher its pages? And another to actually understand it?

And when he finally did, everything changed.

After the revelation, Saad simply could not attain enough children. He was insatiable. Adults were fruitless, already too broken to provide accurate pictures of what the energy had shown them—just as the ancient book had indicated.

Thousands of years had shown that children were the only viable option. Children were young, intelligent and still largely untainted, which made Saad's idea of orphanages the perfect solution in harvesting children no one would miss.

Visions from the desert energy had proved stunningly prophetic and decipherable, allowing Saad to amass an extraordinary fortune from his prescient and opportunistic timing that no one could ever understand, not even his greatest adversaries.

But those visions were merely the tip of the iceberg. Saad's true wealth was hidden much deeper within the book, buried millennia before in the tomb of King Akhenaten—the last of the book's living scribes. King Akhenaten had added the last pages before his untimely death.

Before he could use it.

A king who, along with several others living before him, had ultimately shaped and accelerated every aspect of Egypt's youth. Agriculture, medicine, and of course, language. Creating one of the most advanced and longstanding cultures the world would ever see.

Now, Mido Saad was about to follow in Akhenaten's footsteps. In all of their footsteps—those who had used the book to live, again and again, using the mysterious and everlasting energy of the glass desert.

All he needed now was the child who could survive the binding.

66

The hotel room door burst open, startling Angela Reed and Leonard Townsend, who both whirled around to see Joe and Mona enter with a young girl between them.

"We're leaving," growled Rickards.

"What?"

He moved directly to the closet and pulled the door open, retrieving pieces of clothing. "I said we're leaving. Now. You have five minutes to get your things together."

A startled Angela turned to Mona for an explanation but got none. Mona carried a dreary expression as she knelt in front of the girl and spoke to her in Arabic.

"What happened?!" Angela asked.

Rickards motioned in Mona's direction. "Everything she said is true about Saad. They were waiting for us downstairs."

"So, you never made it to the police?"

"We're lucky we made it back up here. And it won't be long before they're back—especially for her," he said, looking at the girl.

For her part, the girl answered the questions Mona asked her quietly but willingly, all the while staring up at Rickards, who moved to the bedroom after finishing with the closet.

After briefly disappearing from view, he returned to the doorway. "I said get your things!"

"Where are we going?" Angela asked.

"Somewhere. Anywhere but here."

Angela turned to Townsend, then Mona, who was still on her knee, gently touching the girl's tiny shoulder. After another moment, she stood. "Her name is Eshe."

Again, Rickards returned to the bedroom's doorway.

"And?"

"And what?"

"What else?"

"She's as confused as we are. And afraid."

Angela stepped forward, bending down to Eshe's level and smiling softly. "Are you okay, Eshe?"

The girl looked at her without answering, instead staring through the bedroom door to watch Rickards.

Slowly the young girl eased away from Mona and toward the door until she could see Rickards rapidly packing. Without saying a word, she crept into the room and moved to the corner, where she waited quietly.

Both women peered in through the white doorway and watched her standing idly in the corner watching Rickards like a hawk.

He finally noticed and looked at the child, then the women. "What is she doing?"

The women shook their heads.

Angela moved closer to examine several minor bloody scrapes on the girl's legs and arms. "Leonard, can you bring me a damp cloth?"

"Absolutely."

"It was then that Angela noticed something and carefully and gingerly raised Eshe's right arm to study it.

"Oh my god."

"What?"

She looked at Rickards as he zipped his suitcase closed. "You're not going to believe this."

"Too late," he replied sarcastically.

"Joe," she said, watching him cross and leave the room. "Joe."

When there was no answer, she called again, more forcefully this time. "JOE!"

"What?"

"Look at this."

Rickards reappeared. "Look at what?"

Angela raised the girl's light brown arm to reveal what

Eshe had drawn on herself—an unmistakable shape in black ink.

When Rickards saw it, his expression changed.

"Does this look familiar?" asked Angela.

The shape on Eshe's arm was instantly recognizable to both of them.

The *spire* in Bolivia.

Behind him, Townsend pressed into the room and handed Angela the cloth, which she used to dab at Eshe's wounds.

"How about you, Professor? Notice anything familiar?"

Townsend's expression was just as stunned as Joe's, quickly turning to fascination.

"Well, well, what do we have here?" he said, moving past Rickards to bend down and study the drawing.

Mona was still in the dark, looking back and forth between the three and waiting for an explanation. "What is it?"

Rickards shook his head. "We really need to get out of here."

He started to turn when Eshe's dark eyes caught him, and he stared back, softening his gaze and lowering himself onto one knee. For a long time, the two looked at each other without saying a word.

"What… is going on?"

The women had no idea, prompting Mona to ask Eshe in Arabic.

"She says Joe looks familiar to her."

"Like—who?"

"She didn't say."

Angela looked at Rickards. "Joe?"

He breathed in before looking up. "She looks familiar to me, too."

"You said you hadn't been here before."

"I haven't. But there's something very familiar about her." He inhaled again, eventually smiling at Eshe and pushing himself to his feet.

"We have to go," he repeated.

"Where?"

"Anywhere but here."

Angela and Leonard moved quickly to the room's outer door and immediately crossed the hall.

When Townsend disappeared into his room, Angela paused momentarily at her own door, turning around to look back. No one else in the room could have known except Joe, but he was too close to see it. Even with her darker complexion... Eshe bore a small resemblance to Joe's daughter.

67

They were inside Mona's car in under fifteen minutes, packed shoulder to shoulder within the modest sedan with Rickards in the driver's seat and Mona next to him. Angela and Townsend occupied the back, with Eshe securely strapped in between them.

"Find us the nearest police station."

Mona raised her phone and presented it to Rickards. "You turned off my phone."

"Right." He reached into his pocket. "Use mine," he said, handing it over.

Rickards started the engine and backed out the car, then turned and drove forward, carefully scanning the parking lot through the windshield. He glanced down when Mona started the navigation on his phone and targeted an ENP address two kilometers away.

It was past ten o'clock, and most of the traffic had cleared, allowing them to reach El Wahat Road and smoothly merge with a long stream of other cars as the large numbers on Rickards' phone decremented to 1.8 kilometers remaining.

"Tell me again why we're doing this," said Mona.

"Telling everything to the police no longer makes you Saad's sole liability. Once other people know, his problem gets bigger, and hopefully, ours gets smaller."

"Then what?"

"Then we find another place to hide."

"Such as?"

"Another hotel. While we come up with a new plan."

"What about Eshe?"

Rickards looked at the girl in the rearview mirror. "I'm

working on that."

He slowed and glanced back, moving over a lane, preparing to turn as instructed by the voice on his phone.

The exit was called *Dream Land*, and they followed the road as it curved left and rounded into a lengthy boulevard, heading for a cluster of buildings in the distance.

"Should we tell the police about Eshe?"

"I'm not sure," said Rickards, considering the question.

The investigator in him said yes. Best to provide all relevant information. But he also knew how bureaucratic organizations worked, especially law enforcement, which tended to act first and ask questions later, making it entirely possible Eshe could be taken from the outset.

No, he decided, *she should stay in the car with Angela and Townsend. Better to—*

Without warning, there was a loud screech and multiple bright lights on them as two silver SUVs roared past on either side and abruptly slowed in front of them, together coming to a stop in a V-shaped angle.

Rickards slammed his foot against the brake and brought the sedan to a swerving stop, immediately shifting into reverse when men opened the doors and stepped out of each vehicle.

"Hold on!" yelled Rickards, throwing an arm over the back of Mona's seat and accelerating backward.

He barely made it twenty feet before two more vehicles screeched to a halt behind him, sending black smoke rising from the pavement in front of their headlights.

Rickards checked either side and found nothing but long concrete walls lining both sides of the street. There was no place to go.

Through the windshield, he could see the four men in front of them approaching the car.

And four more men behind.

With eyes fixed forward and both hands clutching the steering wheel, all Rickards could think to say was, "Lock your doors."

He then reached for his handle and pushed the driver's door open, stepping out with Badawi's gun tucked into his belt at the small of his back.

Once out, he tossed the keys to Mona and locked his own door, pushing it shut with a loud *thunk*.

The four men stopped several feet away while Rickards checked over his shoulder at the others. One of the men in front was Badawi himself, glaring through seething eyes while all eight men slowly surrounded him.

They were after Mona and the girl. That much was clear. But the real question was how badly Saad wanted to involve Americans, giving some hope to Rickards that he was simply in the way. It was a good reason to leave the gun in his belt and not make their decision easy for them.

"Give them to us," said Badawi flatly.

"And then what?"

He cocked his head and let out a wry grin. "You get to go home."

"And if I say no?"

The man turned his head, motioning to the barren landscape around them. "You stay here."

Rickards twisted and glanced through the car's front windshield at everyone inside, with the last being the young girl.

Those surrounding Rickards had an enormous physical advantage. Eight strong men against one. It was simple math.

But their American target had an advantage of his own.

Two, actually—the first being that he was a man who knew how to fight. The second was purely emotional. Joe Rickards had lost everything in his world. Everything of any meaning. Which left a man with deep internal rage…and absolutely nothing to lose.

Badawi attacked first through a desire for revenge, lunging in a single movement of raw power and speed.

Yet Rickards had maintained enough distance, beyond a single step, requiring an extra stride and slightly more time. This allowed Rickards to move at nearly the same time, a smooth step out and around Badawi's advancing frame. Rickards wrapped his right arm around the man's neck like a clothesline, momentarily lifting him from his feet then suddenly down onto his back with a cracking thud.

Never fight from within a circle.

It was the first tenet in any multiple attack scenario, highlighting the ridiculousness of action movies. Instead, Joe had to find an exit.

The next man's attack was just as fast, rushing and swinging, but he was too wide and his blow glanced off Rickards' left jaw as the man stumbled forward, receiving two successive hits to the side of the head. The man grasped futilely for the American as he fell, causing the next two to navigate around him.

Smoothly, Rickards retreated, forcing them to compete for a straighter angle. The first earned a three-punch combination followed by two punches over the top into the next man's face.

Behind Rickards, Badawi was back on his feet and moving quickly, advancing on Rickards as he backed up, attempting to funnel his attackers.

He landed two more strikes before he took another impact, and then another, sending him reeling backward trying to catch his footing as one man threw his entire body at Joe, grasping around Rickards' arms and taking them both to the ground rolling.

Rickards' fingers found the man's eyes and caused the man to scream as he scrambled back to his feet just in time to be hit again over the back by something hard and metal. With barely enough time to spot the object as it made another swing high and overhead.

In a split second, Rickards stepped in and closed the gap against his attacker's body and grasped the man's swinging arm, working an elbow free and smashing it into his assaulter's chin.

A powerful strike sent Rickards stumbling forward, dropping to one knee before pushing back up to his feet and turning to find the rest of the men advancing.

Secretly, he gripped the weapon in his right hand and readied himself, realizing he couldn't see through one eye— not for lack of function, but because one side of his face was covered in blood.

With a quick swipe to his eyes, he blinked through the streaming blood and lowered his head.

Before another could attack, a powerful gunshot erupted through the night air, causing the men to stop and turn.

Badawi was standing next to the sedan with a handgun raised over his head. When Rickards turned, Badawi slowly lowered it and pointed it through the glass directly at Mona.

"Stop!" he yelled. "Enough!"

The men continued to converge around Rickards as Badawi used the butt of the gun to smash the sedan's side window, showering pieces of glass over Mona. He then reached in to unlock the door and yank it open.

He grabbed her arm and forcefully dragged her out onto the pavement.

Losing sight on one side again, Rickards finally relented and reached behind himself for the gun.

It was gone.

Badawi would have liked nothing more than to kill them all, especially the American standing in front of him. But Khoury had been very clear. No one was to be harmed— particularly the girl, when found.

But he could still *threaten* to shoot. Which he did, until his men had surrounded and restrained Rickards face down on the ground.

Four held him down with a large foot against the side of his head while the others extracted both Mona and Eshe, dragging them each to one of the SUVs and climbing in after them.

From the ground, Rickards watched through one eye as the truck doors slammed closed, just before one of Saad's men brought down the missing gun on top of Rickards' head.

Blackness.

68

"Joe... can you hear me?"

It took Rickards a long time to finally hear the words, which were followed by a blinding glare as he tried to open his eyes. With an audible groan, he closed them again and reached up a hand to touch the back of his head, which was swollen, painful and damp.

He tried to speak, but his mouth struggled to form the words, leaving him to acknowledge the others through a simple grumble.

He tried his vision again, wincing at the bright light of a lamp high above him. At least both eyes appeared to be working.

Rolling his gaze to one side, he found Angela's worried face leaning over him. Townsend was on the other side. Behind them were more he didn't recognize.

"Can you hear me?"

He nodded and carefully tried to move his jaw. "Yes."

"Good. Do you know what your last name is?"

Rickards blinked his eyes, trying to adjust to the glare. "Presley."

Above him, Townsend peered worriedly at Angela, who simply shook her head. "Very funny."

"Where am I?"

"On the street. You were knocked out."

Rickards managed a nod and with a groan, rolled onto one side of his body—searching.

The SUVs were gone, replaced by several other cars. Passersby who had stopped to offer help.

"Are they gone?" he murmured.

"Yes," Angela answered.

"Shit."

"Yeah."

He rolled back and gazed up at the night sky past the glare of a streetlamp, feeling exasperated. "How bad is it?"

Angela dabbed just above his eyebrow. "You've got a good-sized cut, but the bleeding has stopped."

He nodded. "So now what?"

"I don't know."

Kneeling with them, Townsend's phone rang and he stood up as he answered.

"Hey, Will."

After listening, he peered up at the night sky along with Rickards before looking back down at him. "My friend says he has a live satellite feed on us."

"Great. Hope he enjoyed seeing me get my ass kicked."

Townsend grinned. "He thinks you did pretty well."

"That's why I'm the one lying in the street."

"He says he's watching the SUVs."

Rickards' gaze shifted, and he forced himself up to his feet in a wave of pain. "Right now?"

"Yes."

"Where are they?"

Townsend waited. "Headed back toward Saad's estate."

"Then that's where they'll be."

Townsend held up a finger, slowly shaking his head. "They're not stopping there."

"What do you mean?"

The older man looked at him. "They're heading out. Due west, into the desert. Toward the glass."

Rickards turned and gazed westward, into the darkness. "What in the hell is Saad doing out in that desert?"

Townsend replied solemnly. "I'm not sure. But if I'm right and that place is somehow connected to quantum energy… part of me may not want to know."

Rickards took a deep, painful breath. "I need a map."

69

The four vehicles came to a stop in the darkness next to two waiting silhouettes—Saad, dressed in a long white gallibaya, and beside him, Khoury, wearing dark fatigues like the rest of his men.

Badawi and the driver both exited from the second SUV, allowing Khoury and Saad to take their places, and opened the vehicle's rear door to check on the females. Mona and Eshe sat together in the back seat, bound with plastic ties around their wrists and ankles.

Badawi tugged on each binding to ensure they were secure, and once satisfied, leaned out and closed the door again.

In the driver's seat, Khoury turned off the headlights and all interior lights before reaching down to retrieve a pair of night-vision goggles and pulled them over his head. Within moments, all the lights on the other trucks also went dark.

As the small convoy again began to move, Saad looked back from the passenger seat.

From what he could see, the woman was more attractive than he was expecting, even beneath her disheveled mess of dark hair. His eyes then moved to the girl, who, surprisingly, appeared to be nothing special above the endless other children he'd dealt with over the years. Nevertheless, it was a profound and meaningful moment for him, staring at her shadowed face, quiet and dirty, like her clothing, along with what appeared to be skinned elbows and knees.

It wasn't until he noticed her arm that he held up a small handheld penlight to view the image.

Just like the drawings from his jet.

Saad lifted his own pair of goggles and pulled them over his white hair, which was partially illuminated by the glowing moon.

"So, you're the one," he said, staring back at her white outline in his goggles, "that's been causing so much trouble."

"I think you have it backward."

He chuckled and glanced at Khoury. "Ah, the innocence of youth."

"You won't get away with it," said Mona.

He let the chuckle fade, still staring at her like a strange android. He grinned with an air of amusement. "Get away with what?"

She didn't answer.

"Please. I would love to hear what exactly you think you know."

"I know everything."

"Everything?" Saad looked at Khoury again. "Well, I guess it's all over, then. Let's just turn them all around."

Her eyes narrowed contemptuously. "I'm not afraid of you."

"Of course you are," he replied without a hint of doubt. "Everyone is."

He turned his attention forward through the front windshield, seeing the enhanced outline of the SUV in front of them.

"Let me guess—you believe you've found something important about me. Earth-shattering, even. Scandalous." He turned around to retrieve something Mona hadn't noticed him climb in with and tossed it onto the seat next to her. "You've been looking for this, no?"

She looked down at the seat. It was the rest of the papers.

Her evidence.

"Would it surprise you to know that I had no idea who Abasi Hamed was until just a few hours ago? One of Egypt's great air force pilots, I hear."

"A hero."

Saad feigned a look of admiration. "How wonderful.

314

But like I said, a complete unknown until today. And do you know why?"

Mona didn't respond.

"Because I didn't care. He was merely another serf in this great scam we call *the free world*, run by powerful elites around the planet benevolent enough to allow the rest to believe they live in a free and just world. At least occasionally. A world just a revelation or two away from becoming the fair and equitable system of which they all dream. People like you. And Colonel Abasi Hamed."

"He was a good man. Better than you."

Saad laughed. "I should hope so. I didn't know who he was because I didn't need to know. But in retrospect, I wished I had, so I could thank him. Because if it weren't for him, I would have been stopped a long time ago."

"What?"

"Oh, come now. Surely you know about the children."

"I know a lot about the children."

"Then you must know about the children Hamed killed. And the truth, that Hamed saved me a lot of anguish without ever knowing it."

Mona smirked. "He figured it out."

"Some of it. But thankfully, shooting down my jet back then was the best thing he could have done for me. It was flown by one of my own pilots, who suddenly grew a conscience and attempted to save a shipment of my children—from me."

Mona stared at him with disdain, as if wanting to spit. "You make me sick."

"The price of naïveté. Idealism while lacking the ability to understand the world around you. What's the English phrase? Ignorance is bliss?"

When there was no answer, Saad shrugged. "I suppose Colonel Hamed was vindicated in the end. Perhaps even forgiven by Allah for compiling his information and giving it to someone who would actually believe him and find a way to take down the great and evil Mido Saad."

"And I will," Mona said, bouncing in her seat from the rumbling dirt road beneath them.

Her remark brought a devilish grin to Saad's lips. "Oh, my naïve child, it is far, far too late for that."

70

Rickards made it to the entrance of Saad's estate in twenty-five minutes, a massive sprawl that stretched a quarter mile in both directions. But before reaching the heavily fortified gate, Rickards veered off into the dirt, following a trail along the property's western edge, rumbling loudly over rougher terrain.

When he reached the end, he brought Mona's sedan to a stop and looked forward into the darkness at the clouds of dust billowing past his headlights.

He studied his phone and the overhead image Townsend's friend had sent. Taken during daylight hours, it showed the same trail traveling west into the desert Rickards had spotted from the air. He hadn't known at the time that it ended at Saad's estate. The same road the SUVs carrying Mona and Eshe were supposedly now on—on their way to the glass desert.

Townsend was right. Something was happening within that energy field. Just like Bolivia. Something of which Saad was obviously aware. In Bolivia, the experience occurred just once for each person. If this side of the planet were similar, Saad would need a different subject each time to invoke it.

He'd apparently been using children for a long time— and now he needed Eshe. Only God knew what for. Rickards guessed that it had something to do with the spire drawn on the girl's arm, as if Eshe was aware of both ends of this phenomenon.

Now Saad and his men were ahead of him by at least thirty minutes. Maybe more, with nothing between them but flat open desert.

Contemplating, Rickards stared forward through the

dusty windshield and into darkness, only slightly illuminated by the partial moon above.

Townsend's friend said the vehicles were traveling with no lights— obviously to avoid being seen. Which is what Rickards would have to do as well, unless he wanted them to see him coming.

But even if they didn't see him, what the hell was he going to do? He had no gun or weapon at all, against what—eight to ten men?

Nor did he have a plan, except to reach them in time. Because if he were right about Saad's intention of using Eshe, it would be too late to stop once the phenomenon began.

His only plan, his only hope, was that Angela and Townsend would be able to do what he told them to before he'd driven off in Mona's car.

Find help.

Rickards took a deep breath, forced himself past the fear and took his foot off the brake, moving it to the accelerator and in one powerful motion, mashing it down.

The car's front two wheels spun wildly before gaining traction and leaping forward over the rumbling dirt road. At the same time, Rickards turned off the headlights.

71

Another wave hit Saad, and he leaned forward in a violent bout of dry heaves, keeping his hand over his mouth and reaching for his rag to catch any blood.

"Sounds as if you're not feeling very well," said Mona from the back seat.

Saad didn't respond. Instead, he kept his head and goggles forward, running through his plan again.

He'd thought of everything. The hiding of the money. Amassing the children. Safeguarding the secret book. And, of course, preparations for the binding—a careful protocol he would reveal to Khoury at the last minute before it happened.

In truth, it was his succession plan, more carefully planned and crafted than any other plan he had ever before developed, something to ensure his wealth and belongings remained for him, much like the pharaohs had done.

There was no way to know to whom it would ultimately go, either a boy or a girl. The latter introduced more challenges in this part of the world, but it would still work. The trust was airtight. Even without knowing who it would be, Saad was confident in his failproof process to validate and transfer his wealth to the new inheritor through a careful process of cryptic codes and cognitive assessment until the trustees were forced to accept the results—even if they didn't understand how or why.

And, of course, there was the security. An independent and highly rated security team had been paid extraordinarily well from Saad's trust to protect the child at all costs—not merely their health, but their sovereignty and control over Saad's vast network of assets.

It was complicated, with a multitude of protections and hundreds of individuals standing to gain handsomely by keeping the child alive and in control of his empire.

Because in the end, who they would really be protecting

was *him*.

He continued staring from the front seat in a last-ditch effort to find anything he'd overlooked.

The most critical step in all of it was the binding. After the child had been located, of course. And Khoury's protection while it took place.

As if on cue, Khoury spoke from behind the wheel. "Another thirty minutes." In an afterthought, he rolled his wrist to check his watch. "What about the boy?"

Saad turned. "What boy?"

"The one taken earlier this evening to the glass. They're waiting with him in the shelter."

"For what?"

"Further instructions. What do you want them to do with him now that we have her?" he said, nodding back at Eshe.

"Let him go."

"Into the desert?"

"Who cares?"

***

It was too dark to see either structure until they were almost on top of them, appearing in the moon's pale glow like two obelisks in the middle of an otherwise featureless landscape, one ancient and made of large blocks of stones while the other, over a hundred meters away, appearing more precise and modern.

It was the second structure that showed signs of activity. The simple gray structure's heavy door appeared open, with faint lights moving inside and another SUV parked nearby.

In stark contrast, the stone building in the distance sat dark and idle, abandoned and slightly crooked, with pieces of it gradually crumbling back into the sand and glass beneath it.

Side by side, all four SUVs came to a stop behind the first and were swiftly exited by almost a dozen different men, including Saad, who stumbled at first but caught himself using the vehicle's open door before reaching in to retrieve his cane.

Badawi and another man appeared and reached for the SUV's back door, pulling out first Mona and then Eshe from their seats and into the barren darkness.

When the women had been escorted away, Saad, through a choking fit while bracing against the door, called Khoury to approach.

"Listen to me," he breathed hoarsely. "Carefully."

Khoury leaned in obediently.

"When this happens, it will happen quickly."

"I know."

"No. No, you don't. This time will be different."

Khoury watched him curiously.

"It will start like the rest. Triggered, then the energy, building from the edge and slowly moving inward as it always does. But this time, there will be two in the madhbah—the girl and myself."

Khoury raised his eyebrows in surprise. "We've only used one child at a time here."

"I know that," wheezed Saad. "I know. But the madbaha was designed for two."

"What?"

"Two minds," the old man said, nodding. "And two souls."

Khoury turned and looked out at the dilapidated structure standing alone and silent. "How do you know this?"

"That is for me to know," answered Saad. "But understand this—the time has come to return to our roots, to throw off the bounds of this world that have kept us as mere sheep."

Khoury tilted his head, glaring at Saad. "I don't follow."

"This is not something for you to follow. I know, and

that is enough."

"Know what?"

"That this place is special—more special than anyone knows, not just in the energy release but in its purpose. In its fate for all mankind."

The man blinked at Saad through a set of dark, emotionless eyes. And a sinking sensation in his gut.

"I have arranged to make you wealthy, more than you can imagine," he said, and paused to cough. "As long as you continue to serve me beyond."

"Beyond what?"

"Beyond *this*. A world of cages and nepotism and into a life that transcends."

Khoury stared at the old man, the sinking feeling with him slowly morphing into panic.

Dr. Abo was right. They should not have waited. Saad was going mad.

"What are you planning?"

Saad looked out at the empty building called madbaha— Arabic for altar. The epicenter of the field of glass and the trigger from which the energy was summoned. Where the children were tied down, calling the power that arose and traveled like a wave and increasing in intensity as it approached, kilometer by kilometer, then meter by meter, before reaching the stone house and the soul waiting inside. Then the intense and brilliant flash of light.

"The children's minds were damaged," said Saad. "Because they were alone. Their minds opened to catch that which never came."

"Catch what?" asked Khoury.

"This time," said Saad, lowering his voice. "Two will go in, but only one will come out."

Khoury couldn't believe what he was hearing. The old man was going to offer himself in some deranged act of aintihar.

Suicide.

Only the girl will survive," said Saad. "And you must

protect her."

"Protect her from what?"

"From everyone," he replied. "And everything. Doing so will make you rich beyond your wildest dreams."

"Why will that make me rich?"

Weakly, Saad raised his hand and clapped it on Khoury's shoulder. "Because the girl… will be *me*."

72

The newer building was, in fact, their protection. Painted light gray as a camouflage against the desert sand and glass, the structure was a very different substance than any masonry. This was made of lead.

Solid lead.

It was located far enough away from the stone house, or madhbah, to avoid acting as a trigger itself, and dense enough to survive the intense burst of energy when it reached them, and had initially been designed to allow Saad, then later his men, to safely wait for the event to pass without destroying their own minds. They then retrieved each child and had them quickly draw what they'd seen before their young minds began to permanently degrade.

It was essential that Saad's men remained well inside the heavily protected lead fortress until it was over, and they could safely reprocure the child.

Inside, the small fortress's interior was modest, housing little more than chairs around a table upon which rested several battery-operated lanterns charged on the way to the madhbah. There was also a total absence of even a single window in the two-inch-thick lead walls, with the sole opening being its heavy door that swung outward into the night air.

It was crude but was a reliable harbor from a devastating phenomenon that would last precisely thirty-three minutes.

***

Sitting on the floor of the lead house, Mona rested against one of the cool metal walls, her ankles and wrists still bound. She stared up at the group of men in quiet desperation, completely unaware of what was happening around her.

All she knew was that Eshe was nowhere to be seen. Nor was Saad, nor his top henchman. But Badawi was there—the man who'd attacked them in the parking lot, along with the second man who was now standing right next to him.

All of them were apparently waiting for something.

In loud, crunching steps, Khoury, Saad and the girl marched over the field of glass pieces toward the ancient altar.

Upon reaching it, Saad paused and peered inside through one of the holes in which pieces of stone had long since crumbled away, now resting in a pebbled heap on the ground.

It was just as Saad remembered it from when he'd been here decades ago, while still performing the *christening* himself. And in the middle of the hand-built structure rested the long horizontal stone slab, deeply worn with old, faded leather straps hanging in the still air.

73

Rickards couldn't see a damned thing.

Through the moon's limited glow, he couldn't avoid hole after hole in the roughly strewn dirt road. At forty miles per hour, every one felt like an attack on the car's cheap suspension.

Behind him, the rear window was now entirely covered in a veil of thick dust, leaving the only visibility forward and to the side.

He twisted the knob again, trying to spray water over the windshield and wipers, leaving it only modestly cleaner and barely helpful given the endless darkness before him.

Suddenly, another severe dip resulted in a loud bang of the car's undercarriage as the entire vehicle shuddered in response.

Rickards had no idea how far away he still was or how long the small car would last.

74

After strapping the screaming girl to the stone slab, Khoury watched as Saad readied himself on the other end, easing himself down onto his back with his head less than a half-meter from the child's dark hair.

Through an open stone window, Khoury peered out into the darkness, watching a faint glimmer of light surface far into the distance.

The phenomenon had begun.

The light would take thirty-three minutes to build, approaching section by section and growing ever brighter until reaching the epicenter.

Khoury turned around when Saad began mumbling something with his eyes closed, words Khoury had never heard before, spoken in repeated short sentences through Saad's wrinkled mouth and lips.

Chanting.

In the darkness, he turned back and peered again at the distant glow.

Madness. It was all madness. The sickness had caused the man to gradually lose his mind. And now he was about to destroy it all in an act of utter delusion.

Khoury reached down for his phone and dialed a number, waiting for it to connect. He faced outward as Saad continued to chant and the young girl continued to scream.

When Dr. Abo answered the call, Khoury spoke. "Are you in position?"

"Yes," she answered.

"Do it. Now."

***

Abo nodded and hung up. Raising her head from where she was sitting at the beginning of a long hallway, she peered at the thick door to Saad's underground bunker at the other end. Next to it, the computerized hand scanner waited obediently for Saad's palm print.

Immediately, she stood up and walked toward it.

If Khoury was ready, it meant he believed for whatever reason, getting the information out of Saad was no longer an option, leaving her to execute their fallback plan, something they had practiced dozens of times before.

Reaching the other end of the hall, she lowered a large bag to the tiled floor and withdrew a wide roll of thin aluminum tape along with a pair of scissors.

She took a deep breath and then moved past the scanner to the door itself, where she slowly unrolled a short section from the reflective roll.

Saad was a thorough man—and a man of contingency, leaving her and Khoury certain he would take steps to destroy whatever was necessary should something unexpectedly befall him. Information, property or possibly both.

Which meant this had to happen now.

She held up the piece of tape and used the scissors to cut, then slid them into a pocket while pushing her hand through the remainder of the roll like a bracelet. With both hands available, she pulled the piece of tape taut and took a small step forward.

She carefully approached the locked chrome door handle and lightly wrapped the tape around the top portion, mindful not to press down. Once in place, she retrieved the scissors and tape and cut another piece, repeating each step and methodically applying each new section of tape to the handle until the entire door handle was perfectly wrapped.

Then, waiting several seconds, she just as carefully

removed them one piece at a time, gently laying them side by side with one another on the floor.

When all were in place, she returned the tape and scissors to the bag and retrieved a small plastic bottle.

Unscrewing the cap, she held it over the strips on the floor and gently sprinkled a powder of glistening oxide over them.

Once dry, she lifted the fragments together as one piece and slowly rotated to the correct orientation of Saad's hand and palm, shaking the loose powder free before lowering the single piece down over the scanner, nearly touching it.

Nothing happened.

Abo swallowed and lifted it back up, carefully lowering it again over the entire screen.

Nothing.

Her eyes widened with worry.

One more time. Up and back down over the screen as she prayed for success.

To her relief, the screen finally changed to read *Mido Saad – Authorized*, followed by a loud metal click of the door's robust lock.

***

The Eshe girl was now frantic, screaming and wildly wrestling her hands in an attempt to loosen or break free from the weathered leather straps. On the opposite side of the slab, Mido Saad continued chanting louder and louder, drowning out the girl's screams. Khoury caught something he recognized amid the chanting—a single word that resembled the Arabic version for salvation.

It was all interrupted by a loud sound from a device in Saad's pocket. The old man stopped and reached to withdraw it, staring at its screen. On it read two words:

Access Granted.

Saad's expression froze before his eyes shifted to

Khoury in a look of bewilderment.

His security chief immediately reacted.

With powerful hands, he clamped down forcefully over Saad's feeble mouth and neck, pinning him to the stone bed and causing Saad's eyes to bulge in panic. Saad's body convulsed, and he reached to peel away Khoury's hands, but he was no match for the younger man's strength. He squeezed tighter, a thumb now over Saad's nostrils cutting off his oxygen supply.

Tilting her head, Eshe saw what was happening and exploded in a fit of desperation. While next to her, Saad struggled for the final moments of his life. Under an ever-tightening grip.

Khoury squeezed tighter and tighter, until something popped in the old man's frail neck.

75

Unable to see the groundswell of light behind him, Rickards finally glanced at the two structures ahead of him through his dirty windshield; one, where several SUVs were parked, and another that appeared to be a run-down blockhouse from which a dark figure emerged.

Khoury was less than a hundred feet from the house when he heard the tired sound of a squealing engine.

Stopping, he stared and made out a silhouette from an approaching object. Small and loud, it rumbled over the dirt path leading directly toward them. He withdrew his gun when the automobile's two headlights switched on.

With lights on, Rickards saw the figure before him stopped between the two structures and staring back at him before adjusting his position and raising both hands.

A small flash appeared, and a hole suddenly punched through a corner of the sedan's windshield.

He was shooting!

Rickards momentarily panicked and briefly lifted his foot from the gas pedal.

He had no weapons!

Another bullet tore off the side mirror in an explosion of plastic and glass. Then a second went through the windshield, forcing Rickards to shrink beneath the dashboard.

He then realized. *He did have a weapon—a large weapon. Called an automobile.*

Rickards stomped back down on the accelerator, ducking lower as more bullets tore through the windshield.

Khoury emptied his magazine at the approaching car, now headed directly for him, tearing over the open terrain behind a set of blinding headlights.

Khoury pulled his trigger again and received nothing but a faint click, causing him to instinctively reach for another magazine as he stood in the oncoming spotlight of the approaching car.

He yanked the magazine free but fumbled and dropped it. He searched the ground, but in a panic, Khoury left it and began running for the second building where multiple men were emerging, watching in surprise at Khoury running toward them, followed by a car now careening into their direction.

"Move!" yelled Khoury, racing for protection. He reached and rounded the structure just moments before the sedan crashed into it with incredible force just several feet from the door.

The impact destroyed a large section of wall, tearing much of it from the adjoining corner as the sedan violently lurched sideways.

Men were on the ground, having dived for cover before impact, and were now scrambling to their feet, including Khoury, who reappeared, stumbling, from the side of the small building.

In a cloud of dust and debris, the driver's door on the car was pushed open, and Rickards toppled out on the ground, coughing violently.

When he rose to his feet, his eyes were met by those of Badawi, who was stunned at the sight of the American. He then turned to search the ground for his weapon.

He spotted it, but Rickards was already rushing forward, tackling Badawi and driving him backward into the standing portion of lead wall with an audible groan. Rickards pummeled him, landing several blows before multiple sets of hands grabbed and pulled him off, punching and pounding him repeatedly before throwing him to the ground surrounded by several men. Everyone was shouting in Arabic and beating him with their heavy boots.

One man grabbed a large stone and fell to a knee, striking him repeatedly, forcing Rickards to curl to protect himself. One after another, the rock struck his shoulder and then his arms as he tried to cover his head.

Over and over. The swings were relentless. Repeated. Methodic. Rickards kept his focus by counting first the strikes, then the timing, until all at once, he reached out and grasped the man's hand, holding it like a vice and forcing the man's wrist back in the opposite direction against the joint until the man screamed in pain and dropped the rock.

The distraction of the scream was brief, a moment at most, but it was enough to allow Rickards to spin on his side, kicking and breaking one of the knees of those kicking. He caught a boot, then kicked a second knee, sending another man down and providing an opening for Rickards to scramble away through.

Frantically, he made it to his knees while three men followed. The first again kicked at Rickards, who was now at least ready.

Crossing his arms and catching the kick, he grabbed both ends of the large boot and twisted violently with a snap, punching the man's groin with everything he had as his assailant fell forward.

The man fell screaming. Rickards made it to his feet before being struck hard across the nose by a clenched fist. He stumbled backward, looking for the man but took another to the jaw.

Rickards saw a flash of the third strike and ducked, then instinctively reached up to lock his arms.

The next man ran directly into him and fell away with another broken knee, screaming and causing two more men to pause out of caution, limping forward but now reassessing.

Yet, the person notably missing from the fight was Khoury himself. Instead, Rickards' eyes found him looking not at them, but past them into the darkness.

The glowing ground was getting closer and brighter.

Khoury then turned and stared at the lead building behind him, which now had a large, gaping break in its wall.

Panic riddled his expression.

There was no protection.

One of the two men reapproaching Rickards, Badawi slowed to a crawl as if having a similar thought. Turning to Khoury, his fear was confirmed.

Instantly, he whipped around and peered out into the darkness, seeing the advancing light.

With their lead shield compromised, the phenomenon would wipe them, too!

"Stop!" yelled Khoury. His men turned away from Rickards and looked at him, following the direction of the chief's extended arm. "Move!" he screamed at them. "MOVE!"

In mere moments, everything changed, leaving Rickards standing on two legs and heaving, watching the other men suddenly scramble, dropping everything and running for the SUVs.

Khoury was also running but was farther away, allowing Rickards to charge forward and intercept him on the way to a vehicle.

In his weakened state, Rickards was an easy match for Khoury, but the man had no interest in the struggle. Instead, he quickly scrambled to his feet and shook off Rickards' clutches, continuing to run for the vehicles.

One by one, each truck pulled out, spitting glass out from under their spinning wheels as the thundering vehicles peeled away.

Rickards rose back to his feet, watching them flee. He was puzzled until he saw it himself. The ground was glowing and moving toward him, like a giant, slow-moving curtain of light. Rising high into the night sky, where it became translucent and gradually disappeared.

"Help!" a female voice screamed from behind him, inside the heavy structure into which he'd crashed. He rushed to the open door and looked inside, spotting Mona on the ground scrambling forward on her hands and knees, her wrists and ankles still bound.

"Mona!"

"Help me!" she screamed.

He rushed to her and helped her onto her feet, looking for something to cut the plastic ties. Finding nothing, he led her outside and hopped toward the damaged wall of the building where dozens of jagged edges were exposed. He pulled her over and turned her around, peering behind her to carefully line her up.

He worked the tie around her wrists back and forth until the plastic broke, then lifted her up and used her weight on another edge to break her feet free.

"What is THAT?!"

Rickards turned and looked with her into the desert. The wave of light was growing closer from all directions.

"I don't think that's good," he said.

Mona then turned and peered past him with giant eyes. "Is that my car?!"

"We have to get out of here."

"Wait!" she yelled. "ESHE!"

"Where is she?"

"Out there!" she said, pointing to the rock house.

Rickards burst into a run. Painful and hobbling, but running, with Mona behind him. Both took less than a minute to reach it.

Inside, Eshe was still squirming, trying to get free. And next to her, on the opposite end of a giant rock slab, was the still body of Mido Saad.

Unstrapping Eshe, they ran back outside, standing in the darkness and searching for a place to go.

"We have to leave," said Eshe.

"I know," said Rickards. "But where?"

He ran back to Mona's car and ducked into the driver's seat, trying to start it. The dashboard lights lit, but there was no sound from the engine. He tried again, turning the key and giving a short pump of the gas.

Still nothing.

Rickards pushed himself out of the car and stared at the lead house with its two giant gaping holes.

It didn't matter. There was nowhere to go.

Nowhere to hide from what was coming—which was moving faster and was now only a few minutes away.

"Something's going to happen," he warned.

"What?"

"I don't know, but I don't think it's good."

What he was sure of was they were about to experience what thousands of Saad's test subjects already had.

"Run!" he suddenly shouted.

"Run?"

"Now!"

"Where?"

"AWAY FROM HERE!" he bellowed and led them in a sprint in an attempt to put as much distance between them and the stone house as they could. It was all he could think to do, not knowing just how far the effects would reach.

76

Dr. Layla Abo found it within minutes—the switch for Saad's secret room, revealing nothing but a table, chair, lights and strange book protected under a pane of protective glass.

In the corner was a container of gasoline and matches.

Was that his contingency plan? Gasoline? And was that to destroy the book, or the entire bunker including the thousands of children's drawings spanning decades?

She eased closer, afraid of making too much noise in case a microphone was hidden nearby, leaning in to examine the book, open and displaying strange writings on two of the many delicate pages—pages appearing to be gradually crumbling away around their edges.

Abo raised the clear glass and propped it in place, examining it, then touching the book's pages with her fingertips. She then turned one over and studied again.

She couldn't understand any of it. Nor could she identify the language, except that it was not hieroglyphics. But very old, nonetheless.

This is what Saad had been hiding for all these years? She lightly ran a finger down along the edge of the book's cover. All of this couldn't be about the book itself. It had to be about its contents.

With careful hands, she lifted one side and smoothly closed it, then lifted it off the lighted table and waited for something to happen.

Nothing.

Abo turned and faced the narrow doorway before stepping through, where she turned to examine the larger room again and all of its pictures from so many children.

All were somehow related to the ancient book.

Her eyes scanned again, looking for anything relevant,

until they stopped on a large computer monitor atop a simple desk on the far wall. The screen was illuminated and displaying something that took only a moment for Abo to read for all blood to drain from her face.

Signal received.
Commencing expunge.

And below the words was a number, counting down.

...7
...6
...5
...4

77

Traversing the glass was difficult, like running over wobbly rocks in a riverbed, slowing them all considerably.

Rickards stopped when Eshe tripped and fell, grabbing her hand and lifting her back onto her feet.

The energy was almost on top of them.

"Wait, wait. What are we doing?" called Mona, panting.

"Getting away from it!"

"How far away do we need to be?"

Rickards shook his head. "I have no idea."

Still gripping Eshe's hand, he lumbered forward over the field of loose rocks.

The truth was that whatever was about to happen… would either reach them or it wouldn't. And his guess, judging by the panic in Saad's men, was they wouldn't be nearly far enough.

He didn't hear it at first. None of them did until Rickards paused again to look for Mona.

A low buzzing sound.

At first, Rickards paid no attention. He was still focused on getting as far away from the epicenter as possible. But when the sound became louder, it also became more distinct, until it was loud enough for Rickards to hear it.

The sound of an engine.

After several more seconds, he recognized the pitch. A Pratt & Whitney Canada turboprop.

He turned around but saw nothing in the darkness, so instead, he closed his eyes and used his ears to identify its direction. When he reopened them, he spotted a faint outline beneath the moonlight, a few hundred feet from the ground.

All at once, it appeared like a small bird emerging from

a cover of shadows. A white, glowing bird in the form of a Quest Kodiak high-wing utility aircraft.

Frantically, Rickards began waving his arms and yelling, immediately joined by Mona and Eshe, all waving and spreading out.

The plane banked left and angled itself straight toward them, dropping in altitude, and several moments later, buzzing over their heads as it lowered itself farther into a harrowing descent, pulling up at the last minute and bouncing upon the endless field of glass fragments.

But the plane didn't stop. It continued forward, forcing all three to break into a run just as the ring of energy finally converged upon the small rock house behind them.

"Run!" hollered Rickards. "Get in!"

All three were moving as fast as they could, chasing the moving plane when its side door burst open and Angela Reed's head appeared.

"Hurry!" she screamed over the noise of the engine. "HURRY!"

Behind them, the small ancient structure absorbed the total concentration of light and energy, turning the stone a bright white before exploding into a prism of thousands of swirling colors.

"FASTER!" Angela continued screaming before Leonard Townsend's head poked out beside hers. He was yelling along with her and reaching out with one hand upon the plane's right wing strut, stretching as far as he could while Angela wrapped her arms around his waist to secure him.

As they closed in, first went Eshe, up into Rickards' hands as he continued running, lifting her out to reach Townsend's outstretched hand. He firmly gripped her and pulled the girl onto the strut's arm and into the plane's cabin.

Next was Mona, who reached, grasping the older man's hand and bounding in a desperate leap onto the metal strut before losing her balance and nearly falling backward, saved by Townsend's second hand.

A mighty thundering erupted behind them, and Joe glanced back, still running and reaching, missing Townsend's outstretched hand not once but twice.

A rift in the ground appeared in the distance, and the plane's engine suddenly roared, accelerating the aircraft, causing Rickards to lose his brief grip on the strut and forcing him to run harder with everything he had.

"Faster!" screamed Angela.

Rickards could see the plane pulling away, and sensing his last opportunity, he leaped with everything he had, reaching desperately for the strut, hitting it and wrapping both arms around it like a vice.

Together, Angela and Townsend both reached out, grabbing his clothing and pulling him toward them inch by inch until Townsend managed to get a second hand on him, pulling as hard as he could just as the Kodiak's wheels left the ground.

78

Inside, the pilot's instrumentation suddenly blinked out, bathing the cabin in complete darkness, returning minutes later while both Angela and Townsend struggled to heft the top half of Rickards' frame through the open door, accompanied now by Mona and Eshe. All four pulled together until Rickards finally clumsily tumbled into one of the passenger seats.

Exhausted and panting, he crawled forward and collapsed on top of the vinyl cushion, turning on his side and looking at the others. "Everybody okay?"

Angela smiled and laughed, while at the same time crying. She nodded her head and fell into the seat next to him. Behind him, Eshe and Mona looked over the top and laid their hands on him reassuringly.

With a heave, Townsend pulled the door shut and locked it, then beamed at Rickards. "You, my friend, like to live dangerously."

He grinned and shook his head, lying it back down on the cushion while trying to recover his breath. After several seconds, he frowned and raised it again, looking at the pilot.

"How in the hell did you manage that?"

"You won't believe it." Townsend grinned, then turned forward. "Our pilot knew Abasi Hamed. Didn't you, Mohammed?"

Hearing his name, the pilot glanced over his shoulder, thrusting a fist overhead and yelling over the noise. "Abasi Hamed is great man! Hero of Egypt!"

Mona's eyes widened, and she pointed excitedly. "I TOLD you!"

Rickards laid his head back down… and simply laughed.

"So, what happened with Saad?" asked Angela, buckled into her seat like the rest. Rickards was the only one who wasn't, remaining sideways and outstretched to relieve pressure from his injured leg.

Mona put a supportive arm around Eshe. "Saad is dead," she answered.

Angela couldn't hide her surprise. "What happened?"

Mona turned to Rickards and shrugged. "We're not sure."

"It was the other man," said Eshe. "The man who drove us there. He killed him."

Mona translated and thought back to the SUV. "His name was Khoury. Part of Saad's security detail, I think."

"So they turned on him."

The group was suddenly interrupted by their pilot, who called to them from the front.

Townsend and Rickards both moved forward to look while Mohammed pointed toward the ground. In the darkness were several outlines traveling on the dirt road beneath them.

"Saad's men," said Rickards. He turned to the women. "They're escaping."

"Oh, I don't know about that."

He raised an eyebrow at Angela, who was quietly grinning, as was Townsend.

Rickards turned back to the professor, who pointed straight ahead, far in the distance, where a faint glow of colors could be seen, soft and pulsating back and forth from light blue to light red.

"What's that?"

"The police," said Townsend. "Seems a lot of people didn't like Saad, which I'm guessing also extends to those who worked for him." He looked out the side window as the last of the SUVs disappeared from view behind them, then back up to the approaching police lights. "I'm guessing Saad's men have another five or ten minutes of elation."

EPILOGUE

I

Four days later

The high-pitched whine of the engines eased as the Boeing 767 reached its cruising altitude and began to level off. Above an unobstructed sky, a bright afternoon sun radiated through the plane's long row of cabin windows.

In their seats, Angela turned to Townsend. "Can I ask you something?"

The man in the seat next to her nodded.

"Joe said Saad was dead in that structure when he got there."

"Yes."

"And that Saad was lying on a slab next to Eshe."

"Right."

"Why do you think that was?" she asked. "What do you think he was trying to do?"

Townsend thought about the question. "What do *you* think it was?"

"Something to do with the energy, I assume."

"Same here."

She remained thoughtful a moment before continuing. "If there is some kind of quantum effect at the spire in Bolivia, it stands to reason it could also be happening here."

"As we suspected."

"Something Saad was obviously aware of. And given where he was found, next to Eshe, it makes me think about what you were saying before. About energy and entanglement. And neurons."

"I've been thinking the same thing."

"You said neurons have electrons in them, and therefore neurons themselves can be entangled."

The older man nodded.

"Do you think that's what happens? That this energy somehow entangles things? Or people?"

"I think," he said, "many different things can cause entanglement. To what extent, I don't know. But I think the desert *and* the canyon in Bolivia may be two places where it occurs to a much greater degree." He smiled at her. "But that's just a guess."

Angela nodded, thinking about his answer. "Why do you think no one noticed the lights in the desert over all these years?"

"I don't know," shrugged Townsend. "My friend says whatever it is, it doesn't show up on satellite."

"You're probably right," she answered pensively. "I guess the big question is what happens now?"

He shook his head. "Like Bolivia, more and more people will undoubtedly find out. After that, who knows?"

Townsend closed his eyes, and Angela turned forward, troubled. A few moments later, he reopened them.

"Now, can I ask you a question?"

She turned. "Of course."

"Why do you think Joe was so taken with that young girl?"

Angela thought about it, then answered in a low voice. "Joe lost his wife and daughter in an accident he couldn't do anything about. He wasn't there, and had no chance to try to protect them, which I think has haunted him for a long time." She paused, blinking. "I suspect saving Eshe and Mona helped him with that. Not healed him, but I think it certainly helped him."

Townsend gave a somber nod before quietly leaning forward to peer past Angela to the window seat where

Rickards was leaning uncomfortably against the interior wall, the side of his face still black and blue and dead asleep.

II

The room was dark when Omar awoke, illuminated by a single fluorescent light above the door and leaving little for the rest of the room under which everything else was still.

On top of him, the bed's sheet and blanket were neatly tucked, with railings up and a tube running from his left arm to a machine above him, while the gentle ticking of a clock could be heard high on the wall overhead.

Soft snoring came from the chair next to his bed.

His gaze moved to the chair and he found a sleeping Mona Baraka curled up and leaning against the padded arms, her hair strewn loosely around her face with an outstretched hand wrapped tenderly around his on top of the sheet.

He studied her for a long time before finally stretching his hand and fingers.

The movement immediately woke her. Her brown eyes fluttered open and stared forward, then at him. Excitedly, she straightened and lowered her feet. "You're awake!"

Omar smiled and nodded, keeping her hand in his while he examined the rest of the room. After a long pause, he reached with his left hand and pressed lightly against his sore chest, wincing. "Did I at least win?"

Mona laughed at the joke and stood, leaning over the rail and hugging him. "I am so glad you're okay."

"Me too. Maybe you can tell me what happened."

"It doesn't matter," she said. "All that matters is that you're all right."

"I agree with that."

Mona lowered the rail and sat on the bed, picking up his hand again. "Are you in pain? I can call the nurse."

Omar tried to adjust to a better position and abruptly

grimaced. "Only if I move."

"Then don't move," she replied coyly.

He looked down to see her gently stroking his hand. "Are *you* all right?"

"Yes."

"Good. So, are you going to tell me what happened?"

She inhaled and tilted her head. "Well, what do you remember?"

Omar thought it over before smiling broadly. "I remember we're engaged."

Mona grinned warmly. "When you're up to it, I'd like to introduce you to someone."

He raised an eyebrow. "Should I worry?"

"Hardly. She's eight years old."

III

The Pacific winds were no calmer or warmer than his last visit, still blowing dust clouds over the plains of Baja and the miles of barren scrub brush until eventually reaching out and over the Gulf of California.

The scene was barren and desolate, with nothing to hear but the sound of the howling wind blowing through the remains of the old, dilapidated house.

The damage and debris looked precisely as it had every time he'd come.

"This is it?"

Solemnly, Rickards nodded, then raised his head to gaze out at the nearby bluffs. It took him several minutes to finally start talking.

"I was young," he said. "Just out of the Army. I was celebrating with some buddies."

He then turned and began walking toward the bluffs, a mile out before the land disappeared and dropped down toward the gulf's glistening water.

Each of his steps crunched over dried weeds. "We rented a sailboat in La Paz and sailed it up here."

"How long did that take?"

"I don't remember. Maybe a couple days. We were drunk most of the trip."

"So what happened here?"

He continued forward, with Angela walking alongside. "One night we dropped anchor somewhere around here. In a drunken stupor, we decided to go for a midnight hike."

She continued listening.

"When we reached the top, we sat around, still drinking. We were young and arrogant. Boisterous. Constantly trying to best one another."

Rickards slowed to a stop on the bluff, as if deciding it was far enough.

"One of us spotted a cow grazing up here in the middle of the night all by itself. And somehow, we got the stupid idea to catch it and eat it."

"The cow?"

He nodded. "We were drunk—and stupid. Before, a stupid idea turned into a stupid dare that we could slaughter the cow and take it back to the boat."

Rickards frowned and looked around. "None of us were thinking clearly. We weren't thinking at all. Just drunk and full of testosterone. And one of us had a knife. So, we decided to do it."

"And you did?"

He flashed Angela a painful glance. The next part was the worst.

"I remember when we slit its throat and the image of it falling to the ground. We stumbled around trying to cut it up, but it wasn't as easy as we thought."

"Meaning what?"

"For one, we didn't know what the hell we were doing. Eventually, the alcohol began to wear off and we realized…"

Wrapped tightly in her jacket, Angela continued listening.

"It began to dawn on us what we'd done," said Rickards. "Killing a cow over nothing but a drunken pissing match."

"Did you take any of it?"

"No," he said, shaking his head. "We didn't have anything other than the knife, not even anything to carry it with. But that wasn't the real problem."

"What was the problem?"

"The problem was that we'd killed it in the night like a bunch of thieves." He glanced up, looking again at the distant bluffs. "Cows don't exactly roam wild here."

"So, someone owned it."

"Yes. And if we got caught, it could have meant jail

time."

"So, what did you do?"

"We ran back down to the boat and pulled up anchor, sailing off before the sun came up."

"Were you ever caught?"

"No."

Angela stared at him before looking out over the open plain. Brushing a handful of windblown hair from her face, she spoke. "If you got away with it, then why did you come back?"

"Because," answered Rickards, "it didn't take me long to understand the impact of what we'd really done." He looked at her through eyes of shame. "Mexico is a poor country where most people struggle just to survive. Especially in a place like this. That cow was worth several hundred dollars at the time to whoever owned it. And it may have been the only cow they owned, their primary means of surviving in such a poor place."

Angela stared at him, momentarily confused until finally understanding. She turned around toward the abandoned, run-down house.

"Them?"

Rickards nodded.

"Are you sure?"

"They were the only family living here back then—a man and wife and their two children."

"You think the cow was theirs?"

"I'm sure it was."

She continued staring at what little remained of the dwelling. "What happened to them?"

"I don't know," he said. "It took me years to get past the shame. By the time I tracked down the location, the place was empty. Abandoned."

"You don't know where the family ended up?"

"No. Not twenty years later."

Angela now stared at what was left of the tiny house in a very different light.

"This is why you keep coming back to Mexico?"

"I've been coming here," said Rickards, "to try to find them, visiting nearby towns and digging through old records attempting to find out where they went. I pray they're still alive."

There was a long silence while the winds blew and whistled around them.

The man was trying to fix his mistakes, she thought to herself. *Trying to right his wrongs. For reasons only he knew.* Leaving Angela studying him through a pained expression and wondering what exactly Joe was planning to do if he found the family he was looking for.

IV

Three floors below Omar, in Coptic Hospital's Intensive Care Unit, a man in a pair of dark polished shoes entered through double doors and proceeded to the hall's end. Stopping at the second to the last door, the man lowered his head to peer in through the glass window at the still figure lying inside.

Through heavy bandages and feeding and breathing tubes, little could be seen of the person lying motionless except for the gentle movement of their lungs being mechanically inflated and deflated.

The uniformed man stared from outside for several seconds before turning away, satisfied, and leaving the way he'd come.

She was still alive. But it would be a long time before Dr. Layla Abo would be able to speak.

From the Author

Readers often ask how much of my books are based on fact. The answer is 'quite a lot.' In my opinion, the less you need to stretch the truth, the better the story. This also holds true for The Desert Of Glass. Therefore, I thought you might be interested to know the following:

1) First and foremost, the Desert of Glass is real. It has existed for thousands of years between Egypt and Libya and is believed by many to have mystical and unexplained powers. You can travel to Egypt and see it, and even take home a piece as a souvenir.

2) The *Hypothetical Third Party Theory* is true. Leading Egyptologists do indeed believe Egypt's history to be somewhat of a mystery. Developing very suddenly in comparison to other ancient civilizations, and many are still afraid to speak out on the subject.

3) Everything mentioned in this book about quantum physics and 'quantum energy' is completely true. Quantum physics is extraordinary and often referred to as 'Einstein's Nightmare.' No one on the planet understands it, nor how our physical world can exist given the fundamental principles, or perhaps lack thereof, of the quantum world. This suggests that we truly live in a world that should not be possible. And more importantly, what we believe as real cannot be real. And what we believe to be "not real"... may actually be.

4) Music indeed survives the destructive powers of Alzheimer's Disease, as described earlier in the book. Countless studies have shown just how deeply and permanently ingrained our music

memory is. Look for this to be addressed further in the final Monument book.

5) King Akhenaten was, in fact, King Tut's father and a man of immense controversy. Including rumors of unexplained knowledge. He was indeed found in the mysterious and uncompleted tomb called KV55. Verified through DNA identification, deep questions remain around his demise and burial, including the lingering question of who was originally buried with him.

6) Finally, the great physicist Niels Bohr believed that a 'curtain' separating our physical world and the quantum world might really exist. So the question may now be... where is it?

Thank you again for reading The Desert Of Glass. I truly hope you enjoyed it. If you did and wouldn't mind taking a moment to leave a review for the book, this self-published author would be eternally grateful.

Thank you very much,
Michael

Made in United States
Troutdale, OR
09/20/2023

13059644R00199